P9-DEV-300

HOME AGAIN

A Novel

MICHAEL KENNETH SMITH

Copyright © 2014 Michael K Smith
All rights reserved.

ISBN: 1499157096
ISBN 13: 9781499157093
Library of Congress Control Number: 2014914520
CreateSpace Independent Publishing Platform
North Charleston, South Carolina

Chapter 1

EASTERN TENNESSEE, SEPTEMBER 1859

A large sycamore tree projected out of a riverbank ten feet above the water's edge. Zach and his father were perched on the outcropping, Zach fishing downstream and his dad fishing upstream. Between them, leaning against the tree, was a loaded Enfield musket and a can of worms.

Zach's father glanced back up the bank behind them. "Son, we have a big copperhead crawling down over the top of the bank right toward us. Do you want him?"

Zach looked back quickly, picked up the gun, cocked the hammer, turned, instinctively aimed the rifle and fired before the stock reached his shoulder. The sound reverberated down the river valley and the headless snake fell down the bank and hit Zach's father in the back, writhing violently. In his death throes, the large snake wrapped his body around Zach's father's waist, tightening its grip. The snake was trying to bite him reflexively, even though he had no means of doing so.

"Don't know why he's so mad at you," Zach said. "You didn't do anything to him."

"You are faster with that rifle than most are with a pistol," his father said laughing.

"Just doing what you taught me, Dad," Zach said as he pitched the snake into the water.

" Say, we're about out of worms, so I'll walk over to that barnyard we passed a while ago and look for some more. You stay here and fish. We need a few more to have a nice mess to eat tonight."

Zach was fourteen years old. Every September, he and his father took a week to float a river in eastern Tennessee to fish, hunt a little and live off the land. It always marked the end of the summer and it was the highlight. When Zach was two, his father and mother moved from England to Manchester, Vermont, where his father set up a small gun shop. However, the community turned out to be too small to support the business, so they moved to Knoxville, Tennessee, where the business thrived. This year, they had decided to go down the Obed River, which was a little west of Knoxville, near the small town of Crossville.

Zach was adding a nice bullhead to the stringer of fish when he heard the hoot of an owl. Then he heard the neigh of a horse and immediately looked up, scanning the woods behind him. He grabbed the musket and went up the bank looking for the horse. He was very comfortable in the woods by himself because most summers he hunted every day. Just as he saw the swish of a sorrel's tail in front of him, he felt the cold steel of a rifle in the middle of his back.

"You are trespassing on private property," a boyish voice said. "And you are fishing in my private hole. Who are you?"

Zach was shocked that anybody could sneak up on him like that without a sound. He turned around and saw a thin freckle-faced boy with an old flintlock rifle aimed menacingly at him.

"Zach Harkin. We're just floating down the river like we do every year at this time. We didn't know this was your private fishing hole."

"Who's 'we'?" said the boy.

"My father and I. He went looking for more worms just over yonder."

The boy slowly lowered his rifle. "You fishing with worms?"

"Yes, and we've caught quite a few."

"You mean those little things on that stringer there?"

Zach picked up the mocking tone of the boy's voice. "You know a better way?"

"Sure do. Grubs."

"Grubs? Never heard of that. Where do you find them?"

"Keep a whole box of them in the ground just above where you where fishing." The boy studied Zach's face for a moment. "Want to try them?"

"Sure. We just need a couple more for tonight's supper."

"Looking at the size of those you have caught, you could catch a dozen more and you would still starve to death." The boy gave out a hoot owl whistle and the sorrel horse neighed and came right over to where they were standing. "Say hello to Bonnie."

Zach realized he had been outsmarted. When he had heard the first owl call, his attention had been drawn by the neigh of the horse, which allowed the boy to sneak up on him from behind. He was impressed. Together they walked back to the bank just above the sycamore tree. The boy kicked the dirt, exposing a wooden lid to a buried box. He reached in and pulled a handful of grubs. "Here try one of these," he said. "Hook it from the tail to its head. Then cast the grub down on the riverbank and let the grub bounce into the water."

Zach crawled down to the tree outcropping and after hooking the grub as the boy asked, flung the bait on the bank and watched it tumble into the water.

"Get ready," the boy said.

Seconds later the line went taut, the pole dipped down and Zach had to hang on. The line swished through the water as the fish tried to get away. Zach feared the line would break and pulled as hard as he dared until the fish finally came to the surface. The boy scrambled down to the water's edge and expertly grabbed the large black bass by the gills and hoisted it into the air. It weighed at least six or seven pounds.

"Now you have some real supper," the boy said.

The bass was bigger than all the rest of the fish put together. The boy proudly stuck out his hand. "I'm Luke Pettigrew," he said. "That's the way we do things around here."

"Well, I'll be..."

Just then Zach's father came up and stared at the bass. "Guess we have a lot to learn about fishing in this river."

Zach jumped in. "Dad, this is Luke. He lives around here. I, er, we caught this thing with a grub."

"Nice to meet you, Luke."

"He has a whole box of grubs in this box here," Zach said.

Zach's father said, "Its getting late in the day. Care to join us for supper? Our camp is just upstream a little ways. Will your folks mind?"

"Nope. My father lets me go out all the time; he won't care. Whenever I get home, it'll be alright with him."

"Okay, let's get cracking," Zach's father said as he led the way back to the camp.

It was dark by the time Zach dropped the large fillets into the sizzling frying pan. The fish had been cleaned and scaled and Luke had found some wild onions.

"You ever do any coon hunting?" Luke asked Zach.

"Not so much over our way. We pretty much stick to other animals like groundhogs, rabbits and squirrels. Besides, don't you need dogs for coons?"

"Yes, I got a real nice coon dog named Jeff. We like to start out just after it gets good and dark. We walk through the woods and when ole Jeff picks up a scent, off he goes. Some coon hunters like to wait for their dogs to tree the coon, then they ride their horses over to the tree. Me, I like to run with the dog, stay right with him. More fun that way."

"Now that does sound like fun. Ever try a groundhog from five hundred yards?" Zach countered. "I like to go out just before it gets light in the morning and wait for 'em to come out of their dens."

"Five hundred yards? Wow. You must have a special rifle for that. That musket you have won't go that far, will it?"

"No, it won't, but dad's a gunsmith and he has a couple of rifles that are accurate well beyond five hundred yards."

"Hmmm. I could sit on my back porch and shoot squirrels without even putting my shoes on."

The sweet aroma of the fish frying wafted through the campsite as all three dug in. Halfway through the supper, the sound of an approaching horse interrupted their enjoyment. Luke immediately jumped up as if he knew what was happening.

A man on a large chestnut rode right into the camp. "Luke, where in the hell have you been?" the man said, "You know you are expected to be home before milking time. I had to get the cows in myself. You are the most irresponsible boy the world. Get home. Now."

Luke got up promptly and left without a word. He did a back flip onto his horse and rode away.

"Who in the hell do you think you are?" the man said to Zach and his father. "You are on private property and you better not be here when I get up in the morning." He kicked his horse and disappeared in the night.

Chapter 2

ZACH

MARCH 1862

T he sun had just illuminated the far hillside. The spider lines of Zach's rifle followed the two young groundhogs as they climbed from the hole of their den to the top of the hill. The sun's rays had melted most of the snow over the last several days. Lying on the ground, using an old butternut log to steady his rifle, Zach felt the cold dampness of the early spring earth through his long wool underwear. The groundhogs' fur shimmered. They were both healthy and had eaten plenty of corn in the surrounding fields. The distance was about nine hundred yards, and with a muzzle velocity of twelve hundred feet per second, Zach quickly – intuitively – calculated his bullet would take almost two and one half seconds to reach the target. He knew as soon as the first hog was hit, the second would instantly make for his den. Groundhogs could move at lightning speed. His scope was sighted in at five hundred yards; he needed another two feet of elevation to hit his prey. He felt a slight breeze from the left and he moved the scope's cobweb spider lines slightly to correct. As the second hog rose to survey the surroundings, Zach tried to control his breathing as he always did on long-distance shots, being careful not to fog the lens of the scope. The smell of the thawing earth rose to his nostrils, mixing with the fumes of the gun oil he had applied the night before. Pressing his cheek to the custom-made walnut gunstock, he felt the silky coolness of the wood. His right hand tightened on the rifle grip. It, too, had been custom-made to fit his hand. The bill of his hunting cap shielded his eyes and helped him focus on the target. He relaxed his arm and shoulders to be able to hold the spider lines without movement. He rubbed his trigger finger on the side of the gunstock to increase sensitivity. Finger on the trigger now, he went through his normal ritual... deep breath in... exhale... half-breath in... hold. Steady now, he squeezed the hair trigger and the modified Spencer sent a 52-caliber bullet on its way to his prey more than half a mile away. Before the bullet arrived, Zach, with practiced lightning speed, ejected the shell and pumped a new one into the chamber. Anticipating the second groundhog would hightail it to its den, he moved the spider lines to the mouth of the den fifteen feet below. Compensating for the wind and elevation and before the second hog appeared in his scope, Zach squeezed the trigger again. The smoke from the two shots slowly drifted off and the pungent odor of the black powder permeated the air. He held the spider lines on that spot while he waited the two and one half seconds for the bullet to travel the half-mile. Sure enough, the second groundhog arrived at the hole the exact same instant the bullet arrived. Both groundhogs lay motionless as the echoes of the two gunshots reverberated down the valley once, and then again. Zach broke into a wide grin.

Sitting behind Zach were his father, Tom Harkin, and Jim Luttrell. Both had arrived with Zach some thirty minutes before. Luttrell was the mayor of Knoxville and reputed to be a fine marksman himself. They had seen the whole event with spyglasses that were twice as powerful as the rifle-mounted Davidson 4X scope Zach had used.

Visibly impressed Luttrell said, "Let me see that gun, son." He rubbed his hand over the fine finish. "Damn, Tom, you are good."

"Takes more than just a good rifle to hit a target like that, though, Jim. Zach, go get them; we'll wait here," Tom said.

Zach, still smiling, got up. Standing his full six feet, he wiped the dirt off his front and took off his cap. His long dark hair fell down over his brown eyes, and he immediately brushed it back. "I can smell it now…roasted groundhog stuffed with apple, yummmm…I'll be right back." He took off to pick up the dead quarry. He would skin the groundhogs, and his mother would roast them as only his mother could do.

Luttrell turned to Tom. "Quite a boy you have there."

"We are proud of him. Pity any animal he's hunting; they don't have a chance."

"Tom, he'd sure make a good soldier. You going to let him sign up?"

"He sure wants to, but Lizzie and I are dragging our feet."

"He'd make a great sharpshooter."

"But how could we manage that?"

"Got an idea, Tom. Let me work on it. Think you could hold Zach off for a couple of weeks?"

Several moments later, Zach returned with the groundhogs. Both were nice and fat, about ten to twelve pounds. He took out his hunting knife and quickly skinned and cleaned the animals. He used a unique style he had developed over the years that kept him from getting his hands dirty. After depositing them in a gunnysack, Zach joined the two men on the walk back, about a mile away.

Tom Harkin, a noted gunsmith from Manchester, England, arrived in Vermont with his wife, Lizzie, and his only son in 1857. He had worked at the Whitworth Rifle Company as a design engineer. He loved to work on guns, always trying to improve them, to make them shoot faster, straighter and farther. An independent and adventurous man, he tired of working for a large company and decided to move to America, where he'd been told he'd

find great opportunities. He initially chose Manchester, in Vermont, because he reasoned it must have been settled by people
from his own Manchester, and the transition would be easier for
Lizzie and Zach.

Tom built a small workshop in the family's new three-room
log home and hung out a shingle. Their house was right next
to the Charles Orvis home, and to Orvis' tackle shop, and Tom
thought business would be good next to each other. But the village of Manchester turned out to be too small to sustain enough
business, so after working hard for almost a year, the Harkins decided to move to Knoxville, Tennessee. They purchased a small
house near the corner of Gay and Union Streets and set out a
shingle again. The gunsmith commerce was small but steady,
and provided a modest income for the family. The scope mount
Tom had devised attracted a fair amount of interest. The original Whitmore design had the scope side-mounted, with the rear
portion located near the shooter's eye. While quite effective,
this caused a lot of eye bruising from the recoil of the rifle. Tom's
solution was to mount the scope on top of the rifle and slightly
forward, allowing the shooter a clearer field of vision and greatly
reducing the recoil effect on the eyes. The disadvantage of the
top mount was it rendered the conventional open sights on the
barrel useless. The shooter did not have the choice of the open
sight or the scope. Only the scope could be used with the top
mount. As a result, when the target was identified with the naked eye, the time needed to sight in and fire was longer.

Harkin also modified the way the bullets were fed into the
firing chamber. Ideally a Sharps rifle would be better suited for
long-range shooting, however, he liked the Spencer's unique design for more rapid firing. The Sharps was a muzzleloader that
required a lengthy procedure to load, limiting the shooter to two
to four shots per minute, depending on the shooter's experience.
The Spencer, while much lighter, had a hole in the stock from
the shoulder butt plate through to the chamber in which the
bullets could be stored and held ready for rapid shooting. It was

possible to extract a casing and insert another so fast that an experienced user could fire shots every three seconds or less.

The Spencer rifle Zach used had this top-mounted scope. Tom had also installed a longer barrel and forestock to allow for improved long-range accuracy. Also, the barrel was rifled to spin the bullet faster than either the Sharps or the factory-made Spencer. This design change was tested over and over again and proved to be another measurable improvement. Lastly, he added more black powder to the rimfire cartridges, substantially increasing the penetrating power and range. With the mounted scope, the longer, heavier barrel, and increased cartridge power, the gun was limited to prone- or sitting-position shooting. It was a gun ideally suited for fast, long-range shooting. It was a gun ideally suited for a sharpshooter.

That night, the aroma of roasting groundhog permeated the small house as Lizzie Harkin busied herself preparing dinner for Tom and Zach. She was born Elizabeth Medford in Manchester, England, on this exact date forty years ago. Lizzie and Tom were childhood sweethearts. She lived four houses down the street from the Harkin family home and had been attracted to Tom because of his somewhat shy demeanor and independent streak. Lizzie was diminutive in stature and Tom, being slightly over six feet, proved sometimes opposites do attract. She had mid-length auburn hair, dark blue eyes and a beautiful fair complexion. From a very early age, she knew Tom Harkin was going to be the man of her life, and although the job was not too difficult, she made sure he felt the same way. They were married in October 1844. On July 10th, 1845, their only son, Zachary, was born. Complications during childbirth prevented them from having more children, and Zach became the center of their lives.

"When do we eat?" yelled Zach as he sauntered into the kitchen area. "If I don't eat soon I'll shrivel up and die from lack of food." He grinned and hugged his mother.

"As soon as you wash your hands, set the table and pour some water, we will be ready," said Lizzie. "And you might want to call your father and have him wash up, also."

After they were seated around the table, Tom raised his water in a toast and said, "Lizzie, here's to your next forty years." Birthdays were not celebrated in the Harkin house, and Lizzie flushed. She was not surprised Tom remembered. He always remembered.

During the meal, the conversation was stilted. The war weighed heavily on their minds, but no one said anything. Finally, Zach managed to say, "Father?" He desperately wanted his parent's – particularly his father's – permission to sign up.

Tom took a deep breath. "Son, your mother and I dearly do not want you to go off to this senseless war. We do not believe in this war. If some of the Southern states want to secede from the Union, why should we sacrifice so much to keep them in. Some would say they have a clear right to secede anytime they want to."

"I could forbid you to go," Tom continued. "However, you just might run out there and sign up anyway. You would end up serving under some city-bred officer who wouldn't know beans about war and tactics. Jim has a couple ideas and promised to get back in a couple weeks. Then you can decide."

On a rainy afternoon a several weeks later, Jim Luttrell strode into Tom's little shop.

"Hello, Tom. Have any hot coffee? I'm soaked."

Lizzie always kept a pot of coffee on the stove so customers could sit and relax while they talked about guns. Everybody loved to talk guns, and everybody wanted to talk to Tom about guns because he was the recognized resident expert.

Tom poured a mug for Jim and another for himself.

Jim started. "Tom, as our mayor, I have become a friend of John Sherman, who was a U.S. congressman and now has been elected to the Senate, representing the state of Ohio. I have exchanged telegrams with him about Zach and where he might go in the service to best utilize his unique skills, while keeping in mind your and Lizzie's deep concern for his safety. " John sipped some of the hot coffee and continued, "Sherman's brother is an officer in the Western Army and..."

"You don't mean William Tecumseh Sherman, do you, Jim?"

"The same," John said.

"But I thought he was being treated for insanity. Didn't I read a short while ago he was sent back East for treatment?"

"Quite right," said Jim. "However, doctors quickly determined he was perfectly sound. He has some nervous twitches and a lot of nervous energy, but General Grant thinks he is an up-and-comer. The word is, he is a levelheaded general when he is under fire. His twitches go away and he is extremely competent.

"Furthermore, he wrote to his brother not long ago indicating his need for young men with Zach's talents. Tom, I think if Zach would travel down to Fort Donelson or wherever Sherman might be, the general would make him a sharpshooter. That would mean he would not necessarily be in the front lines of this fighting. He would be one half-mile in the rear of the front lines, maybe behind a log, picking his targets one by one."

Tom weighed what his friend had just said. His son was going to war one way or the other, and this idea seemed to greatly increase Zach's chances of survival. On the other hand, he would be so far from home, probably over five hundred miles from home...

"Jim, I don't like it, but it does offer some distinct advantages."

"Sure it does, Tom, and it appears this Western front is going very well. Our men out there might just be able to stop the South from adequately supplying their armies. Why Zach will be home before the end of the year, ready to join you in your business. Next year at this time, he will have found a wife and you'll be getting ready to become a grandfather."

"Okay, okay. Before you have me in the grave, we'll talk it over with Zach. Sure appreciate your help. Lizzie is worried to death."

That evening at the supper table, Zach could tell his father had something to say. Whenever he did, he would be very quiet – as if he were trying to search for the right words and for the right time to say them. He was very quiet tonight.

"Was Mr. Luttrell here today, Father?" Zach asked.

"Yes, and that is what your mother and I want to talk to you about, Zach."

Tom described the arrangements Luttrell had made.

"You mean I'm going out West? As part of Grant's army? As a sharpshooter? Hoorah!!!! When can I go?"

"Just as soon as a letter of passage comes from General Sherman. But I think there is something very important you need to understand." Tom sat back in his chair, glanced at Lizzie and continued, "Zach, you were born with a gun in your hand. You were shooting rabbits before you knew how to spell your name. You shoot birds, squirrels, groundhogs, fox, deer, anything that moves, and you are good at it, better than I ever was. But let me tell you something, Zach. When you put those spider lines on a man, a human being, you will feel differently. A human being is not a groundhog, not a squirrel hiding in a tree. Someday you will have your sights on an enemy soldier, and you will have the power to end that person's life. That enemy soldier will be another human just like you are, with parents at home, maybe a girlfriend or wife. And you, by merely pulling the trigger, will be able to end that life." Tom waited to let Zach absorb what he had just said and then continued, "When you realize what that means, what that really means, you may think differently."

"I understand, Father, but maybe it will be shoot or get shot. I think I will do what I have to do to help quell this rebellion, and if that means taking another's life, I will do it."

Tom stood up from the table, indicating the meal was over. "You might be right, Zach, then again, you might be wrong. Whatever the case, your mother and I still don't want you to go but…"

"I know, Father, but I'll probably only be gone for a couple of months."

"You write us often," his mother said softly as she put her hand on Zach's.

Chapter 3

LUKE

MARCH 1862

Luke could feel the rhythm of the big mare as she galloped full speed down the rain-soaked cow path. As usual, he rode without saddle or bridle, guiding the horse with his feet and body. He urged her, "C'mon big girl, we gotta round up the cows before Pa figures out we've been lollygagging!"

Just as they rounded a slight bend, Luke saw a stream ahead. The heavy rain had swollen the normally three-foot-wide creek to over twenty feet. Luke leaned back, pulling the mare's mane slightly to slow a bit. The horse eyed the swollen stream and Luke could feel her hesitate. With a gentle nudge and a reassuring pat, he urged her on. Luke leaned well forward and she leaped to the other side, rider and horse seemingly as one.

Clearing the stream, Luke tapped the mare's neck on the left side to leave the path and head into the woods. He knew where the three cows were likely to go when it rained. Cutting through the woods would save a couple of minutes. The trees were thick and Luke let the sorrel mare thread her own way forward. She approached a low-hanging limb, and Luke had to slide down to the side of the horse. Hooking his right foot over the mare's back and wrapping his arms around her neck, he gasped. "Gal dang it, when are you going to learn to give me a little more room?" Just as they got past the obstacle, Luke had to quickly right himself to avoid being walloped by another tree ahead.

Luke wasn't sure, but he suspected the horse had done it on purpose. She was always cranky when heading away from the barn. He thought the horse might be a little smarter than he gave her credit. Turn her back toward the barn, and she always gave him more room; she seemed to have reserve speed only when returning home.

Finally they cleared the woods. Sure enough, the three cows were in a small meadow, munching on wild clover. When Luke appeared, they immediately lined up head-to-tail down the cow path and began moving toward the barn, about a mile's walk away. Luke jumped off briefly to relieve himself and give his horse a breather. After several minutes, he remounted using his own peculiar, well-practiced method.

When Luke was about ten years old, his parents took him to a circus that was touring through eastern Tennessee. The circus had a trick rider who, when mounting a horse, stood on the right side facing forward, grabbed the mane with his left hand and somersaulted backwards, landing on the horse's back, facing forward. It was the cleverest thing Luke had ever seen. Back home, he tried to do it, without success. Luke needed time to grow and strengthen his stomach muscles. He did sit-ups, as many as two hundred a day, every day. He learned quickly to do a back flip, but never got up high enough to reach the horse's back. As he got older, he used a milking stool to give him the height he needed. Eventually, when he was about thirteen, he was able to do it without a stool. From then on, it was the way he preferred to mount a horse.

When the cows reached the overflowing stream, they needed a nudge to go into the water. It was not deep, and they waded across without difficulty. Suddenly, Luke saw movement in some low bushes. He pulled up short and waited for whatever was moving to show itself. After several moments, a red fox wove its way into view and Luke's heart started pounding with excitement.

He quickly calculated the cows would get to the barn without any further prompting — it was not far away. In a split second, Luke decided to chase.

He tapped his heels on the mare's haunches, leaned forward and slapped the left side of her neck. She responded instantly. In three powerful strides, she was at full gallop. The fox, hearing the sound of the hooves, quickly turned to run as it saw the large animal bearing down. The race was on.

Luke had no idea what he would do if he caught up with the fox. He had chased foxes before and all he knew was he loved the chase. He loved riding at breakneck speed — turning, swerving, jumping — doing whatever was necessary to stay close to the fox. He was addicted to the feeling he had when he communicated with his horse using only his body. The horse turned right when he leaned right. She would slow up when he leaned back, speed up as he leaned forward.

They zigged, then zagged. They made large circular turns left and right. The fox was wily and fast. Luke knew where the fox's den was, and the fox was moving in that direction. Up ahead was a large briar patch. The fox slipped into it. Luke figured it would exit the briars in the direction of the den, so he veered the mare to the right, toward the far end of the patch. Sure enough, the fox exited the briars just before Luke got there and the chase continued.

Luke could sense the horse tiring. The fox went under a fallen tree. Just as the mare jumped over, the fox made a hard right. Luke leaned hard right and the horse responded. The grass was long and wet from the rain. The mare turned so sharply her hooves slid out from under her and she went down. Luke had felt her slipping, anticipated the fall, and raised his right leg to avoid getting it smashed under her body. Both were down.

The horse frantically tried to get up, pawing the ground with her hooves to gain traction to right herself. She managed to get all four legs under her and stood without moving. She did not put any weight on her right rear leg.

Luke, having been tossed clear, also rose unsteadily. With a sinking feeling, he approached the horse. She had fear in her eyes. As he embraced her head, she calmed a bit. He ran his hands down her right side to assess the damage. Everything appeared normal, with no obvious broken bones. However, she was very reluctant to put any weight on her back right leg. He massaged the area for some time and eventually she was able to hobble forward. They started back toward the barn very slowly. Then he started to think about his father and how mad he would be when he found out about the mare's injury. They had only two horses, an older draft horse and the sorrel. The draft was used to haul the wagon around the small farm and occasionally to take the buggy to town to get supplies. The sorrel was needed for many daily chores.

Their progress was tedious and Luke could tell the mare was in pain. With each hobbling step she sounded a low, guttural groan. When they finally got back to the barn, he was greeted by a red-faced, very angry father. It was ten in the morning and Luke was late by about two hours.

Luke felt very little attachment to the horse. They had named her "Bonnie," but he did not consider her a pet. Farm animals — horses, cows — were an integral part of a farm's operation, much like a buggy or a plow. They were one of the tools a farmer had at his disposal to do his work. The animals were cared for and fed, but they were expected to work and earn their keep. If an animal could not perform those duties, then that animal was a drain on the homestead.

Luke's father took one look at the hobbled horse and another at Luke, who was bruised and scratched. His face turned even redder, "What the hell have you done this time? Do you have

any idea how much we need that horse?" His raised his voice
louder and louder. "How in the Sam Hill can I run this farm
with this kind of behavior? When are you ever going to grow up,
boy?" He pointed his finger at Luke, his hand shaking, his eyes
looking big—ready to pop out. "Get your sorry ass over to the
woodshed. Now."

Luke walked slowly toward the woodshed. He knew he was
in deep trouble. He had never seen his father so angry. To make
matters worse, the cows must not have made it back to the barn
as he had hoped. And he knew his riding after the fox had been
foolhardy and immature. He had put the horse at risk when it
was not necessary.

Luke's father was a hard man who had lived a difficult life.
In the summer of 1840, Jonas Lucas Pettigrew arrived in Crossville, Tennessee, a very small town near the western slopes of
the Appalachian Mountains on the Cumberland Plateau. He was
driving a team of draft horses that were pulling a small covered
wagon in which he had placed all of his worldly belongings. He
had previously worked on various farms and had saved his money, and now he meant to acquire some land and farm for himself.
Jonas had lost his beloved wife and their child to childbirth. He
had wandered aimlessly from odd job to odd job since her death,
trying to piece together his life. The loss had left him withdrawn.

With the cash he had saved over the years, he purchased a
ninety-six-acre plot of land that contained a decent four-room
house near a small stream. He had a plow, two crosscut saws,
hand tools and a bed. He hoped the cash he had left would carry
him through until the farm could provide income.

He worked hard clearing trees and removing rocks to create
tillable fields. He acquired a reputation with the folks in the
area as being a very hard worker. From sunup to sundown, sev-
en days a week, he worked the land. After two years, the farm
started to take shape. And, in time, he met and began to court
Anna Lambeth, the granddaughter of Samuel Lambeth, one of

the first settlers in the area. They married, and in the spring of 1845 Anna gave birth to a strapping young boy, Lucas.

As he sat on a section of log that was waiting to be split, Luke considered what was coming. He tried to see things the way his father would. He knew his father's first wife and child had died a long time ago, but his father never spoke of them to him. Maybe he did to his mother, Anna, but he never talked to Luke about his past.

Luke's dog, Jeff — the one animal he cared about — came over and put his head on his lap, as if he sensed Luke's sadness.

Luke also thought about the farm. The soil was not a rich loam. It had turned out to be thin, with few natural nutrients to grow crops. The soil was shallow, with more and more rocks appearing each year. It was as if the rocks grew during the winters and blossomed in the spring. He wasn't certain, but he suspected that the farm's income was causing a problem. While they had enough to eat, money seemed to be a continuous topic of conversation between his parents.

The farm was home to Luke. It was all he knew, and he loved his life. He tried to do whatever he was asked and, with only a couple of exceptions, he felt his parents were pleased. Every day was different with the kinds of experiences only a farm boy could appreciate. He was happy. He just wanted his life to continue as it was.

Inside the house, Jonas was trying to cool down and figure out what he had to do. He did not want to confront his son when he was angry. He had to give it some thought. On the one hand, the boy was just being a boy, enjoying the horse. His intentions were probably innocent, but he had clearly used poor judgment. On the other hand, he was another mouth to feed, and the farm was providing only the barest profit. He had discussed this situation with Anna, but she could not see or understand the problem. The land was becoming infertile, and either they would have to change from a crop farm to pure livestock, or they would have to move. Jonas, who was now in his late fifties, preferred the latter. But to move and start all over again would be very difficult at his age.

The continuing rift between the Northern and Southern states was an ongoing discussion between Jonas, Anna and to a lesser degree, Luke. Some of their neighbors were strong abolitionists and some very much believed it was all about states' rights. Jonas and Anna deeply resented the radicals from both sides for stirring up so much trouble.

During the past year, most of their neighbors' sons had signed up for Confederate service and Luke felt left out. Many of his best friends had joined up weeks and months ago, and he felt conspicuous, sensing that people might suspect he lacked patriotism, or even worse, was a coward. Luke knew the South had a much stronger cavalry and better riders than the North, and he preferred to become a cavalryman. He had heard of men like Nathan Bedford Forrest, and their swashbuckling daring naturally appealed to Luke.

When Jonas walked into the woodshed, his face was still red and tense, his lips were pinched, and dark bags hung down from his eyes. His jaw was set so hard the facial muscles contorted his appearance. He sat down on an old stool across from Luke and just stared down on the dirt floor for several moments. Finally Jonas looked up with a bereaved sadness.

"Luke, as you probably know, trying to eke out a living on our farm is becoming increasingly difficult. Each year we have had to draw from our now depleted savings just to buy seed for our next crops. We do not make enough to cover what it costs us, and I fear we have to make some changes if your mother and I are to make it through these times. Your reckless behavior this morning," he continued, "has made our situation worse. We will probably have to put the mare down and we cannot afford to replace her."

"But Pa," Luke interjected, "she might be okay."

"Let me finish, Luke. What I am trying to tell you is while your mother and I dearly love you, you are not contributing to this homestead. We have talked about this before...about some of the reckless things you do. Again and again, you act immaturely and put your mother and me at risk. You need to move on, Luke. Maybe when you grow up and become a man, you will come back and we'll work together to make this a respectable farm. But until that happens, you are of no practical use to us. Who knows, maybe a couple of years in the army might just put some sense into that head of yours." Jonas just sat on the old stool, looking down as if he had said all he was going to say.

Luke stared at his father, his mouth open. He was unable to speak. His mind was flooded with emotions. Rejection, sadness, anger, rebellion, all hit him at once. Grasping the gravity of what his father had just said, he let tears flow freely down his cheeks. For a long time, neither said a word. At length, Luke stood up and started walking toward the door. As he did so, he said, "I'll be gone before morning."

Jonas looked down at the dirt floor with his teeth still clenched, not moving.

The sun was high in the sky as Luke started walking toward town. He had not wanted to confront his mother, and walking out seemed the easiest thing to do.

As he passed the local post office, he stopped and looked at both sides of the front door. On the right was a bright new enlistment poster for the Confederate States of America and on the left was an old poster for the Union that had been mutilated and smeared with mud. He studied one, then the other, over and over.

The Union poster said something about saving the Union, while the Confederate poster brightly headlined, "Wanted: 100 Good Men To Repel Invasion." Luke thought about the messages. Yes, it did seem like an invasion, he concluded. What right does the North have coming down here and trying to force us to stay in the Union? Remembering the phrase "independent states..." in the Declaration of Independence, any doubt he had about who was right and who was wrong went away and his mind was made up.

When he walked through the front door, the postmaster recognized him. "Hi, Luke," he said. "No mail for the Pettigrews today." He looked at Luke more closely, noticing his slumped shoulders and red eyes. Luke's shirt had stains from his fall off the horse and was torn at the elbow. His face was covered with dust and dried streaks from his tears. His curly light brown hair was disheveled and caked with dirt. "What's wrong, son? You look like you came out on the bad end of a fight with a polecat."

"Fell off the horse," was all Luke could manage. "How would I go about enlisting?"

The postmaster replied, "The Tennessee 28th is camped just west and a little south of here, and the sergeant is due here in a couple of hours. He's always looking for recruits. We have quite a few boys from here in the 28th, and they're all itching to get a chance to push the Yankees back north where they belong."

Luke sat down on a stool next to an iron stove. He put his head down and covered his face with his hands. His head was reeling from his father's words, "You need to move on..." His stomach started to churn and he felt nausea creeping in. He got up suddenly, walked out to the side of the front porch and vomited. He sat on the bench looking down on the weathered wooden floor, not seeing. He was numb, forlorn, rejected, alone.

As Luke sat, staring blindly, he remembered more of what his father had said, "Maybe when you grow up and become a man, you can come back..." He felt his face turn red and the hurt gave way to anger. "I'll show him," he thought, "I'll go off to this goddamn war. I'll be somebody. I'll do some daring deed, save lives, be a big hero. He will live to regret what he said. I'll prove him wrong, and he'll beg me to come back. Maybe I won't come back even if he asks me. I'll prove him wrong! He will be proud of me and will regret what he said."

Slowly, a sense of determination came over Luke. He'd wait for the sergeant from the Tennessee 28th to arrive.

"You people of the South don't know what you are doing. This
country will be drenched in blood. War is a terrible thing."
–William Tecumseh Sherman to a Southern friend upon
learning of the secession of South Carolina.

Chapter 4

ZACH

Mayor Luttrell had suggested to Zach that to avoid Confederate raiders in central and western Tennessee, the
best route to the Western front would be to ride north
through the Cumberland Gap into Kentucky and to Camp Nelson, just south of Lexington. Camp Nelson was a large depot
from which the Union helped supply the armies operating west
of the Appalachians. From Lexington, Zach would board a train
to Covington, then travel by steamer down the Ohio River to
Paducah, where he hoped he would learn the exact location of
General Sherman.

With his rifle carefully wrapped in deerskin, Zach left home
just before dawn on a large chestnut the mayor had lent him. In
his pocket was the note from General Sherman which read:

"To all concerned:

Please allow passage of new recruit Zachary Harkin.

Signed

Brigadier General William Tecumseh Sherman"

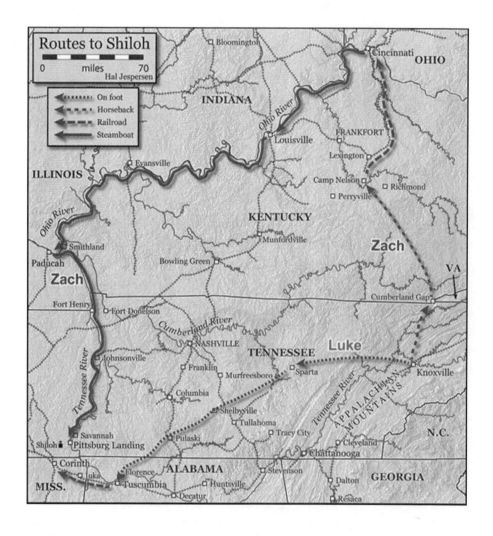

He rode hard the first day. He would turn the horse in at
Camp Nelson and the mayor hoped to get it back some time
later. In the late afternoon, Zach was near the Cumberland Gap.
With the light fading, he decided to make camp near a small
stream and give his horse a rest. He wanted good light to cross
this last big ridge of the Appalachians safely. He tethered his
horse, started a small fire and sat down to eat some biscuits his
mother had given him.

He rolled out his blanket and crawled in just as the last light
of day was swallowed by darkness, leaving eerie shadows from
the dimming fire. He thought about his mom and dad. He had
left so early that morning and was in such a rush to get going,
he'd cut his goodbyes short, giving his mother a quick hug and
shaking his father's hand before he mounted and left.

There wasn't a breath of wind in the air, so the sudden sound
of leaves rustling brought Zach to full alert. Then he felt the
sharp poke of something on his chest. "You from around these
parts, sonny?" an old gravelly voice said.

Zach looked up and the embers from the fire cast just enough
light to see an old man's face standing right over him. He had a
thin face with a long white beard that came down to his chest.
His thin aquiline nose protruded out between two closely set
dark eyes. Zach could not find words. "You a Yankee? Come on,
boy, say something."

Zach felt the sharp poke again. "I'm traveling north," Zach
muttered.

"Well, then, you're a Yankee, ain't ya?"

"I am not a soldier," Zach said.

"You're on your way to sign up, ain't ya? You got a gun in
that there deerskin and you're going north to become a Yankee,
ain't ya"?

Zach could only admit that he was, and when he said it, the
old man sat down beside him. He put his walking stick across
his lap.

"Sonny, I don't really care if you are a Yankee or a Rebel. Makes no difference to me, but all the young boys from these parts are signing up for one side or another and they have no idea of what they're getting into. They think they're off to a road of excitement and glory. Well, they'll get more excitement than they want and no glory. This war is going to be bloody hell. If you want my advice, go home. Go home and hide. Course, you don't want any advice, do ya? Think you got it all figured out, don't ya?" The old man got up slowly and started to walk away. "Don't say I didn't warn ya," he said as he disappeared into the darkness.

For the next two days, as Zach made his way to Camp Nelson, he thought about the old man. Was he a dream? An apparition? Or was he real?

Few passengers were aboard the train to Covington. Zach was bound for a war everyone agreed would be over within a year. It would, in fact, last three times that, and little known to him or anyone else, his participation in the war would have a profound effect on the opposing army of the South.

Zach was impressed with the vastness of the country as the train rambled mile after mile through northern Kentucky. He reached the Cincinnati area on the third day and was amazed at the sheer size of the city, the crowded streets and the overwhelming odor. It was the stench of tens of thousands of hogs roaming freely through the city. He was later to learn that this area was called "Porkapolis" and had become the main pork-processing center for all the Eastern states.

A motley group of wounded and beaten soldiers jeered at the young greenhorn stepping off the train at the Covington station across the Ohio River from Cincinnati. Some of the men were armless, some legless, some were missing an arm and a leg. All wore dirty, torn remnants of their blue uniforms. Their faces were sunken and gray. They were returning home, their lives ruined, all facing the unknown and trying to forget the horrors they had just lived through. They stared at Zach.

Embarrassed, self-conscious and trying not to stare back, Zach walked in front of the men at the Covington station, heading toward the depot. "Hey, boy! They must be sending kids to do men's work, " said a soldier leaning on his crutches, his right leg missing just above his knee.

Another said, "What are you carrying? Your cradle?" The rest of the men guffawed and smirked.

Zach nodded. "It must be hell back there. Fort Henry?"

"No, sonny, a place called Fort Donelson," said one. "You'll find out soon enough."

"What's in the scabbard?" asked the first man again.

The second man jumped in, "Yeah, show us your mother's going away present. You've got a secret weapon in there?"

The rifle was longer than average, and because it had a large scope mounted, it did not appear to be what it was. Zach untied the rawhide laces and pulled out the gun so they all could see. The men became silent. They may not have known exactly what it was, but they were impressed, although they endeavored not to show it.

The second soldier said, "Where does the bayonet go? On the back side?"

That brought a few more snickers. Then a tall man who had been silent until now said, "Is that a Spencer? Let me see that thing."

"My father is a gunsmith uptown in Knoxville," Zach answered proudly. "He modified a repeating Spencer with a longer barrel and mounted this Davidson scope. It's probably the only one of its kind."

The tall man rejoined, "Hmmm, has a nice feel. Accurate?"

From a distance, the Ohio River was visible and Zach could hear the whistle of a steamboat. He quickly sheathed the rifle back in the case. As he was about to leave the men, he said, "I can hit a twelve-inch circle at a thousand yards nine times out of ten." He spoke with a calm conviction that left nobody in doubt he was telling the truth.

"I have to go, boys. I'm headed for Fort Donelson, to report to General Sherman." As he walked away, the men just looked at him.

One said, "Sure could've used him at Fort Donelson."

As Zach headed down to the river he thought to himself, "Did I call those men 'boys'?" He chuckled as the moist air from the river rose up to meet him.

The main pier was located near the bridge that crossed over to Ohio. It was loaded with hundreds of wounded soldiers waiting for transport to the North and East. Again, most were without limbs and had wounds wrapped with soiled bandages. They looked tired, dirty and hungry. As before, several shouted disparagingly at Zach as he walked toward the ticket office, where he learned that the next boat was not due to leave until early evening. He would have to wait most of the day.

Zach noticed a group of young men on the other side of the pier area who were obviously not coming from the war but going to it. They were cleanly dressed, laughing and clearly enjoying each other's company. He walked up to the group, and not addressing anyone in particular said, "You heading to Paducah?"

The nearest responded in a friendly tone, "Sure are, and we hear Grant is having his own way in Tennessee. The war might be over before we can get there, and here we are having to wait all day just to get one step closer to the action."

"Mind if I join you?"

"Sure," said another. "Where you headed?"

"To Fort Donelson, you?"

"We are, too. My name is John Dickson," one said. Zach introduced himself.

"What are you carrying there, Zach?" John asked. "Looks like something serious."

Zach explained how his father had modified the new Spencer rifle for long-range shooting. While all the others were very familiar with guns, they had never seen a scope mount and did not understand the optics. Zach told them the scope was like a spyglass attached to the barrel that, if sighted properly, would allow him to shoot at whatever was viewed in the scope. The boys were intrigued.

"Mind if I have a look?" John asked as he reached out his hand.

"Not at all, here take it. It's a little heavier than you might be used to."

John took the gun and held it up to his shoulder while peering through the scope. He noticed the magnification and said, "You mean, if I put the hairs on a target, this thing will hit it?"

"Exactly," responded Zach. "And if you allow for wind and elevation, you can hit a target a long distance away."

"How far?" asked a recruit named Karl.

"Well, I can hit a relatively small target at a thousand yards and a bigger one at much more."

"Don't believe it," a young man named Vince said.

They passed the gun around for all to see.

"Maybe I can prove it to you. We have some time, let's find some flat ground and give her a try."

"Are you kidding?" Vince asked. "I bet you can't hit my hat at five hundred yards, let alone one thousand."

"You've got a bet, but I'm not going to buy you a new hat when I put a big hole in it."

"My hat is safe," Vince smirked.

They walked southwest along some railroad tracks and soon were in the country. The immediate area was flat and while the tracks gradually curved to the right, visibility was several miles. Zach walked into the brush, found four sticks and pushed them into the ground. He took out his telegram from General Sherman and sandwiched the paper between the sticks. When he was convinced it would not blow away in the light cross breeze, he positioned Vince's hat on top of one of the sticks.

"This is our target. Now let's take a walk," Zach said to the others. "The track is slightly curved, so we will have to allow for that when we figure our distance. Each of our steps will be about one yard and we will add about ten percent allowance for the curvature."

"Sounds about right," Vince said.

The boys were excited as they started counting steps. When they reached five hundred and fifty, they looked back and Vince said, "No way."

Zach continued walking, counting his steps. As they reached seven hundred then eight hundred, the boys started snickering. They finally stopped at eleven hundred yards, which effectively made the distance to target roughly a thousand.

Zach pulled up some grass growing between the rails, held the leaves high in the air and released them to test the wind speed and direction. He then folded the deerskin sheath into a ball, took a prone position between the rails and placed the fore-stock of the rifle on the folded sheath. He then put four bullets in the end of the stock and inserted one shell into the chamber. He again looked to the side at the soft breeze blowing the grass.

As he sighted toward the target, he said, "Sorry Vince, but this first one is headed toward your hat."

"Sure, and cows can fly." All four seemed dubious, as the target was almost impossible to see with the naked eye.

Zach, now concentrating, put the spider lines of the scope on the hat. He intuitively calculated his elevation and wind allow-ance, sighting two feet high and a foot upwind. He rubbed his trigger finger on the stock... deep breath in... exhale... one half-breath... hold. He squeezed the hair-trigger, sending the bullet to its target. He quickly put another shell in the chamber. "The next three are for General Sherman," Zach said as he systemati-cally squeezed off three more shots.

The tension in the group was high as they walked back to the target. Vince started running when they got within one hundred yards. When he got there, he leaned over to pick up his hat. He didn't see a hole and he put it on his head, looked back and said, with a big smug smile, "You missed!"

Zach and the others arrived shortly and looked at the telegram. Three holes in a four-inch diameter! They stared at Zach, impressed.

"But he missed my hat!" Vince yelled as he held the hat up with his hand. "Nary a scratch!"

"Let me see that," Zach said as he took the hat. "What do you call that?" He pointed to a small hole that was partially hidden in the flap.

"I'd call that a direct hit!" Karl said.

Vince looked at the small hole and muttered, "Holy smoke."

Zach took out a pencil and wrote on the back of the telegram, "From a thousand yards."

He asked all four to sign it as witnesses, which they did. He folded it up and put it in his pocket.

Finding General Sherman was proving to be a difficult task. Zach had heard reports the general had gone home to Lancaster, Ohio, to be treated for insanity. Then he learned he was, in fact, sane and had performed well at Fort Donelson and Fort Henry. News traveled erratically. What news he heard could be three months old or three days old. It was now late March, and the news he thought most reliable indicated the general had hastily steamed up the Tennessee River to a place called Pittsburg Landing.

When he arrived in Paducah two days later, Zach saw dozens of steamboats headed up the Tennessee River to Pittsburg Landing. Thousands of soldiers were filing on board the troop carriers. Cannon, ammunition, food and all the things an army needed were being loaded on others. He quickly found a transport about to leave, presented his note from Sherman and boarded.

While on the way, he had a chance to think about what was in store for him, about the fact that he knew he would have to use his sharpshooting skills in the days to come. This meant shooting human beings. His father's warning came to mind. If a man was about to shoot you, why hesitate? Shoot or be shot, that was the difference. A man who was the enemy could and would retaliate. He could, and would, shoot you. Zach had seen the wounded. And he had seen the coffins.

On April 4th, 1862, at an encampment in southern Tennessee near Pittsburg Landing, Lieutenant John Taylor, aide-de-camp, approached General Sherman and said, "Sir, there is a young man here who asks you look at this."

It was the telegram General Sherman's brother had asked him to send to James Luttrell in Knoxville, granting passage for a friend's son to join him on the Western front. General Sherman took the folded telegram, opened it and noticed the three bullet holes. He looked at the piece of paper for a few moments, not saying anything — as if he were trying to figure it out.

William Tecumseh Sherman was a lean, wiry man of medium height, with a receding head of cropped red hair that always appeared disheveled. He had a thin, lined face with sharp features, sunken, steely eyes and a short grizzly beard. The few moments it took him to study the telegram represented an extraordinary amount of time for him to stand in one place, as he was constantly moving, fidgeting, talking. His hands were always in motion, giving the impression that his clothes were too tight or that something else was bothering him. Always with an unlit cigar in his mouth, he usually talked while he chewed on it.

General Grant thought highly of Sherman, who had performed well at Fort Donelson. Sherman handled supplies and reinforcements capably, allowing Grant to concentrate on the strategic elements of the battle. It was a winning combination and as a result, Sherman was given command of the 5th Division, even though he had had no real combat experience since the Federal defeat and rout at Bull Run.

Sherman's face broke into a wry smile. "Let me see this young man," he said to his aide. "If he is as good as he represents, we can use him."

Lieutenant Taylor fetched Zach.

"Sir," was all Zach could muster as he stood in front Sherman with his chest out. Here he was, in front of one of the highest-ranking officers in the Western theater. Not that it mattered much, but he had not shaved for several weeks. His clothes were dirty from his long journey and he felt awkward, diminished.

"So your father is a friend of my brother's," Sherman asked. "How do they know each other?"

"Sir, begging your pardon, sir, my father is a friend of a friend of your brother's, sir."

"Why did you come way out here, young man?"

"Sir, my parents did not want me to volunteer, but I insisted, so they thought I could be of particular use to you, sir."

"Oh they did, did they?" Sherman hesitated, thinking. "Well, they might be right. I do not have much time, but I am going to assign you to Lieutenant McCoy here, who will find a place for you," Sherman said. "Lieutenant, you heard what I said... possibly, he might fit in on our far left side, but you figure it out. Zach, be sure to give your assigned officer your calling card." Sherman handed the safe-passage notice back to Zach.

Zach was still at attention, not knowing what to say.

"Son, you are not going to have much time to get acclimated to this army before you see action. We have a large Confederate presence twenty miles south and in the next week or so, there is going to be a lot of fighting, so get going and get ready."

The general walked away, already gesturing to an aide on another subject, giving orders and chomping on his cigar.

Neither Sherman nor young Zach could have imagined a big battle was only days, not weeks away.

"All we ask is to be left alone."
—Jefferson Davis in response to Lincoln calling up an army.

The Battle of Shiloh was named after Shiloh Church, which was a
one-room church located just outside of Pittsburg Landing. Shiloh
is a Hebrew word meaning place of peace.

Chapter 5

LUKE

The sergeant from the 28th Tennessee pulled up to the general store and noticed Luke, who was sitting under the CSA poster. He leaned forward from the buckboard, buggy whip in hand, as if he were itching to go. "Well, I can guess you ain't gonna be no Yankee, so you must be wanting to sign up to help rid Tennessee of those jackasses. Jump in; we'll talk later. Right now we gotta get across the river. All the rain has caused a lot of havoc, and with so many Union sympathizers around, we best get a move on."

Luke hesitated.

"Hurry up and jump in, boy. We gotta get out of here before we can't!"

The man driving the buckboard introduced himself as Sergeant Bennington Wilmont. He appeared to be in his mid-fifties, with graying hair that probably had not been cut for several years. He wore a striped railroad-style hat and a badly worn Confederate jacket. He was about five feet tall but made up for his lack of physical stature with a booming voice.

Luke got up and walked toward the wagon, wondering what was going on and why the big hurry. He climbed up on the seat beside the sergeant, who quickly drove away. Luke noted the sergeant's beard was full of spittle. He smelled of alcohol.

"Don't you have a gun, boy?"

"No, sir, I left home in a bit of a hurry. Besides, we only have one gun in the family and my pa would never part with it."

"So... you stole off? Did your kin know what you were up to?"

"Yes, they did. But they may not know which side I chose."

As they rode along the muddy road, Luke observed the horse was favoring his back left leg. Gradually, the limp became more noticeable. "You've got a lame horse there, sir," Luke said. "Maybe we should pull up and maybe we can figure out what the trouble is."

"Yeah, she's been getting worse these last few days," the sergeant said as he pulled on the reins.

Luke got off the buckboard and walked around to the front of the mare. "Easy girl," he said as he stroked her head. Keeping his hand on her, he walked back to the leg she was favoring. He faced backward, leaned hard against the horse and picked up her leg as she shifted from the force he applied. He studied the bottom side of the hoof.

"You got any tools? She has a good-size stone embedded into the frog of her hoof, and we'll have to get it out or she won't go much farther."

"All I've got on this wagon is my good looks," the sergeant said. "We only have about six or seven miles to get to our camp, surely she can make it that far."

"Don't think so, sir." Luke released the hoof and walked back to the wagon looking for anything that might help him get the stone out. He found an old railroad spike in the back corner, picked it up and said, "This just might do it." He took the spike, went back to the horse, picked up her hoof and started to pry the stone loose. It wouldn't move, no matter how he tried. "Could you get me a stone to use as a hammer?"

The sergeant crawled off and came back with a rock about the size of a big fist. Luke placed the spike on the lodged stone and hit it hard. It popped out. "There. That'll do it. She will be a little tender for a while but by morning she'll be as good as new." He jumped back up on the buckboard.

"Nice touch with the mare," was the sergeant's only reply as he spewed out brown and yellow juice and then ran his shirt-sleeve over his mouth. They continued on their way.

Luke could hear the river before he could see it. As they rounded a slow curve in the road, the bridge came into sight, or at least what had been the bridge. "Holy Christ, them Yankees blew up the bridge!" the sergeant snorted. "It was here yesterday morning, God bless it, what are we going to do now, God damn them."

As they got closer, they could see much of the bridge's structure remained. The center portion was missing, however, rendering the bridge impassable. The sergeant pulled up and stared at the wreckage. The river was about fifty yards wide and muddy. The light was starting to fade, making it difficult to determine the depth.

"A week ago, this river couldn't have been more 'n three or four feet deep right here. It's probably six or seven feet now and moving much faster." The sergeant got out and walked up to the water's edge, "I know a place downriver a ways where it gets wider. Maybe we can cross there on the buckboard."

They turned the horse, heading downstream. The going was slow because the ground was irregular and muddy; the buckboard strained and creaked. They reached the spot the sergeant had talked about. The banks on both sides were less steep; cattle, seeking water, had worn them down.

The sergeant jumped off the wagon; Luke joined him. The river appeared to be moving faster, but it was wider, and if cattle had crossed here, there might not be any deep, unseen holes. "I think we can cross here," the sergeant said.

Luke wasn't so sure. "This buckboard is not very heavy. With this fast water it just might lose traction and we could get swept down the river."

"Well, it's get across here and get to our camp, or sleep under the wagon tonight. I sure as hell would prefer to sleep in a tent after a nice supper. Boy, you get on the mare and steady her as we cross. She might get excited in the deeper water and you can calm her a bit. I'll stay on the buckboard."

Luke didn't like the idea but hoisted himself up on the horse and they started across. As they approached the center section of the river, Luke felt the cold water soak through the shoes on his dangling feet. He also felt the mare's hooves starting to slip on the gravelly bottom. He looked back and saw the buckboard slip a couple of feet downstream, then grab again. The mare took a couple more steps, lost her traction and started to swim. Almost immediately, her hooves touched the river bottom, and just as quickly, she lost her step again. Luke realized it was too shallow to swim and too deep to walk. He looked back and saw the wagon lose its bite and sweep downstream, pulling the horse down also.

"God damn it, we've got hell to pay now, boy," the sergeant said, his face getting red.

Luke looked back and he could see the panic in the sergeant's eyes. Just then the sergeant jumped off the wagon saying, "Jump, boy, jump for your life!"

Luke responded, but differently. He slid into the cold water, pulled the reins through the yoke loops and started to swim downstream with the panicked horse. The reins were about fifteen feet long and he angled his strokes toward the opposite bank. Now, however, the wagon was pointed backward — directly down current — and the mare was trying to swim straight upstream, which was the only thing she could do. As Luke moved, he started to gain his footing and he pulled both horse and rig toward him. Finally the mare caught her traction, and Luke and the horse managed to pull the wagon to safe ground.

Luke put his arm over the mare's neck and she quickly calmed down. There appeared to be no damage to the rig.   As Luke walked around, he remembered the sergeant. "Sarge! Sarge, where are you?" No answer.

He threaded the reins back through the yoke loops, jumped up on the buckboard and turned again downstream. "Sarge! Sarge! " he kept yelling. Luke told himself to stay calm as he scanned both sides of the creek. Then he saw something in the dim light on the water's edge. He jumped down. It was the sergeant, lying half in the water and half out, with his head face down in the mud.

Luke managed to pull the sergeant out of the water. He put his hands on the sergeant's back and pressed down firmly. Water came forcefully out of the sergeant's mouth. He started to move and gurgle.

Luke smiled at him saying, "Didn't know you couldn't swim; you okay?"

"Hell, yes, I'm okay. I was just resting."

"Sure you were." Luke helped the sergeant up and they walked to the buckboard. Then he gave him a boost up into the buggy seat.

With Luke driving, they headed back to the road.

"Thanks, kid," the sergeant murmured softly.

"Just tell me how to get to camp, you old goat."

It was completely dark by the time Luke and the sergeant arrived at the camp. The first thing that struck Luke was how big it was. He had envisioned possibly ten, or even twenty, tents, and twenty to forty new soldiers. Instead, he saw several rows of campfires, only a few tents, and scores of men huddled, trying to keep warm in the chilly night air. Luke himself felt very cold, as his clothing had not yet dried.

The sergeant instructed Luke to pull the wagon up to a tent set apart, with a flag posted on top. Walking up, the sergeant saluted an officer standing in front and asked to see the colonel.

The colonel, John Murray, came out and eyed the two wet men in front of him. The sergeant had lost his hat in the river. They both looked pathetic.

"What happened to you, Sergeant? You look like you've been trying to ride the north end of a south-bound horse."

Several of the colonel's aides snickered. Luke remained silent.

"The bridge just north of here a couple of miles has been destroyed, sir. We went downstream to ford across, but we got swept away and nearly drowned."

"Hmmm...must have been some Yankee sympathizers in the area. We have reports they have been creating havoc all over eastern Tennessee. What have you here?" the colonel said as he shifted his gaze to Luke.

"Sir, this here is Luke Pettigrew. He's a new recruit from just east of Crossville. He was waiting for me at the general store."

The colonel gave Luke a long, appraising look and without extending his hand said, "Glad to have you." Then he said to his aide, "Take Private Pettigrew to the quartermaster, get him a dry uniform and find someone he can share a tent with."

"Yes, sir," he said, and motioned to Luke, "Come with me."

The sergeant turned to leave with the two of them when the colonel said, "Wait a minute, sergeant, what do you know about this boy?"

"Not much, sir. He left home over some kind of disagreement with his parents. Wouldn't talk about it much. On the ride here, though, our horse was going lame and he handily took care of it. Seems like he has a good way with animals. Also, I might tell you that when we got swept downstream in the river, I thought I was a goner. Luke pulled me out of the water and got me goin' again. He seems to be a resourceful lad, with a cool head."

"You say he's good with horses?" Without waiting for an answer, the colonel asked another aide to go get Sergeant Hayes. "You are dismissed, Wilmont."

Sergeant Buford Hayes was the equivalent of quartermaster for the company. He was in charge of food supplies, what few uniforms they had, as well as arms and ammunition. He was only a sergeant, but the colonel thought highly of him and most people figured him for officer material. He reported to the colonel as requested.

"Sir?" he said as he saluted smartly.

"Hayes, I am assigning a new recruit to you. His name is Pettigrew— forgot his first name already — but according to Wilmont, he shows some talent for handling horses, so you might find him helpful. Assigning him to you will mean he won't have to march and drill with the rest of us, so keep an eye on him. It would not serve us well if he just strutted around bragging to the others. You know how that goes."

"Yes, sir, thank you, sir. He will be working much harder than the boys who only have to march up and down the field all day. We'll see what he's made of."

"I'm sure you will, Sergeant. Let me know how he works out. Now get out of here so I can get some work done."

The next morning after a warm breakfast, Luke, sporting faded gray clothes that were supposed to be a uniform, and having heard he was to report to Sergeant Hayes, sought him out. As he walked over to the wagons and supplies, he noticed a squat middle-aged man with some stripes on his arms. He was moving six horses out into an open area.

"Good morning, sir, Luke Pettigrew reporting. My first day..." He saluted awkwardly.

"Where have you been, boy?" the sergeant retorted. "We start work around here before sun-up, not two hours later. I'm not going to make this a big deal, but from now on, your duties will start one hour before sunup and I expect you to be here promptly."

Luke said nothing. He just stood there, slack-jawed and embarrassed.

"Now take these horses over into that grassy area, stake them out so they can feed all day, water them with those pails over there, curry each one, then report back."

"Yes, sir," Luke said meekly.   He took the tethers from the sergeant and moved off. Luke felt he had been unjustly reprimanded but he was determined to try to please his new boss. He quickly staked the horses at about twenty feet apart and gave water to each. As he curried them, he noticed the horses were in good shape: well fed and cared for and of decent stock. One horse was a large chestnut, and his right front shoe clicked when he walked. Luke went over to the supply tent, found a farrier hammer and secured the shoe.

Finishing up, he looked for the sergeant, but the sergeant found him first. Sergeant Hayes told him to go to the mess tent and carry whatever they needed from the storage area. Luke found out the mess tent was not where food was prepared; it was an area from which food was handed out. Each soldier was in charge of his own meal.

Luke was kept busy all day and into the late evening. When the sergeant told him he was through for the day, he also reminded him to show up the next morning at five. Luke went back to his tent, which was not really a tent – it was a lean-to held up by a sapling strung between two trees over which was draped a piece of canvas. Everybody else had eaten, and most of the fires were flickering out. Luke ate some hardtack, lay down on his blanket and fell asleep.

For the next several days, Luke's routine was pretty much the same: up before light, work all day doing the various duties assigned, and finish in the late evening. The bulk of the new recruits practiced marching all day under the watchful eye of the colonel. Luke did not know the colonel's background, but he assumed he had some military experience. The marching would start in the morning in small groups, then in larger columns, and by the end of the day, the whole camp would march to a fife and drum. They would perform counter-marches — broad sweeping turns to the left and right. They would form lines and march abreast of each other, then fall back into rows, then all over again — and again.

The order finally came down to be ready to leave camp the next morning at four. The rumors flew about where they were headed, but the consensus was they were to join General Albert Sidney Johnston, who was amassing his army near Corinth, Mississippi, several hundred miles west and south of their present location. All the soldiers were issued five days' rations, a job that fell to Sergeant Hayes and Luke. It was well after midnight when the last soldier passed through the line. Then Luke was told to load the three wagons with all the remaining supplies — and to have the teams hitched up and ready to go at first light. He and Sergeant Hayes would be the last to leave camp. Luke was exhausted, but he figured he would be driving one of the teams, so he wouldn't have to march.

For Luke, the reality of war was about to take a giant leap closer.

Chapter 6

ZACH

That evening the mood was relaxed. Zach sat at one of the campfires in the middle of a large array of tents some distance away from Pittsburg Landing on the Tennessee River. The weather was already cool, and he huddled near the fire, listening to the hushed conversations around him. He had been assigned to a group of veterans who had seen action at Forts Henry and Donelson. The men were speculating on what Grant and Sherman were planning, and more importantly, on what it meant for them.

They knew they were headed southwest toward Corinth, where the newly named Army of the Mississippi, under Generals Johnston and P. G. T. Beauregard, was positioned to defend the two main railroads that intersected there. They were on the offensive. They did not expect to be attacked, and had spent no time building fortifications. They had heard sporadic musket fire during the day, but sentries were well posted, as were pickets. The consensus was that the shots heard were merely small clashes between pickets or minor probes.

As Zach listened to the conversations, his thoughts drifted home. So far, his experiences were everything he had expected.

He had seen vast country he had never seen before — large cities with hundreds, even thousands, of busy factories spewing out untold products, and rich countryside abundant with livestock and fertile farmland. He had met other soon-to-be soldiers who shared the dream of going to war. However, he missed his mother's hot dinners and his warm bed. He missed wandering into his father's workshop, peering over his shoulder and talking about his work. He had a slow, longing feeling in the bottom of his gut. He was homesick.

Several weeks ago, General Sherman had been made commander of the 5th Division, but his reception had been lukewarm at best. The regulars worried about going to war under a man who may have used his U.S. senator brother to secure his commission. Additionally, he had been sent home with the suspicion that he was insane. When he returned — with a promotion and a new command —many had wondered whether that was more of his brother's influence.

These doubts had been erased, however, when shortly after he took command, he was ordered to strike south in a surprise attack just across the Mississippi line at the Memphis and Charleston Railroad. Under torrential rains, Sherman transported his men up the Tennessee River in steamships and disembarked around midnight. The rains continued through the night as they sloughed toward their target. Forward scouts had a very difficult time, losing several horses and men trying to cross swollen creeks. With the Tennessee River rising, and the possibility that their return route might be completely flooded leaving no escape route, Sherman ordered everyone to return to camp.

Although the mission was a failure, the men thought their commander prudent. In spite of the potential for glory, he made the rational — and right — decision to stop the mission.

The men of the 5th felt good, both about their general and about themselves.

So, as they sat around the fires, they were at ease. They had a good general. They were well fed and well stocked. They believed they could attack Johnston, drive him south, and destroy the last remaining east-west artery for arms and supplies heading east.

The next morning was Saturday, April 5th, and Zach awoke to the sound of the bugle. The weather was mild but wet. The camp still seemed relaxed, even as sporadic musket fire could be heard from the south.

Zach's orders from Lieutenant McCoy had been to position himself behind the Federal encampments in such a manner as to be able to sight his two major targets, Rebel cannoneers and Rebel officers. This task seemed simple enough, but how, when and where? Zach assumed that he was one of only a few sharpshooters assigned to this regiment. And, as he hadn't met others, he thought he might be the only Federal sharpshooter in the 5th Division. His deployment had been generally left up to him.

The enemy appeared to be somewhere between the camp and Corinth to the south, so Zach reasoned that he would have to fire in that direction. He was granted permission to scout the area to the east and south to get an idea of the lay of the land. He left the camp, heading directly east with the intention of making a big arc, returning to camp from the southeast.

He proceeded behind Shiloh Church, where he saw many officers and horses and a high degree of activity. He got a glimpse of General Sherman and assumed it was the 5th Division's command headquarters. A steady flow of couriers rode in and out carrying messages to various regiments. As he continued east, he found himself in front of General John McClernand's Union camps. The land was a gently rolling plateau, with large trees and bushes, offering little high ground for elevated firing positions.

Continuing even further to the east, he came upon an old, dilapidated cabin set on the north edge of a cotton field and a peach orchard in full bloom. Next to the cabin were a few large hardwood trees. Zach thought they would offer a broad view over the cabin, past the cotton field, and into the peach orchard. Also, the greenery of the trees could provide ample cover from which to fire unseen. Moving on, he now found himself behind Brigadier General B. M. Prentiss' troops, which surely would be moving forward when they marched toward Corinth. He decided this position would have no value because he would be too far from any action that might occur.

Traversing the Hamburg-Savannah Road, Zach continued angling further east and south, passing in front of troops belonging to Colonel David Stuart. After crossing a small creek, he came to Bark Road, on which he proceeded west to the main Corinth Road.

He had not walked more than two hundred yards on this road when he heard horses approaching. Not knowing exactly where he was, he fled into the scrub bushes just in time to watch a formation of mounted troops ride by at a fast gallop. He could hear the sound of their sabers rattling in their scabbards and the panting of the horses. He was within ten feet of the road, but his view was obstructed by the bushes. Finally, after they passed by, he could see the last riders from the rear. Their uniforms were not Union. It was the first time he had seen the enemy. He realized he had walked too far; quite possibly, the Confederate troops were closer than many thought. He remained hidden, trying to gather his senses. He found himself shaking as he realized he most probably would have been shot, had they seen him.

After waiting several minutes, Zach crept back toward the north. After he had crossed a small stream, he got up and started running. He ran until he arrived back at the southern end of the peach orchard he had seen several hours earlier. He found his way back to camp and sought out the first officer he could find.

Zach approached the officer, saluted, and said, "Sir, I just saw a large group of Confederate cavalry just to our south, sir." He had spoken so fast he did not even know if he had said it correctly.

"Now, slow down, boy. Who are you?" the lieutenant asked. "And where is your rifle?"

"Zach Harkin, sir. I am attached to General Sherman as a sharpshooter. I have been trying to get the lay of the land in front of our camps in case we should have any action nearby in the next several days."

"Okay, what did you see and where?"

Zach explained what he had seen. The officer seemed dismissive, saying, "There is no enemy nearby in force, but you should stay closer to camp."

Most of the soldiers in camp were busy marching. It seemed everybody was always marching. Because of his unique assignment, Zach was excluded from this duty, and he was happy for it, but some of the other men in his regiment thought he was getting special treatment. They thought he was a slacker, and some said so.

Zach sat down next to a small cedar tree, his mind occupied: How to deal with the perception others had of him and how to be prepared when they became engaged in skirmishes or battle. He decided to take his gun apart and re-oil all the components. He would be ready for the action to come.

While he was working on his rifle, his unit returned to camp from a full day of marching. The men were tired, sweaty and hungry. When they saw Zach under the shade of the tree, they did not try to hide their resentment.

"Did you have a hard day?" one of them mocked.

Another said, "Did we wake you up? Can we cook you some supper?"

Zach had just finished reassembling his rifle when a feisty soldier hollered from the rear — not to Zach but to the others — "Yeah, just because he has that fancy contraption of a rifle, he thinks he can loll on his ass all day. I bet that rifle can't shoot any straighter than mine!"

Shortly, about a dozen men had gathered around. Someone taunted, "Sounds like a challenge, why don't we find out?"

The feisty one, whose name was Barney, did not back down, but realizing he may have issued a challenge prematurely, said, "You pick a target at 300 yards and we'll see if he's any good."

Another said, "Three hundred yards? Are you sure, Barney?"

"Hell, yes. I can hit a squirrel at more than three hundred yards."

"Okay, if you really want to do this, closest five shot pattern. You go first," said Zach.

Barney took charge, stepping off 300 steps and posting a piece of paper on a low-hanging tree limb. By now, it seemed like the whole camp had gathered around, including a few officers. Barney came back to the middle of the group, loaded his gun, and with a smirk on his face took a prone position and placed his rifle on a nearby knapsack. He pointed his rifle at the piece of paper. He carefully sighted at the paper and pulled the trigger.

Zach could tell Barney was an old hand with a rifle. He drew a deep breath before each shot and squeezed the trigger rather than pulling it. While reloading, he handled the gun expertly and with a high degree of confidence. This was a man who grew up with a rifle in his hands.

After the five shots, one of the men raced out to retrieve the paper target. When he looked at the paper he uttered, "Holy smoke! Barney, this is some of the best shooting I have ever seen!" He showed it to the onlookers and they all chimed in with expletives equally laudatory.

All five shots were in a three-inch pattern.

"Wow!"

"Yeah, nobody can shoot better than this!"

Zach looked at the paper and seconded everybody else's comments. "Going to be hard to beat."

"Should we get another paper target or do you just want to give up?" Barney said with a cocky voice.

"Maybe not a piece of paper. Does anybody have some biscuit flour and a nail?" Zach asked.

No one answered immediately, baffled by the question. One of the camp's cooks said he had both and ran off to fetch them. When he returned, Zach said, "Okay, Barney, if you don't mind, take this nail and pound it into that same limb. Place it so the head of the nail faces in this direction and leave about two inches sticking out. Then, put a bit of the flour on the head so I can see it."

As Barney trotted back to the tree limb, the others slowly figured out what Zach was going to attempt. Murmurs at first, then chuckling, then guffaws. From that distance, most would not even be able to see the small target, let alone come close to hitting it.

Zach inserted five bullets into his rear-loading Spencer and took the same prone position Barney had, using an old log for a prop. After checking what little breeze was in the air, he sighted toward the white nail. He knew after he hit the nail the first time, the white flour would disappear. This meant he had to make sure he knew exactly where it was for his last four shots. This took some time, and the men, who had been very quiet, started to get impatient.

Finally, Zach was ready to fire. He rubbed his trigger finger on the stock, adjusted slightly for the breeze, relaxed, took a deep breath, exhaled, half-breath, hold… He squeezed off the first shot and in the next twenty seconds, fired the remaining four, never taking the spider lines off the target. The smoke lingered as he rolled over on his side and said, "Let's all go over and have a look."

By now, everybody in hearing range was gathered around. They all walked the three hundred yards to the target. The few who got there first just stood looking and scratching their heads. Barney could not find the exact spot where he had put the nail.

"The nail is gone," he snipped. "Looks like it must have flipped out. Anyway, there is only one hole here; you must have missed the whole limb with four of your five shots! You had better learn how to march. Maybe I can be a sharpshooter and lie around all day."

One of the officers drawn to the melee was Colonel David Stuart. The men separated as he approached Zach, Barney and the others. All were silent. They did not know if they were in trouble for making noise, and all thought silence was the best defense. The colonel looked at the single hole in the limb, then he looked down on the ground, saw the nail and picked it up. He held the nail next to the hole, thought about it and said, "Boys, we have a real sharpshooter here. This nail has been driven through the tree limb as if it'd been hit with a hammer. The shot pattern is no wider than the bullet itself! Son, come over and see me before daybreak tomorrow morning. You'll find us on the far left flank." He disappeared in the crowd.

Disbelief and silence. Nobody could find words.

"Damn," a soldier said.

"Some kind of shooting!" said another.

The crowd broke into a cacophony of praise. Many came up to shake Zach's hand, others to pat him on the back. Zach felt his face getting red with embarrassment.

"Guess this means no marching for you. I thought I was pretty good, but you are too much for me," said a sheepish Barney.

After all the excitement wore down and the evening mess was over, Zach was again thinking about the coming day and how best he could prepare for whatever was on the horizon. He wondered what Colonel Stuart had in mind. On a hunch, he walked over to a sutler's wagon and obtained a small hatchet and a light rope. He just might be able to use an old trick he had learned while hunting turkey back home.

That night Zach had trouble sleeping. He had a feeling the next day would offer some of his first action and that thought was both exciting and frightening. He finally dozed off, thinking of being home again and of a warm cozy bed.

Sherman, although not anticipating an attack, had studied a map of the area and noticed a possible weakness on the far southeast corner of the plateau. He reasoned — correctly — that if an attack occurred, it would be logical for Johnston to try to turn the Union away from the Tennessee River, so he placed Stuart's brigade south of General W.H.L. Wallace on the far left, even though it split his own command and put Stuart over a mile east of his commanding officer.

Colonel David Stuart, born in Brooklyn, New York, graduated from Amherst College, studied law and practiced in Detroit. At the outset of the war, he raised two thousand volunteers and equipped them at his own expense. He was commissioned a lieutenant colonel, then became a full colonel, and on this morning he commanded the 2nd Brigade in Sherman's division.

On the morning of April 6th, 1862, the entire Union Army was under strict orders not to engage or incite any action with the Rebels. General Henry Halleck, commander of the Department of Mississippi and all forces in the Western theater, wanted Grant to hold off any action pending the arrival of General Carlos Buell's Army of Ohio, which was marching overland from Nashville. Buell's army of thirty thousand seasoned veterans would give Grant numerical superiority, and upon his arrival — expected any day — Grant would then move on Johnston toward Corinth.

Zach arrived at Stuart's headquarters well before dawn. He was surprised at all the activity in the tent. The colonel was sitting on a makeshift bench, writing dispatches that were being picked up by riders who were to deliver them to several officers in his brigade. Stuart wanted to be certain that his officers did not initiate any action.

As dawn broke, Zach could hear sporadic gunfire west toward Shiloh Church. The men in the camp seemed to be used to it, assuming it was the same kind of picket firing that had been going on for several days.

"Son, I have cleared it with your commanding officers. You are temporarily assigned to me. After seeing your marksmanship yesterday, I think you may be able to help us. The Rebs are to the southeast, and I want you to position yourself to target their leaders. We do not expect to be moving from this area anytime today, but get ready. Report to me again this evening."

Knowing he was being dismissed, Zach mumbled, "Yes, sir," and walked away. The camp was on the edge of a small apple orchard, with clear views of several hundred yards from the southeast to the southwest. His best method of obtaining a longer distance view would be from a tall tree.

Despite the belief that the Rebel Army was still at Corinth twenty miles away, Stuart's brigade had formed defensive lines slightly to the southeast of their camp. Early that morning, Stuart had allowed his men to make sure their weapons were in good working order by firing at a small hill on the other side of a creek called Locust Grove Branch. The discharging of the muskets had masked the sounds of an initial attack by the Rebels on the division next to Stuart, which was commanded by General Prentiss. When Stuart received a message from Prentiss stating he was being attacked, he deployed his men, while still maintaining a company to guard the Lick Creek Ford. Controlling the road over Lick Creek Ford would help prevent the Rebels from rolling up the Union's left flank and eventually deny access to the Pittsburg Landing.

As the morning progressed, the sporadic gunfire from the south and west intensified, sounding like vast amounts of popcorn popping over a heated fireplace. It sounded as if they were being directly — and closely — attacked. The heavy gunfire and the men screaming just to the south confused Zach. The camp

•

was nearly vacated and he stood there, stunned, not knowing what to do. He had not been given specific orders.

Suddenly, a wounded man staggered back to the camp. He did not stop – just kept moving to the rear. Then Zach saw two more, then ten more, bloody and bleeding, all rushing to the rear. The men were running for their lives. The noise increased; the firing intensified, sounding like the tearing of heavy fabric, slow then fast then slow again. Zach, shaken into action, ran to the tallest hardwood tree on the northwestern edge of the camp. He quickly roped his rifle to the cedar boughs he had cut the previous day. He took one end of the rope and climbed up as high as the limbs would allow. When he reached a spot where he could perch and see, he pulled up the bundle. Sitting on the limb, he stuffed cedar branches, one at a time, into the legs of his pants, his sleeves and under his belt. Then he took the remaining branches and tied them around his waist so that the ends of the limbs extended over his face. Moving was difficult, but he placed the gun on his lap and started to wait, hoping he was hidden well enough.

He would be up in his tree much longer than he anticipated.

As the flow of wounded soldiers increased, the carnage taking place on the front lines became more and more apparent. This was the real thing, happening under his tree. Men running without hands or arms. Men crawling without feet or legs. Men screaming with belly shots and neck wounds.

At first, the retreating Federals were the wounded and the occasional able-bodied men helping them. Next came able-bodied men, many screaming, "Run for your lives!" "We've been outsmarted!" "Johnston's whole army is out there, run to the river." At the same time, Northern officers were bringing up reserves. As the retreating soldiers ran north, the fresh soldiers ran south. When the reserve soldiers, who were exuberant and anxious to get into the fray, met the retreating columns, it was like a second tsunami hitting the back flow of the first. Most of the forward momentum of the second wave was lost. The result was chaos.

The reserve soldiers slowed up the Confederate advance for a while. While the flow of the retreaters ebbed a bit, the intensity of the gunfire increased. Zach thought the resistance was holding. His line of sight was nothing like he had hoped. He could see directly down into part of Stuart's camp, and he could see way out in the distance, but his near field of vision was limited to the orchard, which was bordered by scrub and trees.

The din of battle, the carnage and the confusion was overwhelming. The cacophony of gunfire, cannons, horses and wounded men stopped time and thought. This was not the kind of war he had envisioned. His poorly conceived notions had been naive. Zach wanted to flee but he could not move. He could not think clearly.

It was a full-blown rout. Federal lines broke completely. Officers tried to make the retreat orderly. "Fall back, men. Slowly, now. Follow me to reform!" Some of the bluecoats were running in full panic. Some threw their rifles down so they could run faster; they threw down their canteens and knapsacks, anything to lighten their load. Other officers were in full retreat and had no ability to control the panic sweeping across the Northern soldiers.

Looking to the south over the top of the trees and brush that bordered the orchard, Zach could see an even more harrowing scene. Rebel lines were moving rapidly in his direction. In addition, horse-drawn Rebel caissons and cannon were being rushed into action. Evidently, Johnston was in full attack, for it seemed his whole army was moving toward the camp being vacated by Stuart's withdrawing brigade, over which Zach was hiding.

Then he saw the first Rebels running into the camp, a few at first, then masses of them converging like ants drawn to sugar. Some of the campfires were still burning; the food intended for the routed Union troops was still cooking. For most of the poorly furnished Rebels, the hunger in their bellies far outweighed their thirst for blood. Many had not eaten for two or three days, and the temptation to eat was irresistible. Without talking, they greedily grabbed up anything edible and consumed it. As others came up, they laid their rifles down and started looking into the tents for more.

Zach could hear the hungry men tearing into the food, and he wondered how soldiers could fight so fiercely on empty stomachs.

That thought was brief, however, as more and more Rebels stopped at the camp. When the food was gone, the men started pillaging, searching each tent for whatever valuables they might find. They took diaries, letters, keepsake pictures — anything. One Rebel soldier found a small strongbox, evidently belonging to the brigade's paymaster. The soldier threw the box against the very tree up which Zach was hiding, and the box flew open, sending piles of new U.S. dollars floating into the air. Then, from Zach's right, he saw a small group of Yankees approach carrying a white flag of truce. When they were within easy range, they fired their muskets directly at the Rebels who were ransacking the camp. The looters immediately fired back en masse and killed the entire squad.

To the west, Zach saw an officer enter a tent looking for booty just as a mounted Confederate rode into camp on a tall, stately bay horse. His sword was sheathed on his left side and a pair of binoculars hung around his neck. A gold, braided rope around his waist told Zach he was a very important man, a general.

As the general approached the tents, the officer who had entered one of the tents came out with an armload of plunder. When the general saw him, he said, "None of that, sir. We are not here for plunder." The young officer dropped his loot, embarrassed that he had reduced himself to such low behavior. Sensing his discomfort, the general rode over to a table, picked up a tin cup, held it high and said to all, apologetically, "Let this be my share of the spoils today."

With his right index finger through the handle, he held the cup up high to rally his troops. He rode off, and slowly the looting stopped. The Rebel advance continued. Zach could see thousands of Rebel soldiers heading north, and the thought now hit him: He was behind the enemy lines!

Through all of this, not one soldier had looked up toward Zach.

Perched in the tree, he could not move for fear of being seen. He had tree boughs stuffed into his clothing and the cedar next to his skin had caused a rash that itched, but he could not move to get relief. He had no food or water. His gun rested on his lap, but he could not use it.

The gunfire seemed to be moving north, and he was positioned looking south. Sporadic waves of gunfire spread out from east to west. He could hear cannon fire, but he could not tell whether it was from Rebels or Yankees. The camp below became a gathering point for the Rebels, and one officer made his command post right under Zach's tree.

Zach sat in the tree, alone — wondering how this would end.

Throughout the Civil War, the Union had approximately 1,300 surgeons in the army. The Confederacy had 300.

Chapter 7

LUKE

Spirits were high the next morning as Luke was teaming up horses. Most soldiers were eager to see some action because they did not think the war would last long, and they did not want the war to end before they had a chance to shoot some Yankees. They also felt proud of the training they had received and were confident their unit would preform well.

Rumors were confirmed: They were headed for Corinth, Mississippi. They marched fifteen miles the first day and camped near a small village called Sparta. The men were tired, hungry and thirsty, and all the cheering and yelling had long disappeared. The biggest problem was blisters. A small stream flowed near the camp and many sought relief by soaking their feet in the cool water. The colonel issued announced they would depart again before sunup the next morning, and the groaning sounded like a wave running through the camp as the word spread. The men built small fires and slept in the open, wrapped in their blankets.

Shortly after the march resumed the next morning, the first stragglers started to fall behind. As Luke drove the last wagon, he could see soldiers sitting up against trees with their shoes off, massaging their feet. Later in the day, dozens more fell behind. Sergeant Hayes started to notice some of the stragglers, and if they had problems other than blisters, he would order them to ride in one of the wagons. By the end of the day, ten men with ailments from dehydration to cut feet were riding in Luke's wagon. They did not have a doctor, so each man had to do the best he could to nurse his own wounds.

That evening, after Luke had tended the horses, he noticed a couple of the men who had been picked up were still in the wagons, unable to walk. One young man was lying on the wagon bed with his foot propped up on the wagon seat, his sock and shoe bloodstained. Blood had puddled on the bed of the wagon, so Luke asked, "What happened to you, soldier?"

"My shoes had holes in them before we even started this god-forsaken march," he said. "I cut this foot on a sharp rock this morning and the bleeding will not stop."

It was almost dark and Luke could not see the laceration well, but he knew that the man needed help. "Wait here, I'll be right back."

"I sure ain't goin' nowhere," the wounded man said.

Luke went over to Hayes. "Sarge, that man in the wagon will probably bleed to death by morning if we don't do something about his wound."

"And what in holy hell do you want me to do about it, Pettigrew? I can't babysit these men. We have no surgeon; each man has to help himself."

"But, Sarge, he won't make it. If we could sew his wound shut, it would stop the bleeding."

"Look, kid, I've got a lot to do here just to get ready for tomorrow's departure. If you want to play nursemaid, well so be it, but only if you have all your regular duties finished." He walked away. Luke felt he just couldn't let the guy die right there on the wagon. He remembered seeing his father sew up one of their cows after it had been kicked by another.

"Hey, Sarge, do we have any needle and thread?"

The sergeant stopped, turned around and appeared to be about ready to explode. He saw the look of compassion in Luke's eyes, changed his expression slightly and muttered, "God damn it! You don't give up, do you? Okay, we have a needle or two around here but no thread." He motioned to a haversack near the wagon and said, "You might find a needle in there."

"Thanks, Sarge." Luke found a needle. He took a small bucket and went to the stream, filled it and returned to the wounded soldier.

"What's your name?" Luke asked. "If I am going to sew you up, at least I should know who you are. If I screw this up and you kick the bucket, we will at least have some record."

"Just call me Willie. I heard you talking to the sergeant, and I sure appreciate your help."

"Maybe thanks will be uncalled for. If we don't stop this bleeding, you won't be alive to thank me. I'll be right back."

Luke went over to the area where the horses were staked and pulled several hairs out of one of their tails. He walked back to Willie. "I need a piece of your shirt," Luke said and tore off a small section. He dipped the cloth into the water and washed the bottom of Willie's foot until the wound was visible. There wasn't enough light so Luke asked several men to carry Willie from the wagon to one of the fires nearby. Luke could see a trail of blood across the ground.

The other men started to gather around. All were quiet, but were interested in what Luke was going to do. Luke did not let on that he was unsure how to proceed; he did not show any hesitancy. Threading the needle with a long strand of horsehair, he squatted down and propped the bleeding foot on his thigh. After washing the blood away again, he said, "Willie, this will hurt a bit, but not for too long."

Willie said, "What is your name?"

"Luke."

"Luke, somehow I get the impression you may not have done this before."

"You've got that right. Okay?"

"Have at it, Luke."

Luke blotted the blood away again. The cut was on the ball of Willie's right foot and extended from the root of the big toe almost to his arch. He started near the arch where the skin was thinner. Willie winced as Luke pushed the needle through the first time, and he had trouble not instinctively withdrawing his foot. Luke pushed the needle through on the other side of the cut, drew it up and tied it off. He did it again. As he got to the thicker skin on the ball of the foot, he had to push hard with the needle, but by then Willie was steadier and did not wince. Luke made the last stitch and tied it off, then washed the whole area. The bleeding stopped.

A murmur of approval passed through the dozen or so men who were standing around. "Nice work, kid," one said.

"Okay, Willie. Let's wrap your foot up real tight and you should be good to go. You will need some sort of crutch to walk, because it will be a while before this suture can take your walking on it."

Willie, who could not see the wound or the job Luke had done, said, "Don't know how to thank you, Luke. I owe you."

Standing in the background was Sergeant Hayes. When Luke was finished, he walked away, not saying anything.

The next day, after traveling very rough and hilly terrain, the troops crossed the Tennessee River and boarded a Memphis & Charleston train bound for Corinth, Mississippi. The train was long and was carrying thousands of soldiers who were joining General Albert Sidney Johnston's Army of the Mississippi.

The little town of Corinth had been thrown into chaos. Thousands of soldiers spread out almost as far as the eye could see. Men yelling, horses neighing, creating a visual and audible chaos. Luke attached himself to Sergeant Hayes, who seemed not quite as much awed as he proceeded through the maze of confusion. Hayes had been told the 28th Tennessee Regiment was to camp to the northeast just outside the town. Finally, both Luke and Hayes saw Colonel Murray standing up in his saddle, waving his regimental flag and yelling for his unit to gather around him. As the men came together, they were ordered to form up columns and wait for the colonel to get his orders. It was quite some time before the colonel returned and notified his officers they were assigned to the 3rd Brigade under the command of Colonel Winfield Statham, which in turn was assigned to the Reserve Corps under Major General John Breckinridge.

As various new arriving regiments started forming up lines, a semblance of order began to appear amid the confusion. Luke, standing well behind the columns, could see the huge number of soldiers being assembled. Rumors were rampant about what was going to happen, and they all agreed the battle was going to be big and happen soon.

Colonel Murray made it clear to Hayes that his job was to work with the regimental quartermaster in the requisitioning of all the materials they would need. This included seven days of rations, ammunition, wagons, horses and rifles for any men who did not have them yet. Hayes started walking toward the quartermaster's staging area, which was southeast of Corinth, near the train depot. As he approached the area, he was surprised to find an old friend from his hometown near Nashville. John Herbert had married his sister and was a practicing medical doctor in Nashville. Hayes did not know he had enlisted, but knew he was a very good man and an excellent doctor.

"John? What the hell is someone like you doing in this god-forsaken place?"

"Guess I could ask you the same question," John said as he extended his hand good-naturedly. "Looks like we have a hell of a storm coming."

"Yeah, rumors are a flying, but looks like Mr. Grant wants this little railroad crossing right here, and Mr. Johnston ain't about to give it to him," Hayes said, gesturing toward the depot.

"It's all or nothing in this little spot all right. They say these two rail lines are the vertebrae of the Confederacy, and if we lose them, we lose the whole Mississippi Valley."

"Pretty damned scary, if you ask me. I hear Grant has hundreds of large steamers coming down the Tennessee and is amassing one hundred thousand men at Pittsburg Landing," added Hayes as he spit on the ground. "What are you doing here?"

"I volunteered when the army left Nashville. I figured my services would be needed badly, but little did I know when I signed up how bad this was. We have around forty thousand men right here, ready to do battle, and I am one of only three surgeons I know of to possibly handle thousands of injuries. Shit, this is going to be a bloody disaster. I can see a field hospital in a couple of days with hundreds and hundreds, maybe even thousands of wounded just lying out in the sun with the flies."

"Sure wish I could help you, John. But at least you won't be on the front lines getting shot at, and I'm sure my sister is relieved about that."

"Thanks, Hayes. Didn't mean to cry on your shoulder. I've got to go. Are you still the quartermaster?"

"Yeah. Safer, though. Good luck, John."

They shook hands again, and as Hayes started to walk away, he had an idea he thought might help his good friend and brother-in-law. "John, could you use a good helper? Somebody comfortable around the wounded and pretty good with a needle?"

"Hell, yes."

"Okay, I'll need to do some talking, but let me see what I can do."

They parted. Hayes continued to the depot area and searched for a man in charge. He finally found somebody who knew what he was doing, loaded a wagon with the supplies he needed, and told him he would send a soldier named Luke to fetch the remaining goods and another team and wagon. As he was driving the rig back to the regiment, he could hear musket fire far ahead.

A general mobilization was taking place that he had not noticed just hours before.

Back at the 28th's bivouac area, the men were all gathered, nervously awaiting some word from command on what was going to happen. Rumors were rampant. Many predicted that the anticipated arrival of Grant's Army of the Tennessee, thought to be one hundred thousand strong, would mean Johnston would be forced to retreat further to the south. Johnston had been retreating for weeks, giving up Kentucky and most of Tennessee, and very few thought he would make a stand here. In addition, they heard General Carlos Buell and his Army of the Ohio was near Savannah, just across the river from Pittsburg Landing, which was even more reason for Johnston to retreat.

After several hours of waiting, word finally came. Colonel Murray rode his horse into the middle of the crowd and everybody quieted down, intently interested in what the orders were going to be.

"Men! We have been called upon by our country and God to preserve our rights as a free nation. To protect our homeland from this immoral deprivation of our liberty. To reject this invasion of scoundrels who would impose their way of life on us. To protect our women from the rape and pillage of those huns from the North. To seize the day and push these dastardly encroachers back into the Tennessee River and then drown them in their own blood!"

The men started to cheer, getting louder and louder. They were tired of running away, and in their colonel's voice they could hear redemption as an army. They knew that their march the next morning would be toward the Union camps about twenty miles northeast in the direction of Pittsburg Landing. After several minutes of raucous cheering, the colonel unsheathed his sword and held it high. "Tomorrow, before first light, we move. Not in retreat to the south, but north to meet the enemy on the field of battle. We will have a glorious victory." With the last words, as if on cue, came a bolt of lightning. Another crack of thunder gave the whole scene an almost divine aspect that inspired all who saw it.

Luke was spellbound. The colonel's logic and condemnation of the Northern invasion made perfect sense to him. He wanted to do whatever was asked of him, to do his part to make victory possible. The rain started, and as night approached, the men were issued rations for three days and as much ammunition as they could carry. They tried to build campfires, but the wood they found was too wet. Most did not have anything waterproof and just lay down and tried to get some rest before they had to march again in the morning.

The rains had just let up when the bugle called reveille, raising the men out of a restless, wet night. In spite of the conditions, spirits were high as the men formed into columns. They would begin a fifteen- to twenty-mile hike to meet the enemy. The marching soldiers quickly churned the rain-soaked roads into muddy quagmires, slowing progress down to a crawl. Small streams had turned to rivers, each taking extra time to cross.

They were two days late in reaching the area from which they were to launch the attack, having taken three days to travel what should have been accomplished in one. Rumors were that General Buell had already crossed the Tennessee at Pittsburg Landing, and that they were severely outnumbered. Most thought they would just retreat again.

On the early evening of April 5th, Confederate Generals Polk, Braxton Bragg and Beauregard held an informal meeting less than two miles from Shiloh Church and the Union camps. Beauregard had developed a plan that would sweep to the right along the Tennessee River, forcing Union troops away from Pittsburg Landing and thus denying them the ability to use the river for reinforcements, supply and escape. The intention was to drive them into the swamps to the north. The delay, however, made them change their minds. Beauregard thought the delay had cost them the element of surprise, and he knew General Buell was near Savannah with an additional thirty thousand troops to boost Sherman's forces, which would give them numerical superiority. Polk and Bragg agreed the attack should be canceled. Then General Johnston rode up and joined the discussion in what was later to be called the "council of war." Johnston listened to Beauregard's arguments for calling off the offensive, however, he overruled and said they would attack at daylight. "I would fight them if they were one million," he famously said.

Beauregard, after agreeing not to delay, put one hand on his scabbarded sword and with his other hand pointed to the distant Federal camps. "Gentlemen, we sleep in the enemy's camp tomorrow night," he said.

Beauregard's battle plan was approved by Johnston and issued to all the commanders. Three corps under Generals William J. Hardee, Polk and Bragg would fan out to form a broad front pushing north. Breckinridge's corps was initially held in reserve but was quickly deployed to the right of Bragg.

Luke wasn't sure of the date, but he thought it was April 6th. The one thing he was sure of was it was very early in the morning and he had not slept a wink all night. Already, sporadic gunfire could be heard well to their front, which added an eerie uncertainty to what the day would offer. Luke's job that morning would be to follow his regiment in a wagon pulled by a team of horses to supply ammunition, water and medical needs.

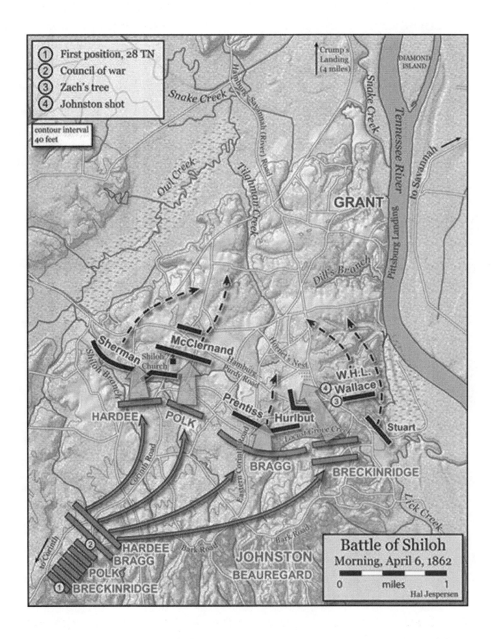

Battle of Shiloh
Morning, April 6, 1862

The widely sporadic musket fire rapidly turned into sweeping waves of intense staccato rifle discharges. The early morning light made the battle more visible, and Luke's brigade started moving forward, ready to fill in as needed. The Confederate surprise attack appeared to be working as the Federal lines sagged and fell back. Soon, wounded soldiers who could still walk started streaming back through the reserve ranks. The first wounded soldier Luke saw had his right hand shot off. His bones were exposed and his clothes were blood-soaked. The man just held up his arm, looking at his missing hand with terror on his face, incredulous. One instant his hand was there, and the next it was gone. He fainted. Some other soldiers tried to assist him, but they were strongly rebuked, told in no uncertain terms to stay in line, no matter what.

Luke had his orders, but this was a fellow soldier. He looked over at Hayes, who was also looking at the fallen man. In an instant, he jumped off the wagon, ran to the wounded man, tore and section of his shirt off, wrapped it around the man's arm just above the wound and pulled it as tight as he possibly could. He then tied it off and ran back to the wagon. The whole thing did not take two minutes.

As Hayes watched him, he was reminded of his idea to transfer Luke to the Medical Corps. He would try to get that done the next day. The way it was going, however, the battle might be over by then.

The 28th kept moving forward behind the advancing lines of the first three corps. With little wind, the smoke from the musket fire shrouded the field. At times the opposing lines of battle could not be differentiated. Then the order came to move up. Colonel Winfield Statham's troops, which included the 15th and 22nd Mississippi and the 19th, 20th and 45th Tennessee, in addition to the 28th, were ordered to fan to the Confederate right. Alongside Statham was the brigade of John Bowen, who had just been promoted to brigadier general six weeks prior. Bowen's brigade consisted of the 9th and 10th Arkansas, the 1st Missouri and the 2nd CSA.

The two brigades marched abreast, heading forward and to the right. They crossed several low areas and by about eleven reached a higher elevation that looked over on a cleared field. As different units moved forward and engaged, the fighting was intense, with musket fire reaching a crescendo, diminishing, then rising again. Engagements did not happen simultaneously across the field of battle, and the sound gave the impression to Luke of waves rippling across water. When the action in front of him would die down, he would take boxes of ammunition to the rear of the front lines so each soldier could access what he needed. Being the only ammunition wagon for the whole brigade made him very busy, and the time flew by.

As the brigades moved forward, the severely wounded and dead would be left in the field, and Luke would have to carefully weave his wagon between the bodies to avoid running over them. Men would be moaning or yelling for water. He wanted to help each one, and to ride by without being able to help made him feel cold-blooded and most of all, guilty – guilty that he felt obliged to obey orders rather than help relieve the men's suffering.

Around noon, Luke was out of ammunition and water. He saw Hayes a distance away and rode over to him to ask where he should go. Hayes said he wasn't sure where the supplies had been moved up, but he should proceed to the rear until he found them. Traveling back through the areas that had been contested earlier in the day, Luke saw more wounded, dead bodies, dead horses.

After replenishing the supplies, he quickly returned to his regiment's lines. By the time he got back, Statham's brigade had advanced another three or four hundred yards to the open field just across a road that extended to the northwest. The Union forces could be seen on the opposite side of the field, with lines of cannon lined up, firing directly into the Southern lines. The Confederate's advance appeared to be bogged down. Casualties were heavy. Just then, Luke saw a tall officer on what appeared to be a thoroughbred bay horse ride in among his own 28th Tennessee. The men were facing north toward the enemy and the officer, who appeared to be a general, rode out in front, exposing himself to the Union line. He rode all along the line, holding a tin cup and tapping each soldier's extended bayonet. The men cheered their commander and started moving forward. The general rode behind the line and proceeded toward General Bowen's brigade, where he raised his tin cup again. Bowen's Arkansas men also began to advance.

The general was risking his life to rally his men, and it seemed to be working. Slowly, the whole line moved forward as the spent Union forces begrudgingly retreated under withering fire. Luke rode forward with his wagon, going across the road and to the edge of the open field. Off to his right, he saw the general again, still mounted on the large bay. The general seemed to falter as another soldier helped him off his horse. Luke got off the wagon and ran to the wounded general. Others were gathered around, so he could not get as close as he would have liked. Reading the expressions on their faces, however, he gathered that the general's condition was not good.

"Who is that officer?" he asked one of the soldiers.

"General Albert Sidney Johnston," was the soldier's terse reply as tears welled up in his eyes.

"Well, Grant, we've had the devil's own day of it, haven't we?"
–William Tecumseh Sherman
"Yes, lick 'em tomorrow, though." U.S. Grant
Evening of the first day of Shiloh, April 6th, 1862

Chapter 8

ZACH

The gunfire off to Zach's northeast was so intense the Confederates called it the "hornets nest" because the flurry of Minie balls reminded them of swarming stinging bees. Directly under his tree, the movement of Confederates slowed to a halt as the enemy soldiers went around the campsite instead of through it. Zach was in an ideal spot and he began to form a rough plan. First, he had to get to the other side of the tree. For the first time in the past six hours he moved his muscles. His rear was numb and his feet had gone to sleep. As he tried to shift his position, several of the cedar boughs dropped down to the ground. He froze, but nobody noticed, so he continued.

Sensation in his legs returned but his line of vision to the north was even worse than it had been to the south. His only clear view was to the northwest onto an area that appeared to be an old cotton field. Union cannon were lined up on the southern and western edges, and they were firing so rapidly, Zach could not figure out how they could see through all the smoke.

Over the next hour or so, Zach could not pick out any targets. The batteries were firing with increased urgency, but the attacking Confederates were hidden from his view. He scoped the area over and over again, waiting. Finally, the cannon were moved

back across the field, and the Union troops appeared to be retreating slowly to the north. With a sinking feeling, he realized
unless something big happened, the Rebels would drive Grant
into the Tennessee River.

As Zach looked out over the carnage, he felt detached from
the battle, not a part of it, like a visitor to a prizefight sitting
safely behind the ropes. To the near side of the field were several farm buildings, and gradually he could see a double line of
butternut infantry emerge, hundreds of men advancing slowly
and firing steadily. As Zach scanned through his scope, he saw a
rider on a horse. The horse was a big bay and the rider was wearing a big wide-brimmed hat. He was the general Zach had seen
earlier with the tin cup. As he watched, the officer on the horse
took the cup and touched his soldiers' bayonets as he rode in
front of them. The officer rode the whole length of the line, then
returned to the front center. A flag bearer came up and posted
next to him. The officer turned around toward the line of battle
and was leading forward with the foot soldiers in close.

Zach realized the general was an ideal target. As the second
line came up, the mounted rider fell back behind the line, staying close. The battle intensified, with both the Union and Confederate lines breaking and filling. At one point, the Confederate
line developed a hole and the general was immediately there,
directing his men to fill it. The Northern line started to waver.

Zach sighted through the scope at the general. Even though
it was nearly five hundred yards, he could see him urging his
men forward, raising the cup in the air. The wind was blowing
toward the target from Zach's position. His scope was sighted for
seven hundred to eight hundred yards, so he estimated he would
have to aim slightly low. The target was moving up and back and
side to side. Zach patiently waited for him to stop briefly while
he was facing away, so he would offer a larger target. Back and
forth he moved. Back and forth, pointing here, then there.

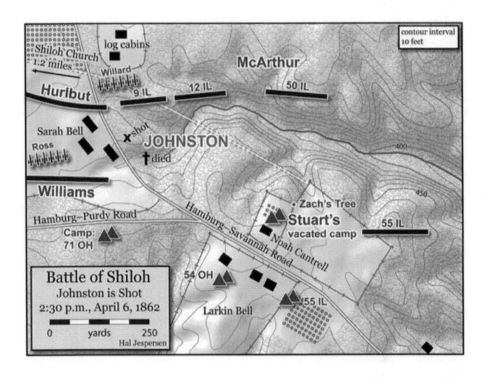

log cabins

Shiloh Church
1.2 miles

McArthur

Willard

Hurlbut

9 IL

12 IL

50 IL

Sarah Bell

Ross

X shot

JOHNSTON

† died

400

Williams

Hamburg–Purdy Road

Camp:
71 OH

Zach's Tree

Stuart's
vacated camp

Noah Cantrell

Hamburg–Savannah Road

55 IL

450

54 OH

55 IL

Larkin Bell

contour interval
10 feet

Battle of Shiloh
Johnston is Shot
2:30 p.m., April 6, 1862

0   yards   250

Hal Jespersen

Zach could see the officer's mouth move as he yelled encouragement to his men. They were evidently inspired by his leadership, because they were moving forward. The general finally stopped and Zach squeezed off a shot, but the general moved again well before the bullet got there. Back and forth. Then he stopped again, facing away toward the battered Union lines, and Zach put the spider lines on the general's hat, rubbed the stock with his trigger finger, took a deep breath, let it half out and squeezed the trigger again. As he shot, he felt a light breeze on the side of his face. The target did not move; he sat in his saddle for a few seconds, seemingly looking off in the distance. Then he rode away and out of Zach's field of vision.

Zach was disappointed, thinking he must have missed his target. The wisp of breeze may have moved his tree just enough to cause the bullet to miss wide. Possibly the wind was blowing more than he'd felt. In previous long-distance shooting, he had at times experienced a phenomenon where a tailing wind would make the trajectory flatter and cause the bullet to strike too low. Whatever the case, it appeared he had lost his chance as the general rode back into the woods.

As the afternoon progressed, Zach could hear the thunderous roar of cannon. He sighted over near the area where he had taken the previous shots, but his vision was blocked by thick clouds of smoke from the fusillades. The roar of the cannon was deafening, even though he was far away. Dozens of cannon were firing at the Yankee lines all at one time. The Northern line was collapsing where it had previously held. Zach had that eerie feeling of detachment again as he watched what seemed to be a rout of the whole left side of Grant's line.

Finally, in the late afternoon, the Rebel advance slowed to a stop. The Federals were out of sight to the north and Rebel stragglers started filtering back into the camp below. It was apparent the Rebels had scored a major victory because the men were upbeat even though they were clearly dog-tired. Zach recognized a few of the men from the morning, though this time they were not looting. Rather, they seemed to be settling in for the night using the Yankee campsite. Bad news for Zach. His body felt numb, as if it didn't belong to him. He was thirsty, hungry, frustrated, and needed to relieve himself.

As time went on, the camp continued to fill with exhausted soldiers. An officer who appeared to be a colonel rode into camp. As he sat astride his large black horse, he said, "Boys, we have done it. The whole Yankee army has been driven back to the Tennessee River, and all the fight has been taken out of them. They have not been reinforced as they expected, and we hold the high ground. We will make camp here tonight, and tomorrow we will finish the mopping up and chase Grant back into Kentucky. What we have done here today is the biggest victory of this godforsaken war and should mean a quick ending so we can all go home to our families and friends."

The cheering men milled around the colonel, exchanging news from the battle. They learned that Union General B. M. Prentiss had been captured and Colonel Everett Peabody killed, and the exhausted men cheered. The colonel told everybody to rest up and be ready to attack again at daybreak. He promised the ammunition wagons would be coming to resupply everybody's needs. As he prepared to leave the camp, a rider approached the colonel. He appeared sober and grave as he handed him a message. The colonel read the message and for a while sat on his horse, not moving, hesitating.

Finally, he sat up straight in his saddle and said, "Men, all has not been perfect this day. I regret to inform you that our commander, General Johnston, was shot and subsequently bled to death. May God rest his soul." The men were silent. "We are now under the generalship of General P.G.T. Beauregard and our orders stand. General Beauregard is confident the Yankees are whipped and we will finish pushing them across the river tomorrow." He rode off.

While Johnston had seen little battle action before Shiloh, he was reputed to be a soldier's general, always just behind the front lines, pushing, encouraging and directing and leading by example. He was an inspiration to the common soldier; he let them know he was not afraid for himself and he expected the same from them. Most of the soldiers in the camp had witnessed his bravery earlier in the day, and his death had a palling effect on one and all. As night approached and they ate what food they could find, a large storm approaching from the west darkened the skies. Those dark clouds would prove to be an omen.

In the darkness, all Zach could think about was the report of General Johnston's death. Could it be? Might his shot have actually hit his target? He reviewed the scene of the shooting over and over again in his mind. Yes, it was possible. As he continued to ponder, he even thought it was likely that his bullet had found its target.

Zach's initial exhilaration slowly ebbed. This man, Johnston, was reputed to be a great general. He had served in the army a long time, probably had a wife and family, and possibly because of him, Johnston was gone. He looked down at his rifle thinking how deadly the weapon was and how one squeeze of the trigger could change lives.

The storm that had been approaching from the west seemed to intensify. The lightning was so frequent it seemed to light up the sky enough to read by. The time between the lightning and the thunderclaps kept getting shorter and shorter. The temperature plummeted. Then the wind brought the rain – giant drops that quickly developed into torrents of water. All the campfires were drenched, and the ground under Zach's tree turned into a blackened quagmire. The wind was blowing so hard the tree started to lean and Zach feared it would break. The cedar boughs he had stuffed all around his clothing blew and twisted, causing them to dig into his skin. He started to pull the limbs out and drop them to the ground. As he shifted his position, he slipped on the wet limb he was sitting on. He grabbed the main trunk of the tree with his left hand but he lost his balance. Instinctively, he reached out with his right hand and his rifle fell from his grip.

Down it fell, hitting several other limbs on the way down until it hit the ground. He could see it lying there as the lightning lit up the sky. Fortunately, the sound of the gun crashing to the ground could not be heard above the din of the storm, and none of the soldiers in the camp, most of whom were under Yankee tents, moved.

Zach straddled the limb, put his arms around the trunk and just held on for dear life as the storm unleashed sheets of water like a fire hose aimed directly at him.

Then a new noise. The sound of cannon. But it wasn't like the cannon he had heard throughout the day's battle, it was a deep-throated roar that sounded like shells exploding. As much as he could tell, the roar was coming from the north, and the combination of the thunder, the cannon fire and the torrential rain made Zach feel like he was at the gates of hell. Zach's parents were devout Methodists, but he had never quite embraced the idea of an all-powerful God. He loved nature and believed his world possibly had a divine order but had not quite figured out what that meant. Maybe now the God he didn't know very well was punishing him for what he had done.

Hours later, the storm passed and the wind died down. The rainfall continued, now coming straight down instead of horizontally. Zach could loosen his grip on the tree and not worry so much about being blown away. He could still see his rifle at the foot of the tree during the lightning flashes. The cannon continued to roar hour after hour. He did not know who was firing the cannon or where they were aimed, but the noise had to be keeping the soldiers on both sides wide awake.

The rush of adrenaline Zach had experienced started to wear off. The temperature dropped down well below fifty degrees and he had no way of warming himself. He was open to the elements, no rain gear, no blanket and no shelter. He started to shiver. His chin began to quiver uncontrollably and his entire body shook. He moved his hands and feet back and forth to try to keep his blood circulating. He took deep breaths, trying to calm his shaking with no success.

He weighed his options. He did not feel he could stay in the tree until daylight, which might still be four or five hours away. By then, who knows, he might find he would not be able to hang on.

He had to do something.

He took his rope and tightly tied one end around his waist. His fingers were so cold, tying the knot tightly took time. He then he put the rest of the rope over the limb he was straddling, reached under the limb and grabbed the rope from the other side, slid off his perch and slowly, hand over hand, let himself down using the wet limb as a pulley. He threaded his way between the limbs. Any noise he made was masked by the rain, thunder and cannon fire. When he reached the ground, he paused for a moment, not knowing whether his legs would support him. Slowly the feeling came back, and he pulled the rope down and coiled it up. He put the rope on the ground and stepped on it, forcing it into the mud, then he scattered some old twigs and leaves to cover it completely. Next he picked up his rifle, noting it had dropped muzzle first, because the barrel was filled with mud. Damage seemed minimal, but he would have to check it all out in the daylight, if it ever came. He laid the rifle on the ground and covered it with the very boughs he had used for camouflage.

He thought about what he would do. He had no idea how far he would have to go to reach the Northern lines. If the reports he heard from the camp earlier were accurate, the lines could be all the way across the Tennessee River. He did not know how far that was, but he knew the Confederates would have a lot of pickets out and if he was sighted, he would certainly be shot. Even if he did make it through the Rebel pickets, he would probably be shot by the Yankee pickets.

With his heart pounding he walked over to the nearest tent. He opened the flap and in a shivering voice said, "Boys, I just got off picket duty. I'm cold and wet. Could I spend the rest of this godforsaken night with you?"

One of the soldiers looked over at Zach, saw a miserable looking young man and murmured, "Only if your teeth stop chattering; you'll wake the whole Yankee army." The soldier rolled over, and Zach lay down in a corner. There were four others in the tent. He tried to stop shivering.

Sleep never came. As he lay there, Zach tried to figure out a plan for the morning, but nothing came to mind. He thought of home and how his life had changed in the four weeks since he'd left. He wondered what would happen in the morning. He thought that if he ever saw his mom and dad again, he would tell them of this day. He was sure nobody would ever come close to believing him.

The lightning storm moved off, leaving the tent in total darkness. However, the cannon fire continued. Gradually, light started to filter in from the east, and the camp started to stir. The men in Zach's tent awoke, and two of them walked outside. Everybody seemed irritable from lack of sleep, spewing profanities about the wet wood and their inability to start a fire. They had little to cook, but a fire would have been nice to warm up and dry out. Zach just lay in the tent with his face buried under part of the bedroll of the soldier next to him. He could hear the sound of regular cannon with increasing intensity. It came from the north. Then he heard the musket fire, creating a din that sounded like the ripping of a piece of heavy cloth.

Just then a rider came into camp at a very fast gallop. "Buell is here, he and his whole army are coming fast. Run! Run for your lives!" He rode off again, heading south. Behind him, some other Southern troops came running through. They had no rifles and were running like scared jackrabbits. "Get out of here, boys. They must have one hundred thousand men out there coming this way. Run or get slaughtered."

Some of the men in the camp grabbed their muskets before they ran, others did not bother. Within several minutes, Zach was the only man there. He smiled to himself as he sat in the tent, wondering what really was happening. Thinking he was out of immediate danger, he got up and walked over to where his rifle was hidden. With one of the blankets, he started to clean his rifle, waiting for the Union troops to show up.

"This horrid confusion, these wet, muddy graves, this reeking mass of corruption, of rotting corpses... How can a man look upon such a scene and still take pleasure in the war seems past belief."
–Berry Benson, Rebel Sharpshooter.

Chapter 9

LUKE

The air was full of pink snow! A peach orchard was in full bloom, and the cannon and musket fire caused the blossoms to fill the air. Like a pink blizzard in April. By four that afternoon, Statham's and Bowen's brigades had advanced further and to the left near a pond and the peach orchard. The Northern position was strong, with lines of cannon firing from the other side of the orchard directly into Bowen's brigade. However, the Confederate troops, with the momentum behind them and the taste of victory in their mouths, just kept pushing forward, the beautiful peach blossoms dropping down on dead or wounded bodies, covering their bloodstained wounds like rose petals on top of a pyre. It was heaven and hell in one picture.

The intensity of the cannon and musket fire reached a crescendo. Statham's and Bowen's men pushed across the peach orchard and around the pond, and by five in the afternoon had helped capture more than two thousand Union soldiers. Even though the Confederates appeared to be in a position to actually push Grant back across the Tennessee, Beauregard ordered a halt to their advance. The fighting was over this first day of the Battle of Shiloh.

Luke sought out Hayes as the firing slowed to a stop.

"We have to help these wounded," Luke pleaded to Hayes. "We cannot let them lie here and die. We can save a lot of them."

"We have work details coming up to take care of these wounded men," Hayes said. "Luke, I think you may be of more use tonight and tomorrow with my brother-in-law, Dr. John Herbert, working at the hospital."

Luke just stood there.

"Get a move on, boy. You can do much more good for us there than you can here." He pointed west, "You'll find the hospital about a mile in that direction. Remember, Dr. John Herbert. He'll be looking for you."

"I saw General Johnston go down today."

"Major loss, but all we have to do tomorrow is mop up, and Beauregard can handle that."

Luke turned to go. "What should I do with the wagon, Sarge?"

"Leave it. You can walk to the hospital in about an half hour."

"Thanks, Sarge. Good luck tomorrow."

The field hospital was just north of where the brigade had started in the morning and just west of General Beauregard's headquarters. A wall tent had been set up in a clearing, and next to it was a gray tarp held up with poles with two tables underneath. Outside were hundreds of wounded soldiers, some sitting up, some lying down on the bare ground, all waiting for the attention of two busy surgeons. Wagons were disgorging more wounded as Luke made his way through the bodies to the tent.

"Doctor Herbert?" asked Luke to the first person he saw inside.

"Yes, what do you want?"

"I am Luke Pettigrew, sir. Sergeant Hayes told me to report to you and said you were expecting me."

The doctor was in the middle of sewing up a soldier who had a gash from his rear buttock to the calf of his right leg. Next to the surgeon was a basin of pinkish red water. John Herbert's white smock was covered in blood, as were his hands and face.

"What makes Hayes think you can be of assistance here, Luke? What experience do you have?"

"None, sir. I have no experience at all. Maybe he sent me over because he thought I had a good way with wounded people."

The doctor extended his suture needle to Luke. "Can you finish this man up?"

Without hesitation, Luke took the hooked needle and began stitching the remainder of the wound. He hadn't worked with a hooked needle before; it made the task much easier. He hooked through the skin and flesh on one side then the other, drew it tight and tied it off and then did it again and again as the doctor looked on.

"You'll do. I have a lot of these kinds of wounds, and you can do them while my partner and I handle the more critical patients." Both of the doctors looked tired. They had been working since the fighting began early in the morning.

Herbert ordered one of the stretcher-bearers to set up another table in the back of the tent. They gave Luke a couple of needles, some suture material, a basin of water and some surgical wrapping. "What's your name?" Luke asked the carrier.

"Name's Horace."

"Okay, Horace, bring me the worst ones first."

"They are all the worst, doc."

"Don't call me 'doc' and we'll get along just fine. Let's get started. Do we have any candles?"

Horace replied affirmatively and left to get some. The daylight was fading, and Luke noticed the two surgeons had a unique way to illuminate their specific work area. It consisted of a reverse bowl-shaped pan made from a shiny metal mounted on a pedestal. A weak magnifying glass was placed in front of the bowl and a candle was inserted in between. The light from the lit candle would reflect off the pan and light the general area, while the light through the glass would provide more intense illumination of critical areas. All from one candle.

Horace brought in a few candles and laid them on the table. Luke lit one and said to Horace, "Let's go out and take a look."

Horace followed Luke into the crowd of wounded men awaiting treatment. Some were moaning softly in dismay, others were yelling and screaming in delirium. Some called for their mothers or other loved ones and others lay in the stupor caused by shock. Luke did not know what hell sounded like, but he was sure this was close.

Luke pointed to five soldiers and instructed Horace to bring them to the table one at a time. All five had minor injuries, deep gashes or cuts that needed more than just a field dressing. With each patient, Luke took his time and tried to do the best he knew how. He would place a couple of candles near the wounds. Then he would bathe the wound with a rag and feel for bone fragments or debris with his finger. After the wound was clean, he would sew it up. It was all done without chloroform because chloroform was in short supply and only used for the more seriously wounded.

As he worked on another soldier, Luke asked John, "How do you decide?"

"What do you mean?"

"With all the wounded out there, how do you pick the next one?"

"When the wounded are brought in, the ambulance drivers usually divide them into two groups. If they have head, belly or chest wounds, they go in one set of rows. If they have wounds to their extremities, they go to another set of rows. Those are the ones we work on. It might sound harsh, but we have only a limited amount of time and resources, and our objective is to help as many as we possibly can in the quickest amount of time. If we operated on one of those poor bastards out there with a gut wound, it would take maybe an hour or two and we would probably lose him anyway. If it's an arm or leg or finger, we can fix it up in short order and move to the next. When a Minie ball hits flesh, it tends to flatten out, making large variegated holes and shattering bones. It leaves a path of destruction that will never heal. If it is an extremity, we can lop it off just above the wound, but if it is in the gut, we have little chance."

Luke worked on.

A soft rain started falling and seemed to wake some of the wounded up or revive them from their state of shock. Their cries of pain got louder.

Around midnight, Luke could tell he was getting too tired to do his work. He was making mistakes. At one point, he made three sutures in the exact same place before he realized what he was doing. "Doctor, I need some rest. I'm no good anymore."

"Me, too, Luke. As soon as I close up here, let's take a break for a couple of hours."

Luke washed the caked blood from his table, washed his hands and face, blew out his candles and lay down right next to the table. A minute later, John lay next to him.

"Big day," John said with a big sigh. Tomorrow will be worse. You are a big help, Luke. I have a couple of ideas on how we could be more efficient." His voice trailed off and he was sound asleep.

Luke still had the excitement of the day in his mind. He lay on his back with his hands behind his head. Just a few weeks ago, he had been home. Home. It was the first time he had thought of it in a while. Thoughts of his mom's cooking, his warm comfortable bed, of riding his horse through the woods... The rain started to come down harder.

"Luke, let's get going." It was John, shaking Luke's shoulder.

Luke opened his eyes and his first thought was that he had not slept at all. It could not have been more than fifteen minutes since he dozed off. "What time is it?"

"Time to get going. Get up and have a cup of coffee. We slept two hours, so we should be good for a while."

"Oooh, my back is as stiff as a board," moaned Luke.

"Wait 'til you get to be my age if you want to complain about your back," John said good-naturedly. "Get some coffee and let's get started."

It was still raining as John and Luke stood under the tarp drinking their coffee when the other surgeon walked up. "John hasn't introduced us, Luke, but I'm Doctor Ley. My friends call me 'Big Ed,'" he said with a smile and stuck out his hand.

At six foot three and over two hundred pounds, Big Ed was big.

"I heard you complaining about your backache. Mine is in pain, too; I have to bend over more than you shorter fellows."

Horace was nowhere in sight, so Luke wandered out in the rain to the nearest tent and opened the flap. "Horace? Are you in here?"

Luke could not see in the dark tent, but he heard about ten different groans, with one of them in the affirmative.

"Let's go, Horace. Big day ahead."

Horace got up, woke the other stretcher-bearers and stepped out of the tent.

"Same procedure; bring the first soldier in."

So it went for the next few hours. At daybreak, the din of the sound of cannons gave way to waves of musket firing as the battle seemed to start all over again. Many had thought Grant would retreat back up the river after being roundly defeated the first day. From the sound of things, that theory was obviously the wrong one.

After Luke had treated what seemed to be a thousand men but was probably closer to twenty, Horace brought in the next patient and laid him on the table. "Holy shit, John, what do I do with this guy?"

John looked over at Luke's table, "What's the problem?"

"For Christ sake, John, this guy is a Yankee!" Luke said as he pointed to his blue uniform.

"So what?"

John walked over to Luke and looked him squarely in the eye. "In this godforsaken hospital, we do not differentiate be-tween gray or blue. Those are all fellow human beings out there, and we will treat one and all equally. Other hospitals may not feel this same way, but all we can do is treat others as we hope they would treat us."

There was not anger in John's voice, only intensity. Luke stepped back. He looked from John's face to the man lying on the table. The man was looking at him. He had fear in his eyes.

The Union soldier had a deep laceration from his right upper pectoral muscle down to the upper part of his right hipbone. The slash was deep, but luckily for him, it had not penetrated the soldier's chest and abdominal cavities. The wound had been wrapped in the field and the bleeding had stopped, but the wound would never heal without sutures.

Luke started to remove the bloodstained dressing. The man still looked pleadingly at Luke. It was at the moment when Luke looked back into his eyes that he realized John was right. This was a human being, just like everybody else. Luke also realized how totally reliant this soldier was on him, Luke Pettigrew.

"We'll get you fixed up right away, soldier. You lost a fair amount of blood, but you are going to be just fine."

The soldier nodded almost imperceptibly and closed his eyes.

Luke took off the dressing and bathed the area thoroughly, making sure the wound was clean. The wound appeared to be a bayonet slash, and if it was, this guy had been very lucky. One half inch deeper and it would have done much more damage. The soldier winced each time the needle was inserted, but he took it all very bravely, and Luke finished up in ten minutes or so.

"There you go soldier. A little rest and you will be as good as new. Try not to put any stress on those sutures for a few days, or you will open up the wound again."

The soldier thanked him.

As Horace came to transfer the soldier out, Luke told him to keep him dry and to be sure he got some water and food.

As the day wore on, the sound of the battle kept creeping closer. The wounded were coming in much faster than before. John asked for a meeting between the three of them.

"We have to find a way to move these wounded soldiers through here faster, or we are going to lose even more. Last night, dozens, maybe hundreds, died just because we could not take care of them. My estimate is that nearly seventy per cent of all the wounded lying on the ground have traumatic damage to one of their extremities. The process is relatively simple. We make incisions on top and bottom of where we want to sever the limb, leaving a flap of skin on one side. We then saw through the bone, tie off the larger arteries, file the bone to get rid of sharp edges and suture the flap over the bone. After we bandage everything up, we move on.

"Now, my idea is, Luke handles the skin flap and the bandaging while we move to the next patient. How does that sound?"

"What about all the patients with cuts and lacerations like the ones I have been doing?" Luke asked.

Big Ed, picking right up on John's train of thought, said, "Luke, the more we can save, the more good we can do. Most of the patients you have treated in the last twenty-four hours or so have not been critical. They can wait until we have more of the critical cases taken care of."

John added, "Right now, we can amputate an arm or a leg in ten or fifteen minutes from beginning to end. If Big Ed and I are freed up to do everything but the sutures and bandaging, we could increase our efficiency. If you get into trouble with a complication, one of us will move right in and take care of it. My guess is that we will handle twenty to twenty-five per cent more patients."

"Okay. I'll do anything you ask. I like the feeling I get when I see a patient leave here with a much better chance to make it than he had before he came. I will need your help on the first couple to make sure I get it right."

"Then let us get started," Big Ed said as he moved back to his table. He motioned to the stretcher-bearers to bring in two more patients who were likely to need amputation.

The new system worked well enough. However, it turned out Luke could not keep up with the two doctors because he just wasn't that fast. When he got behind, the surgeon would finish the patient completely and by then Luke would have caught up.

On and on they worked through the afternoon, stopping only to relieve themselves or have a cup of coffee and maybe some hardtack. Luke's neck and back ached from standing with his head bent down. He was sure the doctors had the same issues, and all three kept at it.

By late afternoon, the distant cannon roar increased in volume while the musket discharges decreased. Soldiers started to stream around the hospital, heading to the rear. Luke heard one say Beauregard had ordered a retreat. Just this morning, most were saying today would be the day they'd sweep the last of the Yankees back into the Tennessee. How could such a reversal be possible? And if Beauregard actually did call for a retreat, would the Yankees take everybody in the hospital prisoner?

Ambulances continued to bring the wounded to the hospital area. As usual, they were laid on the bare ground, the ones with core injuries in long rows, and those with hand and arm wounds in other, even longer rows.

After the wagons disgorged the wounded, workers would pick out the men who had died waiting for medical attention and haul them off to be buried. They were piled onto the wagons like cordwood. Some had their glazed eyes still open and appeared to be staring up to the heavens in anticipation of meeting their Maker. Some were stiff from rigor mortis, and others were still limp, indicating they had succumbed more recently.

The smell of death was everywhere. It came from men who had lost control of their bodily functions or had exposed and perforated entrails, and from corpses whose decomposition had already started. Gone was the glory of any victory on the battle-field. Gone was any sense of human dignity.

A cold north wind blew, and it started to rain again.

"If the enemy come on us in the morning, we'll be whipped like hell!"
–Nathan Bedford Forrest after first day of battle, Shiloh.

Chapter 10

ZACH

The heavy fighting stalled to the south of Zach's tree as a line of Union soldiers came through the camp. They appeared to be part of a reserve element being called up. A sergeant leveled his musket at Zach, who put his hands in front of his face and yelled, "Don't shoot me, I'm from Knoxville, and I have been stuck up in this tree for the past twenty-four hours."

"Yeah, and I'm Abraham Lincoln," said the sergeant menacingly. "What unit are you from, and who is your commanding officer? And where is your uniform?"

"Well, it's a bit of a complicated story, but I have a piece of paper in my pocket that can explain everything. I am a sharpshooter assigned to General Sherman." He removed the telegram out of his pocket and opened it up, but as he glanced at it, he was mortified to see all the ink had bled together from the rain.

The sergeant, who had strict orders to advance as quickly as possible and had no orders on how to handle prisoners, was red with anger. He doubted this kid was a Federal sharpshooter and he strongly suspected he was a Rebel sharpshooter. He stuck his musket in Zach's face and screamed, "You goddamn Southern sons of bitches have been hiding in trees for two days now, shooting at us like the chickenshits you are. You're afraid to fight in the open. I'm going to show you what it's like to get shot, only you will have the pleasure of seeing who shot you. And I'm going to shoot you in the stomach, so you can die nice and slow and think about those of us you shot yesterday."

He moved the muzzle of his rifle down, pushed it into Zach's gut and pulled the hammer back.

"Zach? Zach Harkin? Is that you?"

The sergeant stared over as a tall private from his company approached. "Zach, it's me, John Dickson from the Ohio 54th. We met in Cincinnati."

"You know this guy?"

"Yeah, met him on our way down here from Ohio, and this young man gave us a demonstration of marksmanship that we are still talking about. He ain't no Rebel, Sergeant."

The sergeant acted like he had been robbed of the pleasure of shooting Zach. "Okay, boy. Get off your ass. You are now a part of my company and our orders are to advance. Load that sorry excuse for a musket and let's move. Now! And you, Mister Sharpshooter, I want you right in front me, and if you so much as look to the rear, you're dead. Let's move!"

Zach made sure the barrel of his gun was free of mud and dirt and loaded it as he walked with the others out of camp, heading southwest. The shooting was in a lull. That seemed to be the general pattern of gunfire – rising to a crescendo then falling off, over and over. With the sergeant right behind him, Dickson came up on the other side and whispered to Zach, "Sarge is having a bad day. We lost over half our company yesterday, and he wants revenge any way he can get it. I will be on your right flank."

They found themselves in a wooded area, surrounded by trees and young bushes just leafing out. The fighting was immediately ahead, but the shrubs obscured their vision. For the first time in Zach's life, he felt he was in mortal danger. Bullets were flying, hitting trees and leaves to both sides. The bullets made a flitting sound, like a bee or a wasp flying. They could hear occasional cannon fire, and it was from the Confederate side. Wayward cannon shells hit the trees, knocking limbs down. Smoke was everywhere as they continued forward toward the fighting.

They came to a clearing and there, about one hundred yards in front of them, was the main Union line. They could see other reinforcements to the left and right. The presence of this second line merging with the first gave momentum to everybody, and a general Union advance ensued. The Rebel line was about one hundred yards in front. Dickson pulled up his gun and fired. Soldiers on both sides were shooting and reloading. Zach could see the Rebels as they reluctantly stepped backward in an orderly retreat. He could not really see why the Rebel soldiers were retreating, but he figured there must be a good reason, and it could only be good news.

The Union line moved slowly forward. Near the center, Zach could see the far left and right flanks were not moving in unison, and that his section of the line was bowed forward like a phalanx.

Off to the right and behind the Rebel line several hundred yards away was a slight rise, and a battery of Confederate cannon was being brought up. As the horses pulled the cannons in place, they were unlimbered, and the cannoneers pushed them into a line aimed directly at the bow in the Northern line about where Zach was with his new regiment. The first fusillade of shot came from the big guns nearly simultaneously. All the rounds appeared too high.

The sergeant, said to Zach, "Take that contraption of yours and see if you can discourage those Rebel cannon. They are about to blow us to smithereens."

Zach looked around for a place to rest his rifle, as he always did. No rocks or trees were nearby. Dickson, who had heard the sergeant, knew what Zach was looking for. Not seeing anything, he sat on the ground facing the target and said to Zach, "Try this." Zach squatted behind him, placed the rifle on Dickson's steady shoulder and sighted through the scope at the first cannoneer to the right of the line. The ground was soaking wet and Zach could feel water penetrate his still-damp clothing. The wind was negligible, and the range was over three hundred and fifty yards. He would be shooting up, and experience always taught him to aim a bit low when shooting up. John was breathing and with each breath, the spider hairs would move up and down.

"John, take a deep breath, let it half out and just hold it."

Dickson did, and while it wasn't perfect, Zach aimed at the first cannoneer's chest, rubbing his finger on the stock... deep breath... exhale... half-breath... squeeze...

"Another breath, John."

Zach squeezed off another shot.

"Again."

Another shot.

Three more times and all six cannons were silent. In less than sixty seconds, the entire battery had been temporarily decommissioned. The other soldiers on both sides were too involved to see or realize what had just happened, but the one who counted, the sergeant, did.

After taking the shots, Zach remained on the ground looking for more targets. He felt something brush up next to him. He looked down. It was a rabbit, trembling and scared. The animal crouched and tried to find shelter under Zach's leg. The miserable little rabbit flinched each time a nearby musket fired.

The sergeant, not seeing the rabbit, smiled, revealing big yellow teeth with a goodly sized wad of tobacco in the corner of his mouth. He spit and wiped the remaining spittle away. "Glad I didn't shoot your ass back there. You are still a goddamn chickenshit sniper to me, but I sure would like to have you in my unit permanently. Now, everybody on their feet; let's chase those sorry sons-a-bitches to New Orleans!"

Behind the line, back near the edge of the woods, Colonel Stuart stood on his horse next to his aide. He had ordered for his artillery to stage some cannon to take out the Rebel cannon that were about to fire. He said to his aide, "Remind me to tell

Sherman what we just saw." They rode off as the Union advance moved forward.

It seemed like the second day of this bloody hell was just the reverse of the first day. The fighting raged on, with the Federals pushing back the Confederates, who had initially offered stiff resistance. In the early afternoon, the fighting and gunfire started to diminish as the Rebels began a full and orderly general retreat.

The good news that the Confederates were retreating had a dramatic effect on the Northern forces. Men who had feigned death were no longer dead. Men who were severely wounded all of a sudden rose up and were in full pursuit at top speed. Men who had hidden behind logs or had burrowed into the ground dramatically appeared and joined the chase. Men who had been running away from the battle and trying to figure out how to cross the river turned around 180 degrees. Some were soldiers who had spent the night back at Pittsburg Landing cowering on the banks of the Tennessee River. Together with the arrival of Buell's fresh troops, a general cascade of blue rushed forward looking for the front lines.

Zach walked out on the vacated battleground. The evidence of the ferocity and savagery of battle was everywhere. Zach looked at one dead Rebel who had his hand up in the air and his mouth open, indicating he had died in great pain. Some of the fallen were still living and, wild-eyed, were screaming insanely for help. Over behind the remains of an old log were six or seven men in their butternut uniforms, all killed with one cannonball. The repulsive odor of decomposing burnt flesh, combined with the spectacle of this carnage, was almost too much for Zach. He started to feel sick. One Union soldier was resting against a tree with his cap pulled over his eyes. Zach went over and shook his shoulder; the cap fell off to reveal his open eyes glazed over, staring into space. He was cold and stiff. Zach walked on. He saw a pile of dead horses killed by cannon fire intermixed with both blue and gray bodies, all contorted in ways unimaginable. He saw a man's severed head, arms, bones and body fragments just piled up. Zach stared in shock.

That late afternoon, Zach tried to find Colonel Stuart to report. He had last seen him two days ago, but to Zach it seemed like two years, so much had happened. At Stuart's headquarters, he reported in with a captain named Hammond, who told him to wait until the colonel had time to see him. Stuart had been wounded the day before, he said, but he would see him. Not long after, Zach was led in to see Stuart, who was sitting on a bench with his shoulder bandaged. He did not get up as Zach approached and saluted.

"Good to see you made it through this hell these two days, Harkin. From unofficial reports, you seem to have distinguished yourself. Word is that you were stuck up a tree while our camp was overrun. Is that true?"

"Yes, sir. I had a bird's eye view of the enemy, but could not do much about it."

"Tell me more."

"Well, sir, those Rebels just came into our camp and acted like hungry dogs. They ate everything, then ransacked the camp looking for valuables. Then General Johnston came in and gave them hell. He wanted them on the front, not loitering around our old camp."

"Are you sure it was Johnston?"

"I did not know it at the time, sir, but later figured it was almost surely him. He had a big broad hat with lots of gold trim on his uniform. His horse was a big bay and looked to be a well bred."

"I also heard that you later shot that man, is that true?"

"I had several good shots at him from a good distance, sir. The first, he moved over before the bullet got there. The second had to have hit him, sir, but he didn't act like it. He just kept on doing what he was doing, rallying his lines."

"You mean he was in front of them? Between his men and our lines?"

"Exactly, sir. Doesn't sound like a general, does it."

"Quite contrary, Harkin, it sounds exactly like something Albert Sidney Johnston would do. I heard he was leading the charge while his subordinate, Beauregard, was behind the lines coordinating the battle. Johnston was evidently shot in the back of the leg. That could only have been done from behind their line, which was where you were. The evidence is strong you were the one. If so, we owe you a huge debt of gratitude. I cannot put this incident in my official report, though. I have to be absolutely sure before I do that."

"No problem, sir."

"I also heard you had a good day this morning taking out that whole battery. That's a fact," he said. "Okay, Harkin, I have a lot to do. However, I have a message from General Sherman that he wants to see you in the morning. I don't know what it's about, but be there."

"Yes sir. Will do, sir."

That night, the men celebrated. Fresh food rations, which included beef, had been brought down the Tennessee from Paducah, along with ammunition and tons of supplies, so the soldiers had plenty to eat as they reveled in their victory.

The next morning, Zach found his way to General Sherman's headquarters and reported in to John Taylor, the aide-de-camp. Sherman was using a small table under a tree to write fresh orders.

"Harkin, sir, as you requested," Taylor said.

"Ah, Harkin, heard some good things about you," Sherman said without looking up. "Seems like you are making my brother look good."

As he finished the last of the notes he was writing, he put his pen down and looked up at Zach. "Never did care for sharpshooters much. Always thought a battle should be engaged out in the open, eyeball-to-eyeball and belly-to-belly. But the reports I got from Stuart say you were effective in knocking out a whole battery yesterday." He paused for a second. "Wasn't my brother a friend of your father's? Yeah, I remember now... Seems like a year ago."

"Yes, sir, sort of," was all Zach could say.

"Well, my brother is a goddam politician, and he can't keep his goddam mouth shut. He's been blabbing to everybody who will listen about what a great shot you are. Hell, it's almost to the point he's bragging about you." He shuffled through the stack of papers on his table, pulled one out and continued, "This here letter is from some goddam friend of John's, a Colonel Hiram Berdan, you know him?"

"No, sir," was Zach's rigid response.

"Well, this goddam Berdan has formed up a regiment of sharp-shooters and through John's big mouth, they learned you might be good enough to be a part of it. So, what does this goddam Berdan do? He pulls rank through my brother, and I have orders to send you back East. Can you beat that shit, I'm going to lose the best marksman in this whole goddam army just because my brother has a big fat mouth."

"Yes, sir, sorry, sir."

"You've got your gun with you?"

"Yes, sir, outside, sir. Want me to get it, sir"

"Private, would you forget about the goddam 'sir'!"

"Yes, sir. I mean, yes."

"Well, my orders don't say when I have to send you back East, so I just might take my good old time."

Changing the subject, he continued, "Okay, I am leaving here to make sure those butternuts keep going south and don't decide to turn around, so I want you to ride along with me. Maybe we'll see how good you are with that goddam rifle of yours."

Sherman looked in his aide's direction. "Taylor? Get Harkin here a horse; he will ride with us this morning. I'll be ready in a few minutes."

As Taylor and Zach walked away from the table, Zach whispered, "Whew, that was tough."

"Think nothing of it, Harkin. He's better today than he usually is."

Sherman and his staff all mounted and started to the south.
Zach followed closely behind, being careful not to be in the way.
Grant's orders to Sherman were to be sure the enemy continued its retreat but not to engage. They proceeded down Corinth
Road. They saw the sign of a retreating army, including several
hospitals in which they found only the wounded and dead. As
they came to a fork in the road, he ordered cavalry to investi-
gate both directions and they found the enemy on both, some
distance ahead.

Sherman then ordered General Wood to advance his column
down the left road while Sherman himself cautiously advanced
down the right with the 3rd Brigade. About eight hundred yards
up the right road was a clear field, and several hundred yards further, an area of fallen timber and brush. Just beyond that was the
rear of the retreating Rebel lines. Extensive Rebel cavalry could
be seen on the near side, all lined up facing Sherman's advance.
The cavalry were preparing to charge the Union infantry. Zach
was close enough to hear Sherman order the Ohio 27th infantry
forward and Colonel T. Lyle Dickey's 4th Illinois to be ready for
a charge.

The Rebels charged – six hundred mounted cavalry racing
across the open area and breaking into the Union infantry. As
they would determine later, General Forrest was in the lead. The
roar of six hundred horses thundering toward the Northern line,
the men with sabers and pistols drawn, screaming a Rebel yell,
made any foot soldier in their path tremble in fear. The cavalry
plunged deep into the defenders. The Union soldiers immediately in front of the charge buckled under the savage onslaught
of the Confederate horsemen. Some of the Northern soldiers
discharged their firearms and ran, others just threw their muskets down to speed their retreat. Finally, as the wave of the
charging cavalry lost its momentum, the bluecoats who were left

and right of the charge quickly rallied and folded around, surrounding Forrest's men and forcing them to return to their lines.
The Rebel color guard went down, but Forrest stayed mounted,
slashing even though he was enveloped. Then he turned around
and forced his way back to the safety of his lines. Just as he did,
he leaned over, grabbed a Union soldier and sat him on the rump
of his horse, effectively shielding himself from gunfire. Sherman
looked back at Zach and said, "Shoot that son of a bitch." But by
the time Zach dismounted, the rider had disappeared behind a
slight ridge.

As this was happening, a lone rider with a white coat came
roaring down the slight hill, straight toward the area that Forrest had just vacated. As the rider drew closer, he slid down on
the side of the horse, presenting a smaller target. On and on he
came.

"Shoot that son of a bitch," yelled Sherman again as Zach
took a position to fire, using a large rock to rest his rifle.

Before Zach could even find him in his scope, the rider swept
down, picked up the colors, rode right through several of the
surprised infantrymen and took off on the same path traveled by
Forrest.

"Now get him," said Sherman angrily.

The target was moving fast, and Zach was only used to shooting still targets. He was able to find the rider's horse in his scope,
but the Rebel rider was lying flat on the horse's back and presented a very small target. The best he could do was aim for the
animal. He shot two quick rounds into the back haunches of the
retreating horse.

Nothing happened. The horse kept going and disappeared
over the rise.

Sherman sat on his mount, observing with his field glasses. If
he was upset with Zach, he did not show it. He did display some
disgust with Dickey's men and the infantry for so easily being
confused and thrown back. He ordered all soldiers to disengage,
halting the pursuit of the retreating Confederate Army.

On the way back, Sherman seemed quiet and pensive. He commented to nobody in particular that Forrest was an extraordinary cavalryman. As they dismounted back at headquarters, Zach said, "General, I am sorry I missed. Everything was happening so fast."

"You didn't miss, Mr. Sharpshooter. I had my field glasses on that horse when you fired, and you hit both times. But then again, I could have done that," he said as he looked back at Zach with a wry smile on his face.

"What are you fighting for, anyhow?"
"I'm fighting because you are down here."
Confederate prisoner to Union soldier.

Chapter 11

LUKE

L uke and the doctors labored all night and into the next day, taking very limited rests and occasionally having coffee and eating whatever they could find. Luke's back and legs continued to remind him he was not used to this type of work. His fingers were numb from the unaccustomed motion of suturing. The three of them decided to take another well-deserved break.

They walked out of the hospital area and up a small grade beyond the wounded soldiers waiting for them. As they looked to the northeast in the distance, they could see columns of blue-coats cautiously advancing to the south. To the southeast, they could see the Confederate lines making what appeared to be an orderly retreat. In the rear of the Confederate lines and closer to them was a line of nearly six hundred mounted cavalry acting as a rear guard supporting the infantrymen.

As the Confederate Army retreated to the south with Sherman making sure that the Confederates did not reform and rally, the Rebels would remind Sherman that the Confederate Army was still a viable and fierce fighting force capable of inflicting significant damage if pursued too closely.

The cavalrymen were all lined up in a single row, facing the advancing Federals, their horses prancing, nervously anticipating the coming action. In the front of this line was a lone rider on a big chestnut, brandishing a sword in his right hand. He moved back and forth in front of his men, encouraging them. He sat erect in his saddle, a cape drawn rakishly over his back. The brim of his officer's hat was tied up on the right. He had the look of a swashbuckler. Back and forth in front of the men he rode, inspiring his fellow cavalrymen. Luke couldn't see well enough, but he imagined the man to have fire in his eyes and smoke belching from his mouth. That daring man was exactly what Luke wanted to be when he signed up several months ago.

On the other side of the field, the Union infantry force was attempting to march through a dense thicket of small trees and bushes. As they tried to navigate through the brambles, their formations broke down. Luke had always wanted to be in the cavalry, and seeing the mounting tension directly in front of him made his heart pound with excitement. He forgot about the hospital and the work that had to be done. He wanted to be a part of this scene in front of him.

Just as the Union line plied through the brush, the cavalry officer saw an opportunity. He pointed his sword straight at the blue line, stood up in his saddle and screamed, "Charge, charge, charge!" The sound carried all the way up to Luke. All six hundred Rebel horses bolted forward at the same moment as if propelled from a slingshot. Luke saw the sun's light reflected off the hundreds of swords pointing straight ahead at the enemy's blue line. The Rebel yell could be heard over the thunderous roar of more than two thousand hooves pawing at the moist soil trying to gain traction. As the horses reached full speed, the officer pulled ahead several yards. The whole column of cavalry streaked forward in a shallow v-formation.

To the Yankee infantry, the onslaught of horses and screaming men must have felt like being in the front of a massive buffalo stampede. On and on the Rebels came, traversing the six hundred yards to the Union line. Without slowing, the whole line of cavalry pierced the Union infantry like an arrow penetrating butter. The infantry gave way, breaking up in chaos and retreating pell-mell. The sound of horseflesh colliding with human flesh, the spectacle of sabers slashing and pistols firing all proved too much for the Union soldiers, who ran. Some fired their rifles without aiming. Others just threw their rifles down, fleeing for their lives.

The dashing officer slashed to his left and slashed to his right with his sword as his horse's momentum carried him deep into the opposing line. The horse carrying the Confederate flag went down hard, sending the flag bearer flying headfirst. As the mounted warriors went deeper and deeper into the infantry, their momentum slowed, and some, having accomplished what they set out to do, started to return to their own lines, which left the big bay and his rider stranded as he continued slash with one hand and shoot with the other.

Luke saw the colors lying on the ground as the battle raged. Impulsively, he looked frantically around for a horse, any horse. He spotted an unsaddled mare tied to a tree about fifty yards away. Still clad in his bloodstained white surgeon's smock, he ran toward the mount at top speed, feeling the excitement of battle. Grabbing the reins, he jumped up on the horse with a fluid motion. With a solid kick, they were in full gallop, headed directly toward the ensuing battle.

Opposing soldiers had formed lines, the Yankees facing forward and the Confederates facing backward. Seeing the cavalry embarrass the enemy, the Rebels who had had little to cheer about that day were yelling, throwing their hats in the air and firing their muskets.

The officer on the big bay was nearly alone now, carrying on the fight almost single handedly. "Shoot him! Shoot him!" one of the bluecoats yelled as they surrounded him.

The officer continued to hack and slash. He aimed his pistol and killed the nearest Yankee, using what had to be his last round. A Yankee foot soldier rammed his musket into the rider's side and fired. The officer flinched in his saddle, his horse reared and they turned back toward the line of gray some distance away. Just before he cleared the still-reeling blue line, the officer reached down, picked up a wounded Union foot soldier, lifted him up on the crupper of his horse behind him for protection, and urging his horse forward, ran full speed back toward the cheering Confederates. The Yankees fired at the daring officer, but he kept his mount at full speed. As he approached his own line, he flung the wounded soldier off his saddle like a useless piece of firewood and was swallowed by the butternut troops who continued their raucous cheering.

At the same time, Luke was charging full speed directly at the spot where the Confederate flag lay on the ground. The blue-coated infantrymen were starting to get reorganized, as several of their officers were encouraging them to form a defensive line. Luke felt the familiar rhythm of the mare as she stretched out in a dead run, her mane whipping wildly on his cheeks. He felt his surgeon's coat flying in the air behind him. He could hear the mare gasp for air with each stride. He was approaching at an angle with the blue line on his left. He slid down on the right side of the horse, hooking his left ankle on his mount's backbone and wrapping his arms around her neck. As he neared the front of the line, he heard rifle shots and felt the horse take a hit, but the horse lost no speed as they swept directly into the men. Luke swung the horse in an arc to the left, trampling a soldier in front of him. He reached all the way down to the flag, picked it up and gave his horse a strong kick in the ribs, hoping she had enough left to respond.

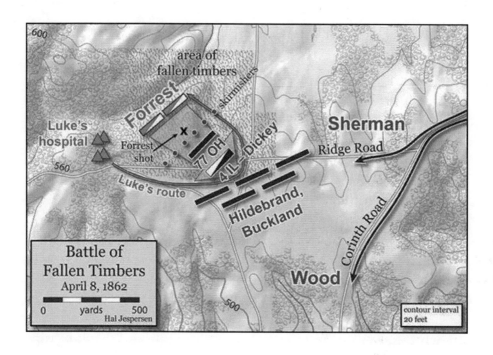

Battle of
Fallen Timbers
April 8, 1862

0   yards   500
Hal Jespersen

contour interval
20 feet

The mare gave him everything she had as they trampled two more stunned bluecoats and bolted out of the Union line. Luke righted himself on her back, lying flat and making as small a target as possible. Shots continued and he felt his horse flinch again, absorbing another shot.

Just before he reached the line, he raised the flag high in the air with a pumping motion. The whole gray line went wild. They screamed the Rebel yell, threw their hats in the air, slapped each other on the back and shot their muskets in the air again and again. The beaten Confederates finally had something to cheer about.

Safely behind the Confederate line, Luke pulled his horse up and spotted the officer who had made the gallant charge. The officer had been wounded and sat leaning next to a tree. As Luke slid off the mare, her legs gave out and she fell mortally wounded. Luke approached the tree, leaned the flag against it, looked at the man sitting there and saluted. The officer was evidently too weak to respond, but looked up at Luke and winked with an almost imperceptible smile. Luke returned the wink, and realizing the officer was being well attended, walked away.

The crowd gave way for him. "Would any of you care to tell me who that guy is?" Luke asked as he motioned back toward the officer.

"Colonel Nathan Bedford Forrest," a soldier responded. He was standing in the middle of a group of soldiers all staring at Luke. "And who are you?"

"Luke Pettigrew, from Crossville, Tennessee," Luke said. As he walked up the hill toward the hospital, he could still hear the men behind him yelling. "If my father could only see me now," he thought.

Luke was later to learn that the action he had just seen was to be called the Battle of Fallen Timbers. As the last casualty of the Battle of Shiloh, Forrest would heal quickly and return to service.

Luke walked under the tent with a smile on his face. John and Big Ed stared at him, not speaking.

"What's wrong?" asked Luke.

"I guess the best way to say it is that we are disappointed," John said.

"Why?"

"What do you think you gained by that little shenanigan you pulled? You risked your life! And why? For a worn battle flag? Is that a good reason?"

"Well, I—"

Ed chimed in. "Are you trying to prove something? Trying to prove you're brave? You were nearly killed out there. And what if you had been?"

"These wounded men need our attention. We are saving lives here. We are not impulsively riding off on some dangerous lark. You can do immeasurable good right here under this tent," John said. "Your work here is far more important, and now you will be a marked man when we get taken over by the Union troops."

"I—I never thought of that."

"Nobody's questioning your bravery, Luke. But your judgment?" Ed added.

John broke the pause. "Okay, enough on this. The problem is that you are going to have to get out of here. The whole Union Army saw what you did, and they are not likely to believe that you are just a non-combatant hospital worker. They will take you prisoner, sure as shooting."

"I guess you're right," Luke said after another pause. "Maybe I should try to leave tonight."

By the late afternoon, all the Confederate soldiers had left the area, including the stretcher-bearers. The hospital was unprotected. A young lieutenant with a blue uniform walked into the hospital and stared at the three remaining workers. He looked at Ed, then at John, and when he saw Luke, he stopped.

"I recognize you," he said as he looked Luke up and down. "You are that wise ass who pulled that crazy stunt today with the Confederate colors. Yeah, you're the one!" He put his hand on his side weapon.

John read the lieutenant's face. "This young man has sewn up a lot of wounded soldiers, including many of your own. We need him here to continue our work. We still have a lot of men who need attention, and some of them have blue uniforms. We do not differentiate between North and South. To us, everybody is the same."

The lieutenant looked out over some of the treated patients and did indeed see some in blue. He walked over to a young Union soldier who happened to be one Luke had assisted earlier. The patient, who had heard the conversation, said weakly, "He sure did a good job with me".

The lieutenant looked back at Luke. "Okay, you continue working, I'll be back tomorrow." He walked away.

Luke awoke from a restless sleep. It was dark. John and Big Ed were having a rest break, eating some biscuits and drinking fresh coffee, which he assumed had been supplied by their captors. "Have something to eat and come over here and tell us what you plan to do," John said.

"My plan is simple, maybe too simple. I am going to borrow one of our Union patients' hats, walk to where the cavalry is encamped, borrow a horse and ride south. The Union pickets are right over there." He motioned to his right. "I will ride around them, gain the north-south road I saw when I came here and head south. If they see me and ask me to halt, I will just keep going. What can they do? Shoot at me? In the dark, I can disappear pretty quick."

"The decision is yours, Luke," John said. "But we hate to see you go. You have sure given us some unexpected excitement, and you have been an immense help. A lot of those poor bastards out there owe you a debt of gratitude. They will go home with handsome scars made by a young kid who's quite handy with a suture needle."

Big Ed walked over to him. "Luke, I have three daughters. You remind me of the son I never had." He took Luke's hand

and shook it. "Now, get the hell out of here and let us get back to work."

"Yeah, before we get all sentimental," John chimed in as he also shook Luke's hand.

Luke flushed; his friends spoke with a warmth he did not expect after the reprimand he had received earlier. "Thanks," he said. Then he grabbed a hat and left.

The half moon was shrouded by a broken layer of clouds. When the clouds blocked the moon's light, visibility was near zero, but when the moon shined through, Luke could see. He quietly headed toward the encamped Union cavalry. Their horses were tethered to a rope that was strung up between two trees. Their bridles had been taken off and the horses were haltered, so with the aid of the moonlight, he found a pile of bridles, took one and approached the end horse slowly. No soldiers were nearby, and by the sound of distant snoring, he assumed most were asleep.

He approached from the front, softly cooing to make sure the horse made no noise. He passed his hand over the horse's head and down the front shoulder, sliding off the halter and slipping the bridle bit into its mouth. Slowly, he eased out, making almost no sound. He looked around. So far, so good. The moon went under, so he waited. Finally, the clouds cleared and Luke continued to walk the horse slowly toward the road to the east. He looked up and saw that he probably had three to four minutes before another cloud, so he mounted and continued. He wove around the camps, keeping good distances between himself and the dwindling campfires.

Once on the road, he could see the remains of a defeated army in full retreat. The road was littered with abandoned wagons, ambulances, limber boxes and other materiel. Luke slowly wove his way as if in an obstacle course. He was approaching the top of a slight incline as the moon went under again.

An unfamiliar sound…

"Who goes there!" The voice was just in front of him.

Luke remained frozen in the darkness, afraid to speak.

"Identify yourself, whoever you are!"

Thinking frantically, Luke blurted out, "Medical Corps, rounding up dead and wounded."

"That's bullshit," said the sentry. "You sound like a goddam Rebel to me."

Luke heard a shot. He did not know if it was a warning shot or one aimed at where the sentry thought he was. He gave the horse a hard kick and bolted straight ahead, running right over the sentry. About fifty feet later, his mount hit something hard. He could hear bones snapping as the horse went down headfirst, catapulting Luke straight ahead into the darkness. A loud thump was the last thing Luke remembered.

Some time later, Luke opened his eyes. He was lying on his back and he could see that it was daylight out. His first sensation was a harsh stabbing pain in his head. It was so sharp he reflexively started to raise his right hand up to his head. As he did, an even greater pain hit him in the right shoulder. "YEOW," he screamed.

"You've had a tough day." John's voice was soothing. As Luke moved his eyes around, he could see he was in a familiar place – right back under the hospital tent. "Take it easy, Luke, you have a broken clavicle and humerus and a severe concussion. We are most worried about the concussion, so we are going to give you some chloroform. When you wake up, we should be able to tell if you have a brain hemorrhage." John poured some fluid onto a piece of gauze and put it over Luke's mouth and nose. Luke was out in five seconds.

"What do you think?" Big Ed asked John.

The upper right side of Luke's forehead was deep purple and starting to swell. When he was brought in on the stretcher, there was an indentation in his skull, indicating his wound was serious. "Hard to tell. If he has a hemorrhage, it won't be good. He should awaken in about an hour, and if his brain has been damaged, we should have some indication either from the way he speaks or moves his good limbs."

"Don't know quite what happened out there last night. Seems his horse bolted into a broken down wagon and threw Luke ass over tin cup. They had to shoot the horse. The side rail on the wagon where Luke's head hit broke clean through. The kid must have a hard head."

"And all for naught," John added. "That lieutenant will not let him get away this time. They will likely send him back north somewhere. He ain't going to like it."

"Yeah, but we've got to make him better, first."

Just then, the same lieutenant walked in, looking around. Seeing Luke, he asked about his status. After John had given him a full report, he said to both doctors, "You two have signed an agreement not to engage in the violence of this war, and I will take your word as professionals. However, this troublemaker here is a different story. I was almost willing to bend a little after I saw what he did for some of our men, but his attempt to escape sheds a whole different light on things. I further want your word that you will keep him here until I come back tomorrow, and if he isn't here, you both become prisoners. We have a new prison up in Ohio, and you two would freeze your asses off up there in the winter, assuming this war isn't over by then. Have I your word?"

"This kid isn't in any shape to go anywhere right now, and yes, you have my word," John said.

The lieutenant looked at Big Ed. "Do I have your word, too?"

"Yes, sir."

"Okay, then. I'll be back in the morning."

It was almost two hours later when Luke stirred. The doctors were just finishing the last of the wounded, which totaled more than two hundred and fifty. They were bone tired. John walked over, put his hand on Luke's good shoulder and waited. Luke opened his eyes as if awakening for the first time.

"How's it going? You have been out for quite a while. Guess I may have given you too much chloroform."

Luke started to smile, but grimaced as soon as something moved. "Where am I? Who are you?"

"You fell from your horse and you have a severe head wound. I am going to ask you some simple questions, okay?"

"Guess so."

John held up his finger in front of Luke's face and asked him to follow it with his eyes. Back and forth, back and forth, Luke was following. The he placed his hand on Luke's leg and asked him to move that leg. Getting a positive response he asked Luke to move the fingers on his left hand. John seemed satisfied with this part of the examination.

"Now, Luke, look at me. Who am I"?

Luke squinted, trying to focus. He looked at John for a few moments, "I don't know you."

"Look around this tent, do you recognize anything?"

Luke's eyes slowly roamed around the ceiling of the tent. "No, nothing."

"One more question, where are you from?"

Luke thought for a while. "Crossville, Tennessee."

"Okay, try to rest, we will talk more later."

In a couple of minutes, Luke was asleep again. "What do you know about memory loss, John? I have very little experience. His motor functions are okay, but memory loss... I don't know."

"Several years ago I had a similar case at a little hospital in Nashville," John said. "We had a patient who had fallen off a barn roof. He had hit his head hard, which knocked him unconscious for several hours. When he woke up he knew his name, his hometown and much about his past. He had no idea what day it was, what he had been doing when he fell or anything that day. Within several days, however, he recovered full memory and was perfectly normal. I can only assume Luke's case is very similar.

At first light the next morning, the lieutenant walked into the tent again and saw both doctors lying on the ground, sleeping. He looked over at Luke, noticed he was awake and approaching the table said, "You are a prisoner of the Union Army, young man, and as soon as you can move, we're taking you out of here."

Luke was wide eyed. He winced at the pain in his head, then remembered the attempted escape and fall. He looked around as the doctors were rising from their sleep. "Before he can go anywhere, we will need to set his arm and try to immobilize his clavicle. It will be at least several days before he can move," John said.

"Still got your word?"

"Yes, sir."

"I will be back this way in a couple days," the lieutenant said as he hurried out.

Whether Luke liked it or not, he was a prisoner of war.

Chapter 12

ZACH

MARCH 1863

The grass was green, and the trees were starting to show their foliage this day near Falmouth, Virginia. The 1st and 2nd Regiments of the United States Sharpshooters Service, along with the entire Army of the Potomac, were encamped on the east side of the Rappahannock River just north of the city of Fredericksburg, which was occupied by the Confederate Army. The camp was abuzz with rumors that President Lincoln would be coming to visit them, the excitement compounded by the anticipation of the upcoming spring offensive.

The man standing in front of Zach was tall and slender, with a receding hairline and frizzy whiskers growing on the side of his face. His colonel's uniform, green with gold buttons, was the unique uniform of the United States Sharpshooters. He stood erect, with his sword hanging from his left side. He had a fair complexion and wore light-colored leather gloves. He looked Zach up and down but did not make eye contact.

"Ah, Harkin, welcome to Camp of Instruction. You have come a long way. I am quite surprised General Sherman gave you up so easily," Colonel Hiram Berdan said.

"Yes, sir. Sorry it took so long for me to get here, but Corinth, Mississippi, is a long way from here," Zach said as he repositioned his rifle from one side to the other.

Looking down at Zach's rifle, the colonel said, "What do we have here? Looks like a Spencer, but not quite. Mind if I look?" Picking up the gun and slowly examining it from end to end, he continued, "One of a kind. Who made this?"

"My dad. He's a gunsmith back in Knoxville, and he's always tinkering, trying to shoot farther and more accurately."

"Nice scope. English isn't it?

"It's a Davidson."

The colonel lifted the gun up to his shoulder and sighted at a distant object as if to shoot. "Handles right smart, and the weight is right. Hmmm... and this breech mechanism..."

"It'll fire every three seconds without losing focus on a target, sir, and it will hold eight cartridges."

Still handling the gun, the colonel asked, "What's your father's name?"

"John Harkin, sir"

"Believe I've heard of him. Yeah, nice work on this design. How straight does it shoot?"

"Got a chance to use it some at Shiloh, sir, and it worked fairly well."

"I've heard a little bit about how well it worked out there," the colonel said as he handed the rifle back to Zach, still avoiding eye contact. "We have a different way of doing things around here though, and we will just have to see. I have a lot of friends in Washington, which is why I was able to have an order sent to Sherman to bring you here. We have certain standards that have to be met before you can officially join the Sharpshooters Regiments. For you, these probably will not be very difficult, but we'll have to do them. I will have my lieutenant... Oh, hell, I will do it myself. We've got a little shooting range out back here, so let's get set up and see how you do."

Zach had learned the colonel was an engineer in private life and had made a fortune in industry, patenting several ideas and later selling them. He also learned he was not a military man but was reputed to be one of the best shots in the world. As they walked back behind the camp, they entered a far corner of a very long, narrow field lined on both sides with trees. It appeared to Zach that the field extended from the camp all the way to a road nearly a mile away.

The colonel asked several soldiers, all dressed in green, to assist. He looked out at some targets already set up and said to Zach, "Our requirement is that you have to place ten shots no more than five inches from a target bull's-eye at five hundred yards, freestanding. We call that a fifty-inch string. That should be quite easy for you."

Zach noted one of the assistants within earshot looked up quizzically when the colonel said "five hundred yards."

"Okay, sounds good to me," Zach said as he loaded his gun with five shots. "I usually shoot from a rest, so this will be different."

The colonel pointed to the target he had in mind and told Zach to proceed. Zach checked the wind, noting the trees on both sides were blocking the left-to-right breeze. He brought the gun up and looked for the target in the scope. As his gun was heavier than any other commercially available rifle, Zach had difficulty holding the spider lines steady on such a small target, but he systematically ran through his routine, rub the side of the stock with his finger, long breath in, exhale, half-breath... squeeze. He shot five times, reloaded and shot five more.

The colonel then told the assistant to put up another clean target. A sergeant appeared from the rear with Berdan's rifle. It was an open-sighted Colt with a revolving chamber and held five cartridges. Zach could tell it was a custom-made rifle because it had special scrollwork behind the trigger and some engraving. "Let me try and then we can compare," said the colonel as he stood and took his shooting position. He fired five shots and then five more in a very practiced, precise way, giving the impression he had been doing it all his life.

"Bring 'em in," he yelled.

The colonel took the two targets and held them up to the light, one next to the other. With an almost imperceptible look of disappointment, he said, "Looks like we have about the same pattern, although mine is a bit tighter." The colonel's pattern was ten within about a five-inch diameter, while Zach's was slightly bigger.

"Pretty nice shooting," the colonel said and pointed to his own target. "With a little practice, you could get your pattern down a bit."

"You are right, sir. That is very nice shooting," Zach said, pointing to the colonel's target. Zach knew the colonel understood that his gun was at a distinct disadvantage when shooting from a freestanding position. For some reason, the colonel was either trying to make himself look good or make Zach look bad.

Zach asked the colonel if he could look at the Colt. As he drew it up to his shoulder, he could feel the quality of the design. It was light and stable. Zach felt like he was in a corner. He knew if he asked to try again with the Colt, the target pattern would be much smaller than the colonel's and that might embarrass him. But then again, he had not shown what he knew he could do.

Finally, he said, "Sir, I would like to show you what this Spencer can really do at a longer distance. It has some tighter rifling in the barrel, and the results might surprise you."

"Sure, what do you have in mind?"

"Have your sergeant ride out toward the road and place a similar target farther out."

By then, additional soldiers had gathered around and were listening intently. These were men who prided themselves on shooting, and this was turning into a shooting match of sorts. They routinely shot in competitions to keep their skills sharpened, but the colonel almost never participated. Usually, he only shot during exhibitions, when dignitaries would visit the camp.

The sergeant mounted his horse and the colonel gave him a target. "How far out?" the colonel asked.

"Go until you hear a rifle shot," said Zach.

The sergeant took off toward the road at a gallop. Zach turned his back and started to reload his rifle. The men would look at the rider, then at Zach, then back at the rider. Eyebrows were raised; men were poking each other with their elbows. On the rider went, the noise of the horse's hooves starting to fade. Zach turned around and looked at the disappearing horse and calmly looked up at the treetops lining both sides of the field, noting the wind speed and direction. He casually held up a tuft of grass and released it, checking the wind at ground level. When the rider was nearly out of sight, Zach pulled up the rifle and fired. The sergeant pulled up, dismounted and pushed a stake into the ground with a target attached. The actual target was a one-foot-square sheet of paper and was nearly invisible at what Zach guessed was about twelve hundred yards.

Zach took a prone position, using one of the rests that were scattered here and there on the range. He sighted down, looking for the target, taking some time.

"Bite off more than you can chew?" snickered one onlooker.

Zach continued to study the target.

"Must be waitin' for rain," another howled as he and others broke into laughter.

"Ten to one he hits the sergeant instead."

"He can't see the sergeant. Might get his horse though," from another.

Closely following his practiced routine, Zach fired five times. As the rider returned with the target, the tension was palpable. Everybody was gathered around in a tight semicircle.

The colonel looked at it, studied it, and then picked up Zach's first pattern at five hundred yards. He held up both targets so all could see. The pattern Zach had just shot was tighter than what

Zach had shot at five hundred yards. Upon closer inspection, it was closer than the colonel's at that distance.

The men cheered while the colonel's expression turned dour. There seemed to be something going on that Zach did not pick up, some reason the men were cheering the colonel's loss.

"Nice job," the colonel said and immediately walked away.

The men then gathered around Zach, patting him on the back and continuing to carry on. "Great shooting, soldier," said one.

"Yeah, and I guess you showed the colonel," said another.

"Nobody beats the colonel," another said.

It started to sink in. After thinking a bit, Zach said, "You mean nobody has ever beat the colonel, or nobody is supposed to beat the colonel?"

"The last time somebody beat the colonel, he was put on the very front line in the next skirmish," a tall soldier said from the back.

"And he is no longer with us. Yep, shot dead in the first hour at Fredericksburg. The colonel posted him one hundred yards in front of everybody else, and he took a Minie ball right through the head."

Zach was deeply troubled by this conversation. He liked to have everything in order and avoid any kind of conflict whenever he could. When he was young, he got into trouble with his father for skipping school to go hunting. His father found out and gave Zach a very severe tongue-lashing. His father had never raised his voice in anger before, and Zach could feel his wrath. Later that night, the memory of his father's anger kept him wide-awake. It bothered him so badly he got sick and could not keep food down for several days. From then on, he had tried to stay on the good side of his father and of everybody else.

He decided he would talk to the colonel and apologize for any embarrassment he had caused him.

The colonel was sitting at his writing table with his back to the opening in the tent as Zach approached. "A word, sir?" Zach said.

"Yes, soldier, how can I help?" said the colonel as he turned around. "Oh, it's you, Harkin. What do you want?"

As Zach approached, he saw that the colonel had been making sketches on writing paper. "Sir, I do not want you to think I'm a braggart or a smart ass. I just want to do the best I can and show you what that is."

As the colonel considered what Zach had just said, Zach noticed the drawings on the table were of a gun mechanism. It looked a lot like a drawing of the design of his own gun.

The colonel denied any offense was taken. He curtly told Zach to report to the orderly to get a uniform, adding that he would make a good addition to the 2nd U.S.S.S.

As Zach left the colonel's tent, some of the soldiers who had witnessed the target shooting were loitering around under a nearby tree. A young man came up to Zach, his hand extended.

"I'm Myron Mansfield from Kentucky. Nice shooting back there," he said in a friendly voice as he motioned back toward the range.

Shaking his hand, Zach said he was from Tennessee.

"Just to get this straight," Myron said as others ambled over. "You are the guy by the name of Harkin who was at Shiloh last year?"

"Yes. After that godforsaken battle, I was transferred here to join Colonel Berdan."

"And you're the guy who single-handedly took out a whole Rebel line of cannons just before they would have blown your regiment to kingdom come?"

"Well, I..."

"And you're the guy who shot Johnston?"

"Well, no... I..."

"Welcome to the Sharpshooters," Myron said. "Hey, boys, can you beat that? Here he is. In person."

Zach shook hands with all the guys gathered. He was greeted warmly, and the soldiers seemed to be genuinely proud he was now a member of the U.S.S.S. As the banter continued, Zach said, "Now, look guys, I am really happy to be here; however, these things being said about me are way overblown. I did no more than my duty, and about the Johnston thing, there is no proof I was the one who shot him."

"But you did shoot at him, right? Myron said.

"Yes, I had two shots. The range was far enough that after my first shot, he moved slightly and the bullet evidently went wide. The second time, he did not move; however, I was high up a large tree and the wind was blowing that day. The tree was probably moving, and I had no way to adjust for it. Word was he got hit in the back of his knee, so if it was my shot, it was just luck I hit him."

"How far away do you think he was? another asked.

"He was quite close. In the neighborhood of three hundred to four hundred yards. I was sighted for about eight hundred, so I had to compensate a bit, but that shouldn't have been a factor." For Zach this conversation was like talking to his father. Everybody was experienced in long-range shooting and he was comfortable discussing the little nuances involved. And everybody loved talking about guns.

The conversation went on for a time, until Zach said, "I am supposed to see an orderly to get my uniform. Anybody know where I should go?"

Myron said, "I'll take you to the quartermaster's area right now. Follow me." He gestured indicating the direction.

As they were walking, Myron said, "You said you were from Tennessee. Is your dad the gunsmith Tom Harkin?"

"How do you know my father?"

"A while back, my dad knew I was going to sign up for the North and he wanted a nice rifle for me to take. He mentioned your father as a possible choice for a gunsmith, but we finally settled on another."

"Who was it?"

"Morgan James, in Utica, New York. Dad said he was one of the finest gunsmiths in the East."

"My father knows him."

Zach was surprised by the large size of the encampment, compared to the one at Pittsburg Landing. Everything was so organized. Tents were neatly arranged in long, equally spaced rows. The mess tents were spread out so as not to create too much congestion during the morning and evening meals. The supply area was huge, with stocks from food to ammunition – all the things a fifty thousand-man army would need on a day-to-day basis. But the most impressive thing about the whole camp was its cleanliness. The main walkways between the tent rows were swept daily, at least on dry days.

He was issued a complete Sharpshooter's uniform, consisting of a green jacket with nine rubber buttons on the front and two at waist level on the back. They were designed not to be reflective so the enemy could not pick a target. The trousers were an almost matching green as was the foraging cap, which had a leather headband and chinstrap. Next came boots, with knee-high leather leggings into which he would stuff his trousers.

He was also issued a leather knapsack, also specially designed for the Sharpshooters. It was brown calfskin, tanned with the hair left on the outside. The sides were bolstered by a thin board on the inside, which added to the knapsack's weight but also prevented it from collapsing. A wooden canteen and cartridge box plus a one-half tent completed the package.

Discarding the clothes he had been wearing for almost a year and donning his new uniform made Zach feel like he was finally a bona fide member of the U.S. Army. He was proud and wished his mom and dad could see him now. He would be sure to write to them this evening.

Zach learned he would be attached to Company H of the 2nd Regiment, which was Myron's, and also that their company would go on picket duty the next morning. The whole encampment extended quite a distance along the river, and the number of pickets required was so great that picket-duty teams had to serve every nine to ten days. The picket outposts were as many as seven or eight miles away, so the practice was to march out, do picket duty for two days and then march back.

That evening after mess, the whole company drew four days' rations. While the men were lounging around, anticipating the next day's march, Zach asked Myron, "Can I see that rifle of yours now?"

Myron went to his tent to retrieve his rifle. "Here it is," he said when he came back. "It is a bit shorter than average. We thought we would need to be able to aim and shoot quickly."

"Yes, I like the weight. And these shoulder guides on the stock fit just perfect," Zach said as he shouldered the rifle. "You bring this up to your shoulder, and you are immediately looking right down the sights ready to fire. Perfect. And the balance... must be a great gun to shoot from a standing position."

As Zach continued to admire the gun, Myron said, "You know, that reminds me about your run-in with the colonel today. He had you stand to shoot a target at five hundred yards. Our normal test for any recruit is two hundred yards prone and 100 yards standing."

"I noticed some raised eyebrows when he said 'five hundred yards,'" Zach said.

"He has a burr up his rear for some reason. Any idea what it is?" asked Myron.

"No earthly idea at all."

"Well, maybe it has something to do with all the notoriety you got from out West," said Myron. "Our colonel has a bit of a reputation for always being in the front of our lines except when the first shot is fired. Then he disappears, never to be found, until the shooting is over."

"Hmmm, didn't know about that. I'm not going to lose any sleep over it. And speaking of sleep, maybe we should call it a day. Tomorrow may be a long one."

Zach was soon to realize that this night was to be the first night he would share a tent with his new friend Myron, and also the last.

Chapter 13

LUKE

LATE APRIL 1862

L uke disembarked the USS Lexington in Paducah, Kentucky. He had been on the steamship for the last three weeks, along with more than two hundred other prisoners of war. Located at the confluence of the Ohio and Tennessee rivers, midway between St. Louis and Memphis, Paducah served as a very important depot for war materiel to supply Grant's army as the Union forces advanced. This was Luke's first glimpse of the massive Union build-up. The shore was crowded with steamships waiting to take supplies upstream. A huge depot stockpiled with whatever Grant needed for the war effort – cannons, crates of ammunition, crates of rifles, pallets of gunpowder, cannon shot, and pallets of food, corn, oats and ground wheat. Hundreds of men, wagons and horses were going in different directions – men yelling, horses neighing, dust, smoke, all merging into a chaotic order.

While onboard the steamer, the prisoners were able to rest and were relatively well fed, so Luke had had a few weeks to recuperate. His collarbone was healing, although he was very careful how he walked, because any sudden movement or jerking sent stabbing pain down his arms. One of his arms was in a sling, and he kept it immobile, wrapped tight with cloth. His headaches were manageable and his condition improved daily.

None of the prisoners had any idea where they were headed, but there were plenty of rumors. The nearest Federal prison was in St. Louis, and Luke had heard that the conditions and treatment there were deplorable. The reports were that men either starved to death, were beaten or died of exposure. The other more favorable possibility was they would continue up the Ohio to the East.

They were not under heavy guard. Luke had counted between fifteen and twenty men serving as watchmen. They carried rifles and kept a distance between themselves and the prisoners. After they disembarked, the prisoners were marched to a makeshift corral on the outskirts of the depot area. They were to sleep in the open regardless of the weather. They would be fed two times a day and supplied plenty of water.

On the first whole day in what was referred to as "the pen," the men tried to get used to their environment. The raw material for making war continued flowing through the depot. The Confederate depot Luke had seen in Corinth, compared to this Union depot, was a harbinger to the eventual outcome of the war.

The days went by slowly. The captives could only laze around all day and talk. They talked about the war, their families and their future. The word spread that Luke was the hero at Shiloh and his ride at Fallen Timbers was a favorite subject.

Four days later, the captives headed up river on a steam-powered side-wheeler. Conditions were better. While many had to sleep on top, exposed to the weather, Luke and a couple of new friends found a cozy spot on the bottom deck, where the engine noise was preferable to the cold. The going was slow as they plied upriver against strong currents. The first major stop was Louisville, Kentucky, where they took on water and additional supplies. Louisville was another staging area for the Western war effort. A depot even larger than the one in Paducah was located near the wharf area where they moored. The prisoners quickly found out they would not stay in Louisville, and rumors about where they were headed were again rampant. Speculation was the next stop was Cincinnati, Ohio.

Luke rested well. The pain in his arm became a dull ache as his bones mended. The prisoners had twenty-four hours per day of idle time, and Luke thought of home frequently. He was more at ease thinking about his parents now that he had arranged to have his service pay sent to them directly. He was sure the money would lighten their financial burdens and make life more comfortable for them. That helped ease the guilt he had been carrying around with him since he left home. As he looked back on his last several years, he realized he had been irresponsible, totally disregarding his duties as a member of the family. In these last few weeks, though, he had begun to see himself differently. Even though many of the soldiers who had seen his actions at Fallen Timbers thought of him as a hero, he recognized that John and Big Ed were right. His actions were impulsive and irresponsible. If he had stayed at the hospital, he could have helped save more lives. And he might not have been taken prisoner.

Three days later, upon arriving in Cincinnati, they were ordered to disembark. The city was well defended from possible attack from the south with a series of forts strategically positioned in an arc on the Kentucky side of the river. The city was immense, with dozens and dozens of industrial smokestacks, all spewing out smoke and soot, further enabling the Union war machine.

Luke and his friends were again crowded into an open, roped-off area about a thirty-minute march from the wharf. They quickly learned their stay would not be long. Several men were being transferred to a prison in Chicago, and Luke was going to Camp Chase near Columbus, Ohio. Nobody could figure out why they were being split up, and they speculated that Luke was being sent to a different place because of his notoriety. The friends promised to get together back in Tennessee as soon as the war was over. Luke was put on a train headed for Columbus along with nine others prisoners who appeared to be officers.

Camp Chase was a large training area for soldiers located on the outskirts of Columbus. A large stockade had been constructed to hold Confederate prisoners of war and known sympathizers. The stockade was in the southwest corner of the facility, where rows of small cabins had been built. However, it appeared most of the prisoners were housed in tents.

Luke felt alone as he gave his name, unit number and hometown to the admitting official. He had struck up several conversations with fellow prisoners on the train from Cincinnati, but most of those men were officers who knew each other and paid little attention to the young soldier. The rows and rows of closely placed tents made the camp look like a small city surrounded by four walls over twenty feet high. He had been assigned to a tent that held a Captain Samuel Cowan but was not told its location, so Luke had to walk up and down the tent rows, asking for directions.

Walking along the second row of tents, Luke approached the first officer he met. "Captain Samuel Cowan. Do you know the man and where I might find him?"

"Who wants to know?" came the reply.

"My name is Luke Pettigrew, sir, and I have been assigned to his tent."

The officer was about twice Luke's age, slightly taller than average with light brown hair extending down over his ears. He had soft blue eyes and his face was tanned. He looked at Luke intently. "You are having the pleasure of looking at him," the man said as he extended his hand. "You from Kentucky?"

"Tennessee 28th, sir." Luke shook his hand and noticed Cowan's firm handshake and affable manner.

"C'mon, this way," the captain said as he patted Luke on the back. "We don't have much room in our tent, but we'll find some space. We are never in there much anyway, unless it rains. You have any belongings? Or are you like the rest of us, totally dependent on these damn Yankees for everything."

"Just the shirt on my back and an empty stomach."

The captain gave him a warm smile. "Well, your stomach may not get full, but at least it won't be so empty. They feed us enough to keep us from starving to death. Here's our tent. I'll take you over to the guardhouse and we'll get you a blanket. By the way, you can call me Sam. We're pretty informal around here."

"Okay, Sam, I won't take up much room, and I don't think I snore."

"Ha, wait until you hear the noise around here at about midnight. It sounds like one of those longhaired symphonies. You know, an oboe here, a bassoon there, with a couple of bass violins thrown in."

Luke liked Sam instantly. He seemed like a long lost uncle. Later, they walked over to the guardhouse to pick up a blanket and eating utensils. The pace around the camp was relaxed and very slow. Nobody was in a hurry to do anything, and most just stood or sat around in idle chitchat.

Mess was served at eight in the morning and five in the evening near the guardhouse. The lines would start forming around four in the afternoon and might extend all the way down one side of the stockade wall. Upon being served, small groups would gather in circles to share stories and exchange rumors. Frequently, the evenings would end in songs about home, loved ones and, of course, "Dixie."

That first night in camp, everyone wanted to ask Luke, the new guy, whether he had any news. Then they wanted to know the circumstances of his capture. Luke, not being accustomed to talking about himself, briefly sketched his Shiloh experience, including his work in the hospital and his attempted escape. He did not mention the episode with General Forrest. Even without that part of his story, all who listened were captivated, especially by his ill-fated escape attempt. They asked many more questions about his home and family, until eventually the conversation died down and the men retreated to their tents to sleep.

It was a clear cool evening, and Sam had pulled his blanket outside his tent and proceeded to lie down and get comfortable. Luke did likewise. As they lay there, Sam ventured, "Luke, you didn't tell us everything about Shiloh, did you? You seemed to hesitate during the story. I got the impression you were editing some things out."

"Some things are better left unsaid. No good can come from spilling out your soul."

"You're probably right about that, Luke. Maybe when you get to know us better, you won't mind sharing the rest of it."

"Maybe."

Luke settled down to his first night in the prison. He thought about the four high walls that penned them all in. Whenever he was in a confined area, even in his room at home, he always had to have the door open or at least a clear understanding of how to exit. A touch of panic hit him. He threw off his blanket and started to sweat. He thought about being cooped up for an extended period of time. He could not get his head around it.

About then, Sam said, "Take three deep breaths, relax and try to go to sleep. If that doesn't work, think of home. Just don't think about being here in captivity."

Luke thought to himself, "How does he know what I'm thinking?" Then he said, "Thanks, I'll try."

It was a long time before he succumbed to sleep.

Chapter 14

ZACH

Reveille was at six-thirty. The morning was cool and dry with a light breeze out of the northeast. The breeze made a soft whistling sound through the firs, which reminded Zach of home. As the camp awakened, Zach busied himself packing his new knapsack.

"You will not need your half tent because of the short stay on the picket line," the sarge had told them, so Zach readied his blanket, canteen, ammunition and rations.

The company lined up for departure by nine, led by their captain, Gilbert Hart. As the Army of Northern Virginia was located near Fredericksburg, on the other side of the Rappahannock, the march was to the pickets on the Union side of the river.

They reached the lines around noon and the company they were replacing left to go back to the general camp. The picket camp was within one hundred yards of the river; it was primitive, with small lean-tos and crude shelters set up as protection from the night's cold air. The other side of the river was visible through a stand of trees and brush. Somewhere on the opposite side were the Rebel pickets.

That night the soldiers gathered around their campfires in good spirits, knowing they only had a few nights on picket before they would return to their camp.

Zach heard a soft strumming of a guitar. "Come on over to the fire and play that thing," Myron said. "We haven't sung in a coon's age. Let's sing ole Abe's favorite song."

"And what might that be?" said Zach.

"John Brown's Body."

The guitar player started to play, and Myron joined in with a deep baritone voice that reminded Zach of his preacher back home. After they sang "Aura Lee," the sergeant stood up. "Time to turn in, boys. We need to be sharp tomorrow."

Zach was comfortable. He felt he was a part of the army, and he was proud of his accomplishments. He went to sleep thinking of home again and wondering how long it would be before he could return.

The next morning, the captain deployed the men, and Zach and Myron found that they were on the extreme eastern end of the picket line. They had had some bacon, hardtack and coffee. Up and down the line, the men passed the time with small talk.

Myron was telling Zach about a girl he knew back home, who he hoped was waiting for him to return.

"What's her name?" asked Zach.

"Her name is Mary Ann, and she has the most beautiful blond..."

"Phfft," a sound came through the bushes.

Zach looked down at his gun. It was covered with blood. He looked over at Myron, who had fallen to his knees. As Zach reached out to keep Myron from falling, he could see a large cavity in the back of his head where a bullet had exited.

"Holy Christ," Zach screamed. "Somebody help!"

Myron had slumped to the ground, and Zach realized it was over. "Everybody take cover, we are under fire," was all he could say. The whole company hit the dirt behind a row of logs set up for defensive purposes.

"Where did it come from," one yelled from down the line.

"Must be from across the river," said another.

Zach was scared. Even though he had been under fire before, he'd never been this close. And he'd never seen a friend fall. "Had to be from the other side," Zach said.

The sergeant crawled over, stared at Myron's fatal head wound, and asked, "What direction was he looking when he got shot?"

"Straight across the river, Sarge."

"Did you see any smoke?" a lieutenant asked.

"No chance, sir. But it had to be from a long way off. I heard no sound."

"Okay, it looks like we have a sniper on our hands, men. Let's not give him another chance. Everybody stay down behind these logs. Don't even so much as peep over the top," said the lieutenant.

"Goddam chickenshit son of a bitch," someone said down the line.

Zach crouched behind a log. Over across the river some-where was a shooter who had just taken the life of his friend. That shooter could have been himself. And it could have been his own life. He felt violated.

A while later, after the initial shock had worn off, Zach placed his gun between two logs, being careful not to expose himself. He scanned the trees and bushes on the other side. Nothing. He tried to triangulate the sniper's position by noting the direction Myron had been facing. The bullet appeared to have entered his head at an angle perpendicular to that direction. He scanned that area, moving ten to fifteen degrees on both sides of an imagi-nary line he drew in his head. Over and over he scanned. Noth-ing.

One soldier asked, "What do you think we should do, Lieu-tenant?"

"Let's just stay here behind these logs for now. Keep your heads down, everyone," said the lieutenant as he crawled over next to Zach. "You got any ideas, soldier?"

Honored to be asked, Zach said, "Well, sir, I agree with you we have to hunker down, probably for the rest of the day. After dark, we could move our little camp back a hundred yards or so and the brush would totally conceal us."

"Yes, but maybe that is what they want us to do. If we are out of their sight, then they would be out of our sight, free to make a move without us knowing about it."

"So maybe we should try to think what the sniper is thinking. He probably thinks we cannot see him at all, and therefore he is probably in the same position as he was when he shot Myron."

"Okay", the officer said. "So what?"

"Well, if he is comfortable in his position, one way we might be able to pinpoint his exact location is to get him to shoot again. If he shot again, we might be able see the smoke from his gun and figure out where the hell he is."

"Okay, then what? We still won't be able to shoot because he still will not be visible. We might know where he is in a fifty foot circle, but killing him in a fifty foot circle would be one chance in a thousand."

"Well, at least we would know more than we know now."

"He could be moving around. Tomorrow, he might be in another tree," the lieutenant pondered.

"My guess is that he is comfortable. He has found an effective position, and he might just want to stay there. He probably comes out of his hiding place at night and returns the next morning, right to his same comfortable spot. Why would he change?"

"How would we get him to shoot again?"

"Come nightfall, we stuff a uniform with weeds and grass, put a hat on it and let him see it. Might be interesting to see how long it takes him to find the target and shoot."

The rest of the day, the whole company stayed hunkered down out of sight. Just before dark, Zach stuffed a uniform jacket with dead grass. Then he cut a long sapling, trimmed off the branches and stuck it through the torso from bottom to top. Then he took his own cap and set it on the top end of the stick.

"From one thousand yards or so, this guy will look real," Zach said. "If we bob this around a bit, he will surely see it and shoot. All we have to do is spread out a little so we can look for his gun smoke from as many angles as possible."

"We'll give it a try," the lieutenant said.

The next morning as the sun rose downriver from their picket camp, the lieutenant gave everybody orders to stay well behind cover and spread out up and down the line. He gave them the general area where they thought the sniper might be located.

Zach squatted behind a large sycamore tree waiting for the lieutenant's signal and when the officer nodded, Zach slowly raised the dummy up over the foliage.

"Phffft," came an almost immediate report, and Zach noticed his forage cap had a hole in it dead center.

"Holy shit," someone said. "Dead center. He must have been waiting all night right in the same spot."

"Anybody see any smoke?" yelled the lieutenant.

Nobody said anything. Finally, Zach spoke, "There is not even a little breeze out there. He has to have smoke. I don't get it."

The lieutenant crawled over to where Zach was squatting behind the tree and looked at Zach's cap, "That guy is one damn good shot. Perfect shot," he said as he poked his finger through the hole. Thinking about it a bit he added, "Now what?"

Zach sat down. He took his hat and again studied the hole the sniper had just put into it. After several moments, Zach said slowly, "Guess we'll just have to go over there and get him."

"You've got to be kidding," the officer said. "And how in the hell would you do that?"

"Let me think on it a bit. There has to be a way," Zach said.

After the second sniper shot, the whole company felt on edge. Anybody exposed to the sniper would be dead. They spent most of the day prone behind logs, rarely looking across the river.

Just before dark, Zach crawled over to the lieutenant, who was writing his daily report log. "Sir, with your permission, I have a plan that might work."

"Let's hear it," the officer said as he looked up at Zach.

"Well, sir, we are not going to be able to continue our picketing here because of the threat of that sniper. We either have to pull farther from the riverbank, which would defeat the purpose of these pickets, or we have to eliminate the sniper. I think I can swim across the river tonight and wait. In the morning, if we can get him to shoot one more time, I will be able to locate him and then nail him."

"Hmmm, I was thinking along those lines too, soldier, but I disregarded the idea because crossing the river is too dangerous. I figure the water temperature is too cold, and if somebody did make it over to the other side, there would be no opportunity to start a fire and dry out. The Rebs would smell you, and it would be all over. Plus the current is fairly strong, and you would be swept too far downstream."

"Yes, sir," Zach came right back. "But I would propose taking my clothes off and placing them and my gun on a log to keep them dry, so that when I made it over, I could put my uniform back on and warm up pretty quickly. I would walk a mile upstream before starting out so I would reach the other side well above the sniper."

"And say again how you would locate him?"

"Put the same dummy up about the same time tomorrow morning. When he fires, I will not only hear him, I should be able to see him. If I see him, he's dead."

"You thought about how you would get back?" asked the lieutenant

Encouraged, Zach replied, "Back the same way. I would wait until dark, walk upstream again and swim across, mission accomplished."

The lieutenant looked at Zach, got a wry smile on his face and said, "You've sure got balls, kid. Your plan probably has less than

a fifty-fifty chance of success, but we have to try to do something, and your idea seems to be the only one we've got."

The two of them spent the rest of the afternoon working out
details. One of Zach's concerns was with the cloudy weather –
he would not have enough light to see where he was in relation
to the camp when he landed on the other side. They agreed they
would start a large fire for him to guide by.

Just after dark, with his rifle and knapsack containing his
clothes resting atop of a six-foot log, Zach eased into the dark
river. He felt the mud ooze up between his toes. But he wasn't
ready for the temperature; the cold shocked him, taking his
breath away. Instantly he knew this job was not going to be as
easy as he'd thought. He hesitated. He could hear the rest of his
company mocking him if he turned back now. He pushed off,
keeping the log in front of him and used a strong kick to propel
him toward the opposite bank. The moon was obscured by thick
clouds, giving him no clue of his direction or his progress. He
kept kicking as hard and fast as possible. The river was about
one hundred yards wide, but he knew he was being swept down
current at a rapid rate.

He could feel the cold penetrating his legs. His kick was losing power as his muscles contracted from the numbing cold. On
he kicked, trying to work across the current. It occurred to him
vaguely that it was so dark he really didn't know if he was swimming across the river or downstream. He thought about how
stupid the whole idea was. He had not thought about making
a reference so he knew what direction to go. Building a little
fire on the bank before he started would have been so easy. He
stopped kicking briefly and let his legs go down vertically in the
water to see if he could touch bottom. No bottom. His hands
slipped off the log and it immediately disappeared into the darkness – the log with his custom-made rifle and warm clothes.
He swam toward where he thought the log might be. With each
overhead stroke, he felt for the log. No log. In near panic, he
propelled himself forward with all the strength he could muster.

Thinking he was off target, he turned slightly in the water. His stroke was losing power and he slowed. Something bumped him from the side. It was his log. In his panic, he had swum past it. He grabbed onto it, trying to catch his breath.

With hardly any energy left, he thought he should turn around and go back. But what direction would he go? He felt like he was lost in the middle of a dark ocean. He kept on kicking in the direction he thought he should, but he knew his kick had little power. The cold wouldn't let him relax. He felt his body heat dissipating into the river. The river, normally a friendly place, benign, serene, now was an unsuspected adversary trying to steal the last bit of his reserve energy, trying to pull him down into the depth.

He kicked in a panicky rhythm. He just kept kicking.

His foot hit something. It was an underwater piece of brush that had lodged itself in the mucky bottom. He swung free of the brush, then felt something again. He let his legs sink down and his feet gained traction. Zach was on the other side. He pushed his log as hard as he could, sliding it up onto the shallow bank. He lay there briefly, exhausted, trying to catch his breath, thankful he was alive.

Zach pulled himself out completely and sat on the bank just above the water line. He tried to untie the knapsack and rifle, but his fingers were too numb. He rubbed his hands together vigorously, and he was finally able to free the ropes from the log. He tried to stand, but his legs and feet had no feeling. He rubbed his feet and legs until his circulation started to come back. He put on his dry uniform and started to walk in a circle to get warm.

He remembered the lieutenant was going to build a fire to help him determine where he needed to be. He looked across the river. No fire.

"Shit," he thought to himself. "Am I upstream or downstream of the picket line?"

Continuing to walk in small circles, he thought about where he might be. Before entering the water, he had walked upstream about a mile to compensate for the strong current. He reasoned there was no way he had drifted down more than a mile, so he started walking downstream. Sure enough, several minutes later the campfire came into view. He knew exactly where he was. Now came the hard part: finding the sniper who had shot his friend. He lay down. He knew sleep would not come, but he curled up and rested. Some time later, breaks in the clouds cast enough light for Zach to find some cover. He checked his rifle to be sure it was dry and loaded and he continued to wait.

Zach figured the sniper would come out of his hiding place in late evening and return just before sunup, so Zach wanted to be in the best position possible. He would wait for the sniper's shot, locate him and take the shot himself.

Zach crawled into a weeded area within a hundred yards west of where he thought the sniper took his shots. He sat and waited. The morning light slowly crowded away the darkness. If he was correct, the rising sun would yield a perfect profile of his target.

He heard some movement on his right. The rustling sounded like an animal moving softly through the woods, maybe a deer. He heard it again. Steps. Somebody walking in his direction, the steps slow and deliberate. Zach strained his eyes trying to make out a form or silhouette. Finally he saw him about 30 yards in front. It definitely was a man. A man carrying a rifle.

The man walked slowly but steadily toward the river and disappeared behind some shrubs. The sound of his footsteps stopped. Zach heard the tinkle of water as the man relieved himself. Next, the soldier appeared above the shrubs. He was climbing up a big red oak to which he had nailed rungs. Up he climbed, clearly visible, to a makeshift platform. The soldier sat down and began loading his gun.

Zach, in a sitting position, shouldered his rifle and sighted toward the rebel. There was just enough light to see his target and make out the scope's spider lines. The man was bearded, with long black hair. As Zach centered his sights on the man's head, he never had the feeling that he was about to take a man's life;

rather he felt like a hunter aiming for his prey. He never thought about the consequences.

To allow for the close range, he centered the spider lines just below the bottom of the sniper's head. He rubbed his finger on the stock. Deep breath in... Exhale... Half-breath... Hold and squeeze. The shot rang out and echoed through the trees. It hit the man's jaw, splattering blood and bone fragments against the tree.

Zach quickly walked over and climbed up to the tree platform. The sniper lay dead against the tree with his eyes still open and the lower portion of his face missing.

Zach stood. Next to him was a small logbook with a picture of a young woman. Zach looked at the picture and felt a strong surge of remorse as he thought about the woman, probably the sharpshooter's wife, waiting at home for his return. He put the book in his pocket. On a whim, he picked up the dead man's foraging cap and replaced it with own, the same cap with the hole from the dead sniper's own gun. The sniper had used rope to mount a tent canvas on the top of his platform. It was why they never saw the smoke from the sniper's gun.

He picked up the Rebel's gun. It was an imported Whitworth with a scope attached. Zach remembered his father talking about these English-made rifles, about how accurate they were and, how expensive. This soldier had either brought this rifle from home or, more likely the Confederacy had issued it to him. If the latter, he must have been the best of the best. Zach lay down and sighted across the river toward his own picket line. Scanning back and forth, he saw a soldier looking right at him, moving his head up and down. It was the same dummy they had used the day before.

Zach climbed down from the platform and quickly hiked back up the river. At a spot about a mile up, he located another log and tied on his uniform and rifle as he had done on his swim over. Although he had agreed with the lieutenant to wait until nightfall, he decided crossing at night was too dangerous.

The temperature of the water shocked him again, but this time the crossing was much quicker. He could ride the current instead of fighting it. He arrived the other side, donned his uniform and new cap and walked back toward camp.

When he got there, the whole company was hunkered down behind the same logs in the same state of siege.

"You boys got any breakfast left? I'm starving," Zach said with a smile.

"Oh my gosh! We thought you were a goner," the lieutenant said. "What happened?"

"Yeah, when the dummy didn't get shot, we knew something happened," said the sergeant. "It appears you got the sniper."

Several soldiers noticed his new foraging cap at the same time. "Where's your hat? The one with the hole in it?"

"All right, give me some of that bacon over there," he said as he pointed to a skillet, "and I will give you the full story."

Zach sat down against one of the logs, and while he ate the bacon and some hardtack, recounted his adventure of the last twelve hours. When he got to the part about the sniper's broken jawbone, several cheered. Finally, he told them about how he had exchanged hats. They snickered. The men liked the idea the Rebs would find their sniper with a Union foraging cap with a hole in the center. For the next several hours, they peppered him with questions. Any one of them would have loved to be Zach that morning.

Later that day, the next company of pickets came in to relieve Company H, and Zach and his group marched to the main camp with one fewer soldier in their ranks.

That night and after all the hoopla about the sniper shooting, Zach retired to his tent. The tent seemed empty to him because Myron was gone, but he lit one of Myron's candles and started to write home. He told his parents generally where he was. He wrote about the rumors that they'd be moving out soon and about the forthcoming visit from Lincoln. He told them about Myron. Thinking of his mom and dad made him realize how much he missed home and how he would like to get home and resume his life.

While reaching in his knapsack to get the sniper's diary, he noticed a tag inside the dead man's hat: "McGowan Brigade." He'd meant to ask the lieutenant if he had ever heard of it. He picked up the dead man's logbook, and with an eerie feeling, he opened it and flipped through the pages. It appeared to have daily entries. He paged through to the last one:

"March 3: Back in my tree. Pickets still across the river. Think I got another. Seems a bit too easy. Two days until I get to go home. God, I can't wait to see her. It's been so long."

Zach stared at the words and sadness crept over him. He crawled out of the tent and sat down on a log next to the fire where several men were still talking.

"I want to read this to you," Zach said.

He read the journal entry in a somber tone, and all were quiet until finally a sergeant said, "War ain't much fun. I know that guy shot Myron, but shit, he was only doing what any of us would do in a similar situation."

"Oh, that's horse crap," came a voice from the darkness. "That guy would have shot us all if he'd had a chance. It's either kill or be killed out here."

Zach sat down and lowered his head. "I was just thinking of his family. Maybe he even was married and with children. They will never see him again. Each time they see a man walking down the lane toward their house, they will think it might be their son, or husband or father. They will get their hopes up, only to be disappointed. Then one day they will get a letter, and their lives will change. Just because of some damned shoot-happy kid."

The sergeant got up and stretched. "You are way too hard on yourself, Zach. You really did a brave thing out there. Who knows, if you hadn't gotten that guy, he might have gotten any of us, including you. Now, get some sleep. You'll feel better in the morning."

As he tried to sleep, Zach could only think about the sniper's words.

"Maybe the sarge is right," he thought. "I was just doing my duty and possibly saving my buddies from the same fate. Maybe if I hadn't shot him, somebody else would have." But then he thought of the soldier's family waiting for him to return, hoping, praying, then getting a letter, and of the anguish they would feel...

He rolled over and closed his eyes. The image of the dead man with part of his head blown off would not go away. The vision of a hopeful mother or spouse waiting back home for him to arrive continued to haunt him.

Chapter 15

LUKE

The weeks turned into months, with the only excitement being the arrival of new prisoners and the departure of old ones. Arrivals meant fresh news, and without exception, all the inmates wanted to know the status of the war. After Shiloh, Grant continued to move south, and the control of the whole Western front, including the entire span of the Mississippi, seemed lost to the Confederate cause. Such was not the case in the East, where General Lee had led the Army of Northern Virginia to repeated Confederate battle victories.

Luke and Sam had formed a close friendship with mutual respect and concern for each other. As a captain attached to General Simon Bolivar Buckner, Sam had been with Buckner during the battle for Fort Donelson and his subsequent surrender to Grant. One evening when several of Sam's friends had gathered, Luke asked Sam to tell the story again of how he became a prisoner, and of his meeting with General Grant.

"Well, General Grant realized he had to take Forts Henry and Donelson to wrest control of the upper Mississippi River from the Confederacy, so after taking Fort Henry, he surrounded Donelson and the little town of Dover, Tennessee. General Buckner was in command of some of the Confederate forces facing Grant's left flank. With the Cumberland River behind them and no navigable method of escape, it was decided between the four Confederate brigadier generals on the field – Buckner, Floyd, Bushrod Johnson and Pillow – to break through the Union lines and ultimately join General Johnston, who was in Nashville. General Pillow was commanding the left Confederate flank facing General Lew Wallace…"

Several prisoners soon came close to Sam's group to hear the oft-told story.

"Tell us again what a chickenshit General Pillow was," one of the men said, interrupting.

"Before the war, Gideon Pillow was President Polk's law partner, and Polk appointed Pillow to be a brigadier general in the Mexican War. He tried to take credit for some victories in two battles, after which Zachary Taylor and Winfield Scott initiated court martial proceedings. Pillow wiggled out. He had no field command experience and had not one idea how to defend, deploy or anything else any general should know. And I can tell you for a fact, General Buckner had no use for him. Didn't trust him, didn't like him, and above all didn't want to be next to him in line of battle.

"On February 15th, Pillow did make a nice advance on the Federal right flank. The weather was fiercely cold, and those Union boys nearly froze to death because they were not equipped for it. Neither were we, if the truth be known, but we were better off than they were.

"If General Johnston made a mistake here, it was because he had four brigade commanders trying to work together with no clear over-all command authority in the field. So the coordination of our Confederate breakout attempt was poor, with each brigade operating almost independently of the other. The other odd thing was that the brigades were lined up in a single column. It made no sense…

"After Pillow achieved a handsome gain, for some unknown reason he decided to fall all the way back to the original entrenchments. Grant took advantage and closed in. Buckner dutifully informed Pillow and the others that he would be unable to hold the fort on his own. When Pillow got the message, he forwarded it to Floyd, whereupon Floyd ceded command authority to Buckner. Instead of supporting Buckner, both Floyd and Pillow tried to avoid capture and led their brigades away from the battle. Floyd had been secretary of war under President Buchanan and before he left that post had transferred many tons of war materiel to the South. For this reason, Floyd feared a severe court martial if Union forces captured him.

"Buckner was left with 13,000 Confederates sandwiched in by Grant, with no alternative but to surrender. He waited until the next morning, giving Floyd time to escape, and then sent a note to Grant asking for conditions of surrender. He was hoping against hope that the terms would be generous and that his forces would be allowed to return South on probation. General Buckner and Grant knew each other from way back. The story goes that in '54, Grant, then a captain, approached Buckner in New York and asked for a loan to pay his hotel bills; he would pay the loan back as soon as he could get a letter to his father in Ohio. Buckner took him back to the hotel and introduced him to the manager, explaining that Grant was a man of honor and asking him to wait until Grant received the funds. The proprietor agreed. Grant must have been very appreciative, Buckner thought.

"However, Grant's reply was brief and to the point: 'No terms except unconditional and immediate surrender can be accepted. I propose to move immediately upon your works.'

"General Buckner was disappointed, but he replied promptly, 'The distribution of the forces under my command, incident to an unexpected change of commanders, and the overwhelming force under your command, compel me, not withstanding the brilliant success of the Confederate arms yesterday, to accept the ungenerous and unchivalrous terms you propose.'

"I was standing near General Buckner when Grant entered the fort to sign the surrender. They greeted each other warmly and chitchatted about the Mexican War and the incompetence of General Pillow. 'I thought Pillow was in command,' Grant said.

"'He was.'

"'Where is he now?'

"'Gone.'

"'Why did he leave?'

"'Well, he thought you would rather hold him prisoner than any other man in the Southern Confederacy.'

"'Hell no,' said Grant, 'If I got him, I would let him go again; he would do us more good commanding you fellows.'

"Both had a hearty laugh. Grant offered his purse for General Buckner to use during his impending imprisonment, but was gratefully refused. Grant departed and left us all under Union control. Our defeat led to the eventual evacuation of Nashville.

"So, here we are. Most of the prisoners went to Chicago, but many of the officers were sent here."

The story about Pillow and Grant was ominous. It always left the question hanging about where the conflict was going to end. Everyone wanted the South to win the war. On the other hand, most also wanted to just go home and get on with their lives. The monotony of the days, weeks and months made them all more homesick than anything else. They wanted the war to be over.

One balmy, clear night, Sam and Luke were under their blankets looking up at the stars. Most of the others were either asleep or out of earshot.

"Luke, what would you do if you got out of here?" Sam asked.

"Haven't thought about it much, Sam. I guess I would try to go back across the river, find some friendlies and get back in it."

"What would you do after you found friendlies?"

"I always wanted to be in the cavalry. Horses and I get along quite well, and I like the idea of riding behind lines, picking up information on the enemy, and making life for them miserable. And you?"

"I don't know; I guess I would just try to disappear into the crowd and get on with life."

"Why the question?" asked Luke.

"I have an idea and will tell you about it another time. In the meantime, I have an old friend who used to be the commander of this prison. He is coming to see me tomorrow. It will be nice to talk to somebody, anybody, from the outside. Want to join me?"

"Are you kidding? Nothing I would like more. Hey, how are you pulling this off?"

"I have family that used to live in this area, and I still have a lot of friends. You will meet one tomorrow."

The next day, Sam got a message he had a visitor at the guardhouse. Luke and Sam had been waiting for the notice, and they both walked into the small room where his friend, Paul Perry, was seated. After a hearty handshake, Sam introduced Luke.

Luke could see Paul and Sam had been quite close before the war, as they talked about old times and some of the great adventures they had shared. Paul looked to be around forty, was well groomed and appeared fairly prosperous. After a while, Paul scanned the two of them and said in a concerned, kind tone, "You two look like you've been through the mill. Your clothes are rags, your hair is long, and quite frankly, you look like you could use a good washing."

"Paul, I haven't changed my clothes for months, and I'm sure Luke is in the same boat. We shave every so often, but this camp is not the cleanest. Of course, Luke doesn't worry too much about shaving, although he does have a couple of whiskers popping up," Sam said as he mockingly pointed at Luke's chin. Luke blushed.

"I might be able to help you with some new clothing," Paul said. "My next door neighbor runs a haberdashery. I'll see if he has any discards."

"Oh, don't go to any trouble on our account. We are just fine. Don't worry about us. How's Katie?" Sam asked trying to change the subject.

"She's great. Healthy and still takes good care of me. We have Katie's niece, Carol, staying with us for a couple of months. From eastern Tennessee. Things are a mess down there, so we agreed to have her visit for a while. She's a great young lady, and spunky. She keeps Katie and me on our toes. She seventeen, but seems like she's twenty-five."

Just then the guard came in. Time was up. They shook hands, and Paul promised to come back soon. As they walked back to their tent, Luke mentioned, "Nice guy."

"I don't think the war has any bearing on our relationship. I do know that if Paul or Katie ever got into trouble of any kind, I would do whatever was possible to help them. I guess that's what true friends do."

Later that night, as Luke was wrapped in his blanket, he had time to reflect on the day. Sam's comments about what friends mean to each other had hit him right in the gut. He thought back to home, his mom and dad, his school friends. With a big empty spot in his stomach, he realized he enjoyed no friendship like Sam and Paul's. He wondered if he had any friends for whom he'd do anything. He knew the answer – nobody, except maybe Sam. How would he feel if something happened to Sam?

About a week later, an order was issued to move half the camp to Johnson's Island. The guards went through the camp and very carefully picked one half of any group of men who hung out together. The emphasis seemed to be on officers, and Luke was scared to death they would pick Sam. However, such was not the case.

The camp was busy. More prisoners arrived, bringing news the Corinth railroad crossing was now in Union control. The litany of Confederate losses on the Western front seemed to be unending. First came the losses of Forts Henry and Donelson, which forced Johnston to cede Nashville. Next came the strategically valuable Island #10 on the Mississippi and then the fierce battle at Shiloh, with Beauregard retreating the second day. Now Corinth. Speculation was Vicksburg would ultimately fall, leaving the entire length of the Mississippi River in Federal hands.

Prisoners from several Tennessee regiments flowed into camp, and as they joined the camp population, some old acquaintances were re-united. One day, in line for the evening mess, Sam and Luke found themselves behind two officers who had just arrived from north Mississippi. One, a captain, looked casually at Sam, but when his eyes shifted over to Luke, a hint of recognition lit up his face. He studied Luke intently for a bit, then asked, "Were you at Shiloh?"

"Yes, sir."

"Were you at the Battle of Fallen Timbers?"

"Don't know what battle that was."

"That skirmish where Forrest gave those Yanks the what-for during the retreat."

"Well, I guess I was," said Luke, sure now of where the conversation was going.

"Did you ever wear a medical jacket?"

"Yes."

"Then you have to be Luke Pettigrew of the 28th Tennessee!" The officer stuck out his hand and pumped Luke's for what seemed an extraordinary amount of time.

The second officer did the same, saying, "We've heard so much about you. All of us have been wondering what happened."

"Well I..."

Before Luke could say anything, the first officer turned to Sam and others who were waiting in line. "Do you guys know who this is? He is the hero of Shiloh! He is the bravest kid in the whole army! He showed those smug, arrogant Yanks they don't mess with us! If you sting us, we will bite hard!"

"Yeah," said the other. "He came out of nowhere, rode like the wind, ran over the whole blue line, picked up our fallen colors and brought the battle flag safely back to our lines."

"You had to be there to believe it," said the first officer. "Colonel Forrest said it was the bravest thing he had ever seen. And that, coming from Nathan Bedford Forrest, is no small statement."

The talk went on. Sam knew Luke had been holding something back, not telling his whole story. Evidently he was a real hero and too modest to talk about it. Luke was not proud of what he had done back at Shiloh. He knew he had acted on impulse. He had never considered the risk; he had just reacted, and therefore he thought he did not deserve the credit he was being given. The men kept on talking about it and finally Luke turned to Sam with a pleading look as if to say, "Get me out of here."

Sam picked up on it right away. "Okay, boys. Let's eat. No sense in beating a dead horse. We can talk more tonight."

And they did, to the wee hours of the morning. But Luke excused himself early.

After mess the next morning, Sam got a message he and Luke had visitors. They went into the guard shack and found Paul and his wife Katie with a very attractive young lady. As Sam and Luke shook hands with Paul, Sam gave Katie a warm hug and looked at the young lady. "You must be Carol, the niece from Tennessee. So glad you came along," he said. Self-consciously, Luke bowed to Katie and then to Carol. As he looked at her warm green eyes, his first thought was of his own appearance. He knew his hair was long and dirty, his uniform tattered, his shoes dusty and worn. He was sure that in her eyes, he looked like a vagabond.

However, Carol's face was radiant as she held his eyes and smiled. Her complexion was fair, and she had added a bit of rouge to her cheeks. Her long brown hair swooped down over her shoulders. Her full dress billowed over crinolines, but it had a snug blouse that showed off her figure. She wore a pleated velvet hat with a narrow brim.

Luke took all this in. He was afraid to speak, lest he would embarrass himself. As Sam, Paul and Katie watched the two of them, they tried to hide their amusement.

"Hello! Luke? Are you still with us?" said Sam as everybody laughed and the ice was broken. They sat around a small table. Paul put two bags on the table and pushed one toward Luke and the other toward Sam.

"Here are some clothes. These are not your Sunday-go-to-meeting clothes, but they should be about the right size. You have some non-uniformed prisoners in camp, so you will not stand out with these mufti on."

Katie wanted to know if the men were being treated well. "Do you get enough food? How about water? I just can't imagine being stuck in this prison with such high walls. Why, you can't even see out, can you?"

"Can't see out. However, we are fed enough, and the day-to-day camaraderie almost makes it bearable."

"Thank you for the clothes," Luke finally stammered as his gaze returned to Carol. "We can finally get rid of some of these rags."

Their eyes met again. "I didn't notice," was Katie's remark. Luke blushed.

"Just found out that Luke, here, is one of the biggest heroes at Shiloh. The rascal never told us, but some newly arrived prisoners did," Sam said and recounted for the guests Luke's feat at the Battle of Fallen Timbers.

"Please, Sam, let's let it go," Luke said softly.

Again Carol's eyes found Luke's, but this time he could not hold her gaze. Then the guard came in and told them their time was up. Luke shook Paul's hand, bowed to Katie and bowed slowly to Carol. Just as they departed, Paul gave Sam a small envelope.

That night, Luke lay awake, unable to get Carol out of his thoughts. He turned the visit over and over in his mind, remembering every detail. Her dress, her hair, everything, but mostly her eyes – those beautiful green eyes...

Chapter 16

ZACH

O n the morning of April 7th, 1863, the division was ordered to prepare for full review. The members of the U.S.S.S. were in their full dress, their green uniforms standing out distinctly from the rest. President Lincoln, accompanied by the new commander of the Army of the Potomac, General Joe Hooker, was to review the entire camp.

Later that evening after mess, the men discussed the visit and the rumors that they would soon be moving out. "Did you notice poor ole Abe didn't even look up?" said a soldier. "He just kept his head down while he rode."

"Must be hell to be president," said another.

"Didn't seem to bother Mrs. Lincoln. She was all smiles and seemed pleasant enough."

"He must be seven feet tall. At least he looks like it, with that big hat of his."

"I hear he keeps his letters and notes stuffed in the top of that thing."

During the following days, the weather continued to warm and the mud caused by the spring thaw started to dry. Rebels on the other side of the river could be seen periodically marching. One day, two balloons were seen rising into the sky just north of the camp.

"Guess that means those Rebs are getting restless and General Hooker wants to find out what in hell they're doing," the sergeant said.

Zach said, "You mean people use those things for spying?"

"No, they go up just to get out of the stink of our camp."

"I'll be damned. What won't they think of next?" Zach said. "Think we could shoot from one, Sarge?"

"Maybe they never thought about it. You probably could, want me to suggest it?"

"No. I don't really feel like shooting anybody right now," said Zach.

"Wait 'til you have somebody shooting at you. You'll change your mind."

Breaking camp meant saying goodbye to the comparatively comfortable, but too heavy to carry Sibley tents. The sergeant had told them to throw all unnecessary items to lighten their packs. Many of the soldiers thought some of the things they had accumulated over the winter were too valuable, so they buried them in the ground, hoping they would be back someday.

The most valuable items in the knapsacks were the rubber-coated blankets. Soldiers slept on top of the blankets on dry nights and underneath them on wet nights. They helped the soldiers stay dry enough to get some sleep even in the worst weather.

In the late afternoon of April 28th, orders were issued to be ready to march. Around ten the next morning, they headed up river on Chattel Road. After several miles, some of the soldiers found out their packs had too much weight, and they began shedding blankets and overcoats along with anything not absolutely necessary.

The regiment bivouacked about eight miles upriver around nightfall, staying there through the next day before moving up the river again. Around nine in the morning on a foggy May 1st, they crossed the Rappahannock at the United States Ford and moved south toward Chancellorsville. They stopped in an area referred to as the Wilderness – more than sixty square miles of wet mire covered with thick underbrush, small scrubby trees and ravines. The Wilderness was crisscrossed by old logging paths, with two main roads that led to Fredericksburg, the Orange Turnpike and the Orange Plank Road.

Since taking over the Army of the Potomac from General Ambrose Burnside after the disastrous defeat at Fredericksburg, Joe Hooker had instilled some pride back in his men. They were well equipped, well fed and well trained, and they were confident their new commander was up to the job. Hooker, knowing that his troops outnumbered the opposition force more than two to one, had developed a bold plan in which much of his army would sweep up the Rappahannock to the far Confederate left and get behind Lee. Berdan's two U.S.S.S. brigades were consolidated into one and became a part of General Amiel Whipple's 3rd Division under Major General Dan Sickle's 3rd Corps.

The Sharpshooters were ordered to deploy in a line facing the southeast. Zach could hear occasional gunfire off to his left, and as the day progressed, the whole line moved slowly forward through the difficult terrain. They spent the night in thick underbrush, with Zach's regiment assigned as pickets. In the morning they discovered the enemy had fallen back. Zach's unit again acted as pickets. However, at midday the bugle blew the advance, and Zach cautiously started walking forward. Rebel skirmishers were scattered in the woods ahead, and he could hear gunfire, but at first could not see any of the enemy. Zach scanned the woods ahead, trying to focus on areas several hundred yards in front instead of the closer spots. The thought went through his mind that what he was doing was like squirrel hunting, except that these squirrels could shoot back. He weaved his way over brush, around trees, constantly scanning. He saw a puff of smoke, and in an instant a bullet smashed into a tree right next to his ear, causing bark fragments to sting his face. He hit the ground, lay flat behind a log and sighted through his scope. He scanned all around the area. Nothing.

Again, he thought about squirrel hunting, about waiting for the squirrel to show itself and remembering how much patience he sometimes needed before a squirrel that knew he was there would finally move. Zach could hear additional firing on both sides of his line, but he never took his eyes off the area where he knew the Rebel was hiding. He had lain in wait many times before, but this was much different. A large black spider crawled down over the bill of his cap, almost interfering with his line of vision. His first impulse was to flick it off with his hand, but that could be fatal. He took a deep breath and blew it off, still not moving a muscle. He waited. The sun moved in and out of the clouds, sometimes shining through the trees around his target. The leaves would quake in the breeze. Zach could see them in his peripheral vision, but his focus was unmoved. He waited.

A glint. Zach saw a reflection like the sun shining on a mirror. He put his spider lines right on the spot, but he still was not sure of the exact location of the reflection. He waited. Zach knew the shooter was aiming directly at him, hoping to get a clear shot, and he was not about to give him one. A soldier crawled up beside Zach and Zach was sure the shooter had seen him. He wondered why the Rebel sniper didn't shoot. As he scanned through his scope, he realized the shooter did not want the soldier beside him. He wanted Zach. He had seen the scope on Zach's rifle and realized that any man with a scoped rifle would be a prized target. He thought back to the groundhogs he had shot back home and how they would have felt if they knew somebody was aiming directly at them. He knew if he made the slightest movement, he was dead. The idea occurred to him that he should not do anything. Just lie there and wait until dark. Sweat formed on his brow. His hands were damp and stuck to the rifle stock. Another glint. Without thinking Zach quickly centered the spider lines on the spot and fired. He waited. Nothing. Others around him where advancing. Zach continued to wait. Other soldiers advanced to the area where the shooter was located. Zach got up and slowly advanced himself.

The Rebel skirmishers were slowly retreating. He approached the Rebel's hiding place cautiously and peered over the bush were he had last seen him. There he was. The left side of his face was blown off. He had not moved since he was shot. His gun was still up to his right shoulder, and his right index finger was still on his rifle's trigger. Zach took a close look at the rifle. The front of the scope had a large dent. Zach's shot had ricocheted off and smashed into his eye.

The sergeant came up and looked at the dead man. "Poor son of a bitch," he said. "Had no idea who he was up against."

"Yeah, I guess," Zach said. He knew the sarge's remark was meant to be a compliment. However, the sight of the man with part of his head blown off reminded him of the sniper with the long black hair and beard he had shot by the river. He reached down, slowly took the man's arm off the rifle and laid it over his chest. He then folded the other arm over the first.

"You ain't getting sentimental on me, are you? asked the sarge. "You can't let shit like this get to you."

Zach wiped his sleeve across his eyes and walked on.

The whole regimental line was ordered to make a big turn to the left when it came across a large building next to a huge trench dug into the ground. Strung out in the trench was a Rebel regiment that quickly surrendered en masse. The men were marched to the rear. The building was a foundry that made artillery shot for the Confederacy. The captured regiment turned out to be the 23rd Georgia.

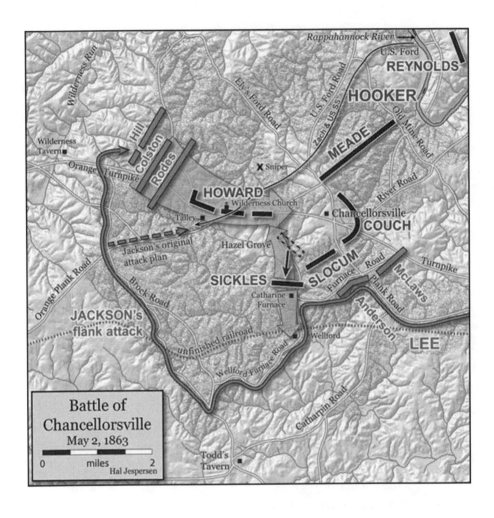

Battle of
Chancellorsville
May 2, 1863

0   miles   2
            Hal Jespersen

Late in the afternoon of May 2nd, Zach's regiment was still in the Wilderness. The musket fire abated as if the fighting was done for the day. Suddenly, there was a noise to their rear. A deer came through the brush on a run. Then another. Birds flew through the trees directly at Zach's regiment, and rabbits by the dozen scurried as if chased by a fire. More deer. Then men. Soldiers. Soldiers with gray uniforms emerged from the brush. Thousands of them. When they saw Union soldiers, they let out a yell and charged.

Zach fell back with those around him as quickly as possible.

"How in the hell could we have Rebels to our right and behind us at the same time?" the sergeant asked as they ran.

"Sounds like a whole Confederate corps charging our right flank," said another.

"Well, that's Howard's 11th Army Corps over there and if the Rebs got behind them, we are all in trouble."

"But how did the Rebels get around our flank without somebody seeing them?" asked Zach.

"Beats me." The sergeant speculated that he and his men were not only flanked but also isolated. "If Howard has been flanked, then our right and rear are controlled by the Rebels. I do not hear any on our left, so we may be all alone out here."

The word spread up and down the lines that the 3rd Corps was, indeed, isolated, and rumors were that they could be captured and become prisoners of war. The Union Army had started the day with an advantage, but now it seemed they were not only about to lose the day but also lose the battle.

General Hooker had successfully moved his Army of the Potomac across the Rappahannock and into a position to attack Lee. However, a major part of his forces were in the Wilderness. Lee, being severely out numbered, saw an opportunity to attack and force Hooker to fight in an environment that neutralized his numerical superiority. Lee and his ever-reliable General Stonewall Jackson developed a bold plan to split the Army of Northern

Virginia.   Stonewall would march nearly half of Lee's army to the west and then up Brock Road to attack the side and rear of General Oliver Howard's 11th Corps.   So in the late afternoon of May 2nd, unbeknownst to Howard, Jackson had nearly thirty thousand Confederates directly behind him.   Even though the hour was late, Jackson attacked.   The Union forces were totally surprised.   Although they fought well, by nightfall parts of Sickles' 3rd Division, including some of Berdan's Sharpshooters, were isolated from the rest of the Union Army.

That night, Sickles gave an order for two brigades to try to silently break through the Rebel lines and connect up with the rest of Hooker's army.   After heavy shooting, they succeeded in forming a passageway for the balance of the corps to go through.

Early the next morning, the order was given for the rest of the 3rd Corps to march through the opening created by the silent charge.   Zach found out how it must feel to run a gauntlet.   As they began their march through the narrow opening, with Rebel lines on both sides, the Confederates opened fire with every cannon they had in the area; the closest Rebels fired their muskets. Very fortunately, the Rebel's aim was off and the 3rd Corps losses were comparatively light.

"We are lucky bastards," the sergeant muttered when he saw that almost everyone had made it to the other side.   Their backs now covered, the men of the 3rd Corps were ordered to about face and fire at the Rebel lines they had just come through.

The Battle of Chancellorsville was effectively over.   Light fighting remained, but over the next few days, Hooker crossed back over the Rappahannock and the Sharpshooters found themselves back at their old campground near Falmouth.

Strategically, the Confederate victory was Lee's greatest; the much larger Union Army had been defeated and forced to retreat. The victory was not total, however, because Lee lost his most trusted lieutenant, General Stonewall Jackson.   Lee mourned his death, and Jackson's absence from the field of battle for the balance of the war was severe loss to the Confederacy.

Once back at camp, the sergeant walked up too the lieutenant and said, "Sir, I have been thinking a lot about Harkin, and I'm worried."

"Why's that, Sergeant?"

"That sniper across the river is getting to him. He picked up the dead man's diary and he's feeling that he has caused the family a lot of grief. He can't let it go."

"He'll get over it. Give him some time."

"Hope you're right, sir, but all of this was compounded when he shot that other sniper two days ago. I'm not sure, but I think he has lost his will to fight."

"Sure would hate to lose him. He is the best we've got, and everybody knows it all the way up to the colonel. Tell you what, Sarge, keep an eye on him and keep me informed. We'll be moving out soon."

"We could give him a furlough for a couple weeks. Maybe a little time away..." the sergeant said.

"If I remember right, his enlistment was by special arrangement through General Sherman. Let's keep him here and see how it goes."

Chapter 17

LUKE

MAY 1863

The next morning, as Sam and Luke were trying on their new clothes, the order arrived for more prisoners to be transferred to Johnson's Island. This time Luke knew the odds that he and Sam would be separated were quite high. Instead, they learned both would go north early the next morning.

Sam motioned to Luke to follow him to a quiet section of the compound where they could speak in private. "Luke, I don't want to go. Johnson's has one access point in and out. To go there would mean being there for the rest of the war."

"What on earth alternative do we have?" Luke thought a second, then added, "You've got a plan, don't you."

"It's not much of one, but, yes, I do. It probably won't work, but it's worth the risk. If we get caught, we are unlikely to be shot; the consequence may be no worse than being penned up again."

"Okay, let's hear it."

"Our civilian clothes are the key. The last time they moved a bunch of men north, they filed everybody out of the prison walls to form lines, presumably to march to the train depot. There were only a few guards, most of them from the guardhouse de-

tail." Sam took out four five-dollar gold coins and gave one to
Luke. "These were a gift from Paul," he said. "I will pass two
coins to one of the guards and ask him if he would let us pass out
of the lines. If he does, we simply disappear."

"Sounds simple, but then what?"

"First thing we have to do is separate. When they find out we
have escaped, they will be looking for two, so we will be better off
apart. With these new clothes, we should blend in and not be so
obvious. The next thing we need to do is find a barber. If we can
get our hair cut and washed, we will blend in even more," Sam
said. "You expressed an interest in heading south to get back to
our lines. Me? I think I will head east and stay with a cousin in
Pittsburgh until the war is over.

"One other thing, Luke. When we escape, the first twenty-
four hours are going to be the hottest. Everybody will be looking
for us. They will be on guard, especially at train stations. So, I
think you should find Paul's house and ask him to keep you one
night. He will be more than happy to do it, and then the next
day you can make your move south." Sam handed him a scrap
of paper with Paul's address. "You will have to be discreet when
you ask for directions."

Luke took a few seconds to think the plan through. It was
simple enough. Finally, he said, "I'm in."

They talked quietly well into the night. After they reviewed
the plan enough times, they started to talk about their lives after
the war and how they would meet again. Luke had formed a
very close bond with Sam. He was like a brother, even though he
was twice his age, or a very best friend. Then he thought about
Carol. He would see her again soon. Luke nodded off after his
heart stopped pounding in anticipation of the next day's events.

The next morning just after mess, one of the guards started
to call off the names of the prisoners who were to be transferred.
Luke and Sam's names were called early, and they exited the prison walls to form up lines, two abreast, for the march to the depot.
Nearly two hundred inmates were to be called, and the process

was taking some time. As the prisoners exited, guards would walk up and down the line, and as the line got longer and longer, each guard had more and more prisoners to watch.

When the last of the prisoners were being called, Sam motioned to a guard passing by. The sergeant stopped, looked at Sam and said, "What do you want?"

Sam flashed the two five-dollar gold pieces, holding them out in his hand with his palm up. "Please, let us pass, sir."

The sergeant first looked at the gold coins; ten dollars gold was a lot of money. Then he looked at Sam with a harsh look, eyes squinting as if he was about to be very angry. Then he looked back at the coins. Then he looked up and down the line. He looked at the coins again, grabbed them said, "Get the hell out of here."

Sam and Luke both casually walked out of the line over to some barracks, turned into the alley between them and, sheltered from immediate view, walked all the way to the end, turned right and exited Camp Chase through the main gate. They walked down an access road and into the outskirts of Columbus. "Remember, Luke, stay calm," Sam said. "They will notice we are gone any time now. Stay in crowded areas where you won't be distinguishable from anybody else. Get a haircut and wash, then work your way over to the Perrys'. Got it?"

Luke looked at Sam. He choked up, gave his great friend a hug and looked at him, unembarrassed, as tears streamed down his face. "How do I thank you?"

"The best way to thank me is to get the hell out of here and stop being a baby. Now go!"

Sam turned one way and gestured for Luke to turn the other. Luke was alone. He started to walk, joining a parade of people and carriages. Whenever he saw a military uniform or a policeman, he would cross the street. He seemed to be entering the center of the town when he saw a barber pole on the other side of the street. He crossed over and went in. The barber had a customer in his chair who was covered with a cloth to keep the hair clippings off. The barber told him he was next and to sit down on the bench by the window. Just as he was about to sit, he noticed the stripes on the trousers of the man getting a haircut. Luke froze. The guy in the chair, who was watching him from the mirror, said, "What's wrong, son, you look like you are hurting."

"Nothing serious, sir. Just my mother has been making biscuits again, and God only knows, she isn't very good at it. They just sort of lie in my stomach."

The guy in the chair laughed and continued his conversation with the barber.

As the soldier left, he glanced over at Luke with a smile and said, "Hope you feel better."

After the haircut and wash, Luke paid the man. He showed him Perry's address and asked where it was. "You know Paul Perry? the barber asked.

"Yes, sir. I just came up from Cincinnati and I don't know my way around."

"It is real simple, son. Down the street that way about two blocks," he said as he pointed to his right, "then left till you get to that number; about a fifteen-minute walk."

"Many thanks," Luke said and walked out of the shop. He felt more relaxed as he followed the barber's instructions. He was clean and his head felt about a pound lighter because of all the hair that had been cut off. He arrived at the Perrys' house around midday and knocked. Katie opened the door and looked at Luke quizzically, registering no recognition.

"Yes?" she said. "Can I help you?"

"It's me, Luke."

"Oh my God. Come right in," she said as she pulled him in and looked up and down the street to be sure nobody was following. "You look different; I didn't recognize you."

"Sam thought it best to cut my hair shorter to avoid being recognized. I hadn't had a haircut in months."

As they walked into their parlor, Luke looked around. The house was the nicest house he had ever seen.

"Paul is at work and Carol is at school. Sit down, sit down. You must be hungry. What can I get you?"

"Had breakfast this morning, so no thank you, m'am. I do not want to be any trouble, but I need a place to stay the night. I'll be off first light in the morning."

"Of course, of course. We have an extra bedroom upstairs. We thought you might come. As a matter of fact, we hoped you might come. Is Sam all right?"

"Yes, as far as I know. We separated as soon as we got out of Camp Chase."

"Excuse me a second," Katie said as she left the room. She came back in a moment and gave Luke a glass of lemonade. "Here, I just made this. Now sit down over here. This is Paul's favorite chair. Here's the paper. I'll be in the kitchen. I bet you haven't had apple pie in some time."

"Yes, m'am... I mean no, m'am. That sure sounds good."

Luke spent some time reading old newspapers from Cincinnati. It was how he first learned of the exploits of Jeb Stuart at the battle of Antietam. With all the Union victories in the West, Luke reasoned maybe it would be a lost cause to go back there. He resolved to go east, where Lee seemed to be having a better time of it. Stuart had a large cavalry and maybe he could join him. First, he had to get out of town, then somehow find Stuart.

Later that afternoon, as the aroma of fresh baked pie wafted through the house, Luke heard excited voices in the kitchen. Then he saw Carol, who pranced into the room. "Fancy meeting you here!" she said with a twinkle in her eye. She walked right over and sat down beside him. "You had your hair cut!" she said in a playful voice. "I loved your long hair... but now I can see more of your face, and I like that, too. And your new clothes! They are handsome."

It was as if she had known Luke all her life. She was so easy. Luke, however, still had trouble finding words to match her enthusiasm. She was so close to him, he felt the warmth of her leg against his. She was toying with him and he knew it. "Why don't you come over here and sit right next to me," he said. "Don't be bashful or anything."

"Oh, I'm not bashful at all." She leaned over and kissed him on the cheek. Her lips were soft and the sensation of the kiss lingered. He smelled her exotic rose fragrance. He flushed, feeling his face turn crimson.

"Okay, you win. I am speechless," he murmured.

She got up, moved to the chair on the other side of the coffee table and said, "Well, now that we got the first kiss over with, maybe we can talk and get to know each other better. The first thing I want to know is, why does everybody think you are such a big hero."

"It wasn't anything, really. But if you tell me a little bit about yourself, I might tell you a little about myself."

She got up and took another chair that was closer and at a right angle to where Luke was sitting. "You have a deal," she said and started to tell Luke about her life.

Carol was born on a small farm near Maryville, Tennessee, just south of Knoxville. She had an older brother, Calvin, with whom she was very close all through childhood. Her parents were farmers and their farm, while modest in size, was profitable and provided a decent life for the family. Calvin loved horses, learning to ride before he was big enough to mount one. His father would perch him on a horse, then slap the horse's flank and away they would go like the wind, with Calvin hanging on to the mane.

The Maryville area was very pro-Union, but Calvin always thought differently. In late 1861, he grew to resent the idea the North could dictate the terms of anybody's life and try to force a state to remain in the Union. It just didn't sit well with him. He had heard a lot about John Hunt Morgan and his Lexington Rifles, and the thought of riding with Morgan had great appeal to him. In early February of 1862, he heard Morgan was encamped at La Vergne, Tennessee, and he asked his father for permission to ride over and join him. After a long argument, his father refused. That night, Calvin left home and Carol had not seen him since.

Word spread rapidly of Calvin's departure, and it was generally believed he had joined Morgan even though nobody knew for sure. In spite of the fact that Carol's parents were pro-Union themselves, they were shunned by the community because of Calvin's action.

On a cold blustery day the following April, Carol and parents took a trip to Knoxville to purchase seed for planting that spring. When they returned a day later, they found their farmhouse had been burned to the ground by marauding Union sympathizers, and with it most of their belongings. While her parents stayed to rebuild, they thought Carol would be safer with her aunt and uncle in Columbus.

As the young people talked, the time flew by. Sometime later, Paul came in from the kitchen.

"Look who's here. Can you believe it? Look at him. Haircut, new clothes... I've been boring him with our life story."

"Not boring at all. Hello, Mr. Perry," Luke said as he reached out to shake Paul's hand. "Sam and I sure are obliged to you. We could not have made it this far without these clothes and your generosity."

"Think nothing of it, Luke. Any friend of Sam's is a friend of ours."

"Thank you, sir. Right now, I would have to say Sam's is the best friend I have ever had."

"Until you met me, Luke Pettigrew," Carol said, unexpectedly.

Luke felt his face turning red again. "Goes without saying," he said with a smile.

At the supper table, Katie and Carol pushed Luke to talk about Shiloh.

"We will not take 'no' for an answer," Carol insisted.

"Well, other than a dumb stunt I pulled taking chances that did not have to be taken, I am proud of my role in the medical corps."

"Medical corps? Are you a doctor?" asked Katie.

"Not even close. I was a stitcher and sewed up wounds after surgery or when soldiers came in with deep lacerations..."

"How did you deal with all the blood? Sounds horrible!" Carol interjected.

"Never bothered me, for some reason. Guess living on a farm and working with animals made me immune to that sort of thing."

"Were there a lot of wounded?" asked Paul. "And did you have adequate supplies? I hear the military hospitals are chronically short of everything, especially the Southern ones. Is that true?"

"Yes, but we had plenty of the basics. When I left the hospital, one of the doctors told me that a lot of the soldiers we treated would go home, look at the scars they had and remember the care they got at our little hospital. I am proud that I was able to help."

"Did you have to saw bones?" Carol asked.

"No, the surgeons did that."

"Why did you leave the hospital?" Paul asked.

"I was afraid of being captured, because of some trouble I may have caused them before."

The questions went on for a couple of hours when Paul said, "I think we have grilled Mr. Pettigrew enough. What are your plans for tomorrow, Luke?"

"First of all, I want to thank you for your generous hospitality. I wish I could stay here longer," he said as he glanced at Carol. "However, I want to get back to our lines and would like to leave tomorrow at first light."

"Where will you go?" Katie asked.

"I thought I would head south, cross the Ohio into Virginia and possibly join up with Jeb Stuart."

"Stuart? That rogue?" Paul said. "We don't know him but we do know one of his lieutenants, General Wade Hampton. If you ever run across him, tell him you know us."

"Will do. Sure seems like you know just about everybody." Hearing no response, Luke added, "Well I better get some sleep. Thank you again. I will be gone before you folks get up in the morning."

After goodbyes and a mysterious wink from Carol, Katie took him up to the extra bedroom and wished him a good night sleep. She closed the door and went back down.

Luke undressed and got into the bed. It was the biggest, softest bed he had ever been in. He lay on his back and tried to think about the day's events. But he was mentally exhausted, and he soon nodded off.

Sometime later, he was awakened by a rustling of the sheets and the movement of the mattress. "Mr. Luke Pettigrew," came a soft whisper, "mind if I share your bed?"

In an instant, Luke realized something wonderful was happening. He was excited but scared. It was fantasy he never dared to think or even dream about. A fantasy he never thought remotely possible, but here she was right next to him. In his bed, right next to him.

"I guess no answer means yes, am I right?"

"Ah... err... I guess so... Sure... I mean yes," he stammered.

Carol leaned over and gave him a full kiss on the lips. Luke, who had had little experience with girls, felt his embarrassment being overwhelmed by his physical attraction to her. Carol took his hand, put it on her shoulder. Luke, I thought and thought about coming into your room tonight – whether I should or shouldn't – but I decided to come. We have only known each other a short time, but tell me if I am wrong: We seem to have a mutual attraction."

She waited for Luke to speak. Slowly he said, "Yes, I can only say that I am very, very attracted to you. I can't say about the other way around."

"Well, I feel that if we just part, you going back to the war and me eventually getting back home to Tennessee, we may never see each other. You will never know how strongly I feel toward you and I may never know how you really feel. I mean, everything between us will be lost in time and nothing will become of this. We have so little time; you will be gone in the morning. I know coming into your bedroom like this is not ladylike. You may even think that I am some kind of hussy, but I just had to tell you how I feel. Does that make any sense to you?"

Luke looked into her eyes and could see she sincerely meant what she was saying. While he didn't know why she felt that way, he was very glad she did. "All I can say is you make me very happy," he said.

"Luke, I'm wearing a muslin sheet, and these are all buttons that hold it on. You have to agree that these buttons will remain buttoned as long as I am here tonight, otherwise I will have to go."

Luke couldn't find any words to answer.

"You promise?" she repeated and little more firmly.

"Yes, I promise."

She put her arms around him and kissed him full on the lips again. He began to kiss her back. He put his arms around and held her close, feeling her warmth. He thought he was in heaven.

At one point, Luke whispered playfully, "And where is my sheet? Do I have to keep it buttoned?"

"Just shut up," she said as she propped her head up on her elbow and ran her fingers through his hair. "I bet you have a good-looking girl back home just pining for your return."

"And I hope it's the good-looking one lying next to me."

A bit later, Carol whispered, "Luke Pettigrew, the next time we do this, you will not have to undo these buttons. I will do it."

She slid out of the bed, gave him one last kiss. " I loved you from the first minute I saw you." And she was gone.

The train station was nearly empty. It was barely light enough for Luke to see the departure schedules. From Columbus, his choices were Cleveland, Pittsburgh, Cincinnati and Indianapolis. The Pittsburgh train was the only one going anywhere near where he wanted to go, but it was not a daily run and the next departure was the following day. He could not loiter around for over a day without a high risk of getting caught, so he asked a passing railroad worker directions to the Ohio River, heading east. The worker suggested an old wagon route that went to Marietta, and Luke thought he could catch a steamer from there to Pittsburgh. Just outside of town, a freight hauler passed heading in the same direction. The driver was a grizzled old teamster and Luke, thinking that he was safe, yelled asking for a ride.

"Where you headed, boy?" the teamster hollered.

"Marietta, any chance you need some company."

"Hop on and hold on, kid."

The wagon never stopped completely as Luke scrambled up on top. As he settled next to the teamster, he glanced back at the cargo area. It was completely covered in canvas and strapped down tight, and judging from the depth of the wagon tracks in the dirt, the cargo was heavy.

Several days later, just before entering the town of Marietta, the teamster turned the wagon onto a little-used lane and pulled to a stop. "Son, I've watched you these past several days, and you are one of the escaped prisoners from Camp Chase, ain't I right?"

Surprised, Luke said, "What gives you that idea?"

"Every time we've met somebody coming or going, you have been on edge, like you wanted to hide somewheres. You are heading in this direction and with no clear destination, I figure you want to cross the river and get into Virginia."

Luke thought quickly. "Well, to be perfectly honest, I thought the same about you. You got a little twitchy every time we met somebody, like you were trying to hide something."

The teamster spat a big wad of spent tobacco out. "God damn it boy, you are smarter than I give you credit for. Let me show you something."

He got off the wagon, went to the rear and pulled up a corner of the canvas covering. "I've got five hundred Sharps breechloaders here. I cannot tell you how I got them, but I am to meet a small ferry just ahead here about a mile and unload. Once I get rid of them, my job is over."

Luke looked at the crate markings: "SHARPS RIFLE MANUFACTURING CO., Hartford, Connecticut."

"Where are they going? Luke asked.

"Don't know for sure," the teamster said. "But I heard they were going to Jeb Stuart. He's getting hammered by the Union cavalry using these same guns."

"Who is picking them up on the other side?"

"Probably another teamster like me."

They rode to the river's edge and waited until darkness fell. The teamster took out a lantern, lit it and started to wave it back and forth. Not long after, they saw a lantern on the other side; then it went out. The teamster sat his lantern on a rock and said, "They'll be here soon."

Luke walked to the water's edge and stared across the river, thinking about what he was going to do. Down deep, he would prefer most of all to return to Columbus. He could get a job; John would surely help with that. Maybe later buy a place, a small farm, get married, maybe go back to school and become a doctor. He liked that idea. Then there was Carol. During these last several days traveling with the teamster, he'd had a lot of time to think about Carol, and each time he did, a warm feeling came over him. He remembered her words, "I've loved you from the first time I saw you..." The giddy feeling overwhelmed him. "The next time I will undo the buttons..." He was consumed by her image, her warm body. He remembered her fragrance and it permeated his senses. But what would she think if he came back? He had a job to do, a duty to perform. Would she think less of him? Why on earth did she love him? What had he done to deserve that? Had she treated other young men the same? What would her family think if he came back?

He had to decide – turn around or get on the ferry and find Stuart.

The square bow of a flat-bottomed ferry slid quietly up on the soft riverbank. The ferry operator spoke in excited whispers to the teamster. Three more men appeared from the ferry, and the six of them made short work of transferring the cargo off the wagon. As the ferry prepared to push off, the savvy teamster looked at Luke and said, "You staying or going?"

"I'll be going with the cargo," he said to the teamster as he jumped on the ferry. "Good luck, and thanks for the ride."

The ferry disappeared in the cool darkness of the river.

Three weeks later, Luke and the cargo arrived at the headquarters of Lee's Army of Northern Virginia near Culpeper, Virginia. The camp and nearby village was a virtual city of horses, wagons, caissons and soldiers, thousands of soldiers. Clouds of dust rose from the feet of the marchers. The smell of mules, sweat, latrines, campfires and cooking food all blended into an assault on Luke's senses.

In the North, impatience with the war and anti-war sentiment were growing, particularly after Lee's spectacular victory in Chancellorsville. Sensing this, Lee wanted to move the war back onto Northern soil to Pennsylvania, then pivot and possibly attack the Union capital, Washington. He thought by doing so, he might just force Lincoln to give up the war.

To do this, Lee needed his movements hidden from Union cavalry, so he positioned Jeb Stuart several miles north along the southern banks of the Rappahannock to make sure Federal

pickets did not cross the river. On June 6th, Stuart had nearly
ten thousand cavalrymen in this immediate area.

Luke, still in the clothes the Perrys had given him, jumped
off the wagon and started to walk toward a large tent that had a
Confederate flag flying over it. He had not gone far when he saw
an officer walking toward him. "Sir, I am an escapee from Camp
Chase, and I'm reporting back to duty."

"Where the hell is Camp Chase, boy?" the officer asked.

"Near Columbus, Ohio, sir."

"Columbus, Ohio? Columbus, Ohio? You mean you came
here from Ohio? How in the hell did you do that?"

"Long story, sir, but after I escaped, I hooked a ride on the
shipment of repeating rifles that just arrived here," he said pointing to the wagon.

The officer looked over at the wagon. "That wagon came all
that way and crossed the mountains?"

"Yes, sir, with five hundred Sharps repeating rifles General
Stuart can surely use."

"You might be right," the officer said. "Wait here. I will be
right back."

The officer returned several minutes later with a lieutenant
who wore a cavalry uniform. The officer pointed at Luke. "This
here soldier has escaped from the Feds and has a present for you
guys."

Luke picked up on the introduction. "Yes, sir," saluting
smartly. "Five hundred Sharps carbines; thought you might find
a use for them."

The first officer excused himself and Luke and the lieutenant
walked over to the wagon where the freight had been uncovered.
Opening one of the cases that had a loose top, the lieutenant
pulled a rifle out and admired it. "Damn. You are right. We sure
could use these. We have a few now, mostly taken from dead
or wounded Yankees. These are the guns we have been fighting
against. Boy, will the general be happy to see these. Where's the

teamster? I want to take these a couple miles north so he can see them."

Luke looked around for the teamster, but he had disappeared. "Sorry, he seems to be missing, sir," Luke said.

"Can you drive the team?" the lieutenant asked.

"No."

"Well, can you ride a horse? I'll drive the wagon."

"Sure can, sir," Luke said.

The lieutenant gave the reins of his horse to Luke and then climbed up on the wagon. Luke admired the sleek chestnut, running his hand along the side of his neck. The graceful horse had a slim build, small hooves and long straight legs. Luke guessed it might be a horse bred for speed. He loved the warm, musty odor of a horse, and the soft skin around the nose. As the lieutenant released the brake on the wagon, Luke grabbed the front haunch of the military saddle with his left hand and hurled himself in the air with his usual back flip, landing neatly astride the saddle.

The lieutenant made note of Luke's ease with horses and his mounting method. Then he asked Luke where he had come from and how he happened to arrive on a wagon loaded with stolen rifles. Luke told him what he had told the previous officer. When he got to the part about being an escapee, the lieutenant asked Luke where he had been captured.

"Shiloh. Well, just after Shiloh..."

"You are here all the way from the Western theater?"

"Yes, sir. When I escaped in Ohio, I had to choose which way to go and decided to come east, because I really wanted to join the cavalry, and I had read about General Stuart in the newspaper."

"You seem to be comfortable on a horse. Why didn't you enlist in the cavalry at the beginning?"

"I'm from a small farm in eastern Tennessee, and I could not supply my own horse."

"How did you happened to be involved at Shiloh?" the lieutenant asked.

"Well, they found out I had some skill treating wounded, so they put me in a field hospital assisting two surgeons. There were so many wounded, after a couple long days, I think I could have sewn somebody up in my sleep. Probably did, actually."

The lieutenant, captivated, continued his questions. "So, if you were working in a hospital, I assume you were overrun by the Yankees..."

"Yes, sir."

"Well, they don't usually take hospital workers to prison, do they? As a matter of fact, I always assumed they let them continue working, even if they were captured."

"After Shiloh was over, Johnston was dead and our men were retreating back to Corinth, Mississippi, followed closely by General Forrest's cavalry."

"Nathan Bedford Forrest? I hear he is one tough son of a bitch," said the officer.

"As our boys retreated, Sherman's infantry got a little too close, and Colonel Forrest charged them with about six hundred screaming, saber-rattling men. You should have seen him, shooting with one hand and wielding his sword with the other..."

"Are you talking about Fallen Timbers?

"Yes, sir. I guess it was the last engagement in the big Battle of Shiloh."

"Is it true Forrest reached down, picked up a Union soldier and put him behind him to use as a shield when he rode back to his lines?"

"Saw it firsthand, with my own eyes, sir."

The lieutenant pulled up the team coming to a stop. He was thinking about what Luke had just said with puzzlement on his face. Then he squinted and looked sideways at Luke. "And you were the one wearing the white coat. You were the one who swept down, picked up the fallen colors and rode back to Forrest's line."

Luke didn't say anything. His face blushed and he just looked down, shyly.

"Did you meet him?"

"Yes, sir. Briefly," Luke replied.

"Wait until they hear about this back at camp," the lieutenant said as he slapped the reins on the backs of the draft horses.

Stuart's camp, located immediately adjacent to the Rappahannock, was a beehive of activity – horses by the thousands, wagons, mules, tents, captured cannon and ten thousand cavalrymen, all under a cloud of heavy dust and smoke.

When Luke and the lieutenant arrived at the southern edge of Stuart's camp, Luke could hear the neighing of the horses, the shouts of the men, the rumble of the wagons, the sporadic gunfire. He could smell the clay in the dirt, the acrid black-powder residue, the sweat of the men and horses, the leather and campfires.

The lieutenant pulled up the team and got off the wagon. Luke dismounted and waited. Despite the seeming chaos of the camp, there was an underlying order to the disorder. Each person seemed to have a goal, a job. Like scurrying ants on an anthill, they were accomplishing a bigger objective, one that very few knew specifically, but to which they were each contributing. Luke thought about his place and what he was doing to help. Which ant was he? He realized something had changed. What? Was it that he'd been in prison and escaped? Or was it Carol? Maybe what had changed was that he cared for somebody and that somebody cared for him. He wanted to go home to her, be with her, love her. Maybe for the first time since he had enlisted, he wanted to be sure he could go home, make a new home, settle down. Carol. Was she real or imaginary? Was her visit to his bedroom just a dream? But for those few moments to be so vivid, so unbelievably heaven-like could not have been a dream. Is this what love was like?

Luke's trance was broken when the lieutenant returned with another officer. "Sir, this is Luke Pettigrew. We were speaking about him..."

Instead of saluting, the officer extended his hand. "Luke, I am an aide-de-camp for General Hampton. Glad to meet you. Nice work escaping from Camp Chase and bringing those repeaters all the way over here. We need them."

Luke shook the colonel's hand. "Just hitched a ride was all, sir. I don't deserve any special attention. Did you say General Hampton, sir? General Wade Hampton?"

"None other. Why are you surprised?"

"Well, when we escaped from Chase, we had some help from Mr. Paul Perry, and he said if I ever ran into Wade Hampton to be sure I mention that I knew him."

"Paul Perry, you say? I will mention it to the general. Meantime, we can surely use you here. We lost a couple of couriers at Chancellorsville, and we'll use you to help fill in. Lieutenant, see if you can scrounge up a uniform for this man and requisition a good horse and saddle from the quartermaster." Looking back at Luke he said, "Welcome to the cavalry, son."

Luke saluted and the colonel walked away, leaving just the lieutenant. "If you like to ride, you will love being a courier," he said. "Can be dangerous, but in the heat of battle, your job will be extremely important. Only the very best of the best horsemen are couriers in this army. Your reputation got you the job."

Luke was thrilled to be in the Confederate cavalry. He was under Wade Hampton. He reflected back to Shiloh and his impulsive ride on the borrowed horse at the Battle of Fallen Timbers. He was happy it got him in Stuart's cavalry, but he realized that he probably wouldn't do it again. So much had changed.

Chapter 18

ZACH

The breeze blew gently over the grassy hillside just south of the small town of Gettysburg. Union Brigadier General John Buford was using his binoculars to scan the Chambersburg Pike, which headed west out toward Cashtown.

"This high ground is one hell of a good defensive position," he thought to himself. He dismounted and walked over to a natural stone wall. "If there is going to be a battle, whoever holds this hill would certainly have a huge advantage."

Buford, a Kentucky native and an 1848 graduate of West Point, was promoted to brigadier general in 1862 and given a cavalry brigade in the 2nd Corps of the Army of Virginia under Major General John Pope. Although he had been wounded in the knee at the Second Battle of Bull Run, his outstanding performance had eventually earned him his own cavalry brigade. On this morning of July 1st, 1863, Buford was a wily, experienced commander, having just three weeks earlier led his division at the Battle of Brandy Station, the largest battle of mounted cavalry in American history.

Continuing to scan, he got the first glimpse of Confederate infantry marching down the road directly toward his brigade.

The road snaked around from behind trees, and as the column advanced, Buford began to realize he was looking at a substantial force. He concluded that it must be the division under his old friend Harry Heth, who had just become a major general.

More to himself than to anybody else, he said, "If that is Heth, what's he doing coming up that road blind, with no Confederate cavalry to scout ahead of him?" Then he turned to Colonel William Gamble, who was mounted just next to him. "Colonel, what do you make of this?"

"Damned if I know, sir. Seems mighty strange. I hear Stuart is on a raiding mission up north of here."

"Yeah, I heard that, too. Must mean that Bobby Lee is running blind and has no idea the whole Union Army is to his south."

"If Heth sees us here, he probably will stop and wait for orders, don't you think?" asked Gamble.

"Hell no," Buford replied. "He won't wait. He will want this high ground just as badly as we do. Harry was in the class at West Point just in front of me, and I remember he always wanted to attack first. He always wanted to be the aggressor, to be on the offensive, not the defensive."

Buford continued to scan, "Yep, Heth will spread out in a line at the bottom of this hill and attack head on, not waiting for anything. He might not even wait for his whole division to arrive before he attacks."

Buford turned his horse and rode over to the other side of the hilltop. He scanned to the south. "No sign of Reynolds," he said. Major General John Reynolds was commander of the Union 1st Corps, under which Buford was assigned. He was somewhere back down the road Buford had just traveled.

Buford turned to go back to observe Heth. The line of Rebel infantry just kept getting longer and longer. It was now about a mile away. He beckoned an aide to come up. "I want you to personally tell General Reynolds that Heth is in force just in front of us with at least two brigades and probably more to come. Tell him we have the high ground, and I will hold it until he arrives. Tell him to hurry at all possible speed. Do you understand?"

Buford thought a moment. "And tell him I think Lee and Heth have no idea where the Union Army is now. Tell him Heth has no cavalry in this area, and if he can think of any way of keeping Lee from finding out our deployment, we will have more time to entrench the whole army on this high ground."

"Yes, sir," said the aide, about to spur his horse on.

"Before you go, repeat what I just said," Buford asked.

The aide repeated the order and took off at full gallop. "Now, Colonel, here is what I want you to do. Take your full brigade, dismount, and deploy all along those rocks there," Buford said pointing at the long line of rocks and rubble on the crest of the hill. "Your men will have to spread out to appear like you are a bigger force than you are, probably three or four feet apart. Make sure your men have plenty of ammunition, because we all might be doing a lot of shooting over the next few hours. Heth will attack and all of Hill's 3rd Corps may arrive before Reynolds gets here. We must hold the top of this ridge."

The two officers dismounted and walked up the line of rocks, placing the men in secure defensive positions where they could fire freely and offer very little exposure. The area would be ideal; they would be shooting down on the advancing Rebels, and both hoped this advantage would be enough to hold until Reynolds arrived, because they could be outnumbered as much as five to one.

Fifteen minutes later, Buford's aide arrived at the front of the Union's 1st Corps and went directly to Reynolds himself. "Sir, an urgent message from General Buford, sir."

The aide repeated Buford's exact message.

"Could you actually see Heth's two brigades, or are you just guessing?" Reynolds asked.

"Sir, we could see them all, sir, right there in front of us coming right toward us."

Reynolds thought a moment. "You go back and tell Buford we will be there as soon as humanly possible." He dismissed the aide with a wave of his hand and ordered his corps to march forward without delay. He pulled his horse to the side of the columns and took a moment to reflect on Buford's message. "What did Buford mean when he suggested we try to keep Lee from finding out the Union positions?" he thought. "How could we do anything about that?"

  He sent a courier back to Major General George Meade, telling him of Buford's report and his own intentions. He continued to sit on his horse thinking about the second part of Buford's message. After several minutes, he got off his horse, took some writing paper from his saddlebag and wrote the following:

To Major General Dan Sickles:
The enemy is in force just north and west of the little town of Gettysburg. We have reason to believe Lee does not know the location of the Union Army, because Stuart is up further north conducting various raids. We need to keep Lee in the dark a little while longer, and this is where I need a favor. I seem to remember that you have the U.S.S.S. attached to your corps. If you could send one or two of your best marksmen out and get between Lee's headquarters and his army with instructions to hit any courier riding north to Lee's position, we may gain a day, and that one day might make all the difference in this major battle that is developing down here. Hope to return the favor sometime.
Your obedient servant,
Major General J. Reynolds

Reynolds motioned for a courier to come up. "Find Sickles and give him this message. This is of the utmost importance, and he needs to get this message as fast as possible. The outcome of this battle may depend on it."

"Yes, sir," said the courier, spurring his horse hard.

Reynolds was born only a few miles from his present location, and he knew the surrounding country well. He also knew almost exactly where Buford was and why Buford thought the high ground was so important. "Wish I had five more Bufords," he said to another aide.

As Reynolds made his way back to the front of the column, General Abner Doubleday rode up along side of him. "What's going on, General?" Doubleday asked. "Looks like we might see some action soon."

"'Soon' is an understatement, General. Let's go up and see what Bobby Lee has in mind."

The two rode off in a gallop, followed by the color guard. Shortly, they could hear cannon fire and then heavy rifle reports. "That would be Heth and Buford going at it," Reynolds said as they picked up the pace.

General Buford was descending the tower of the Lutheran Theological Seminary just west of Gettysburg in the process of directing what was quickly turning into a full-fledged battle. He saluted as his commander approached, "Sure glad to see you, General. As you can see, we are engaged."

Reynolds looked up and down the line. "Mighty fine job here, General. My men are a couple miles back. Can you hold?"

"Well, sir, we have the advantage of our breech-loading rifles. Watch 'em. We are firing three or four times as fast as they are. Also, we have this high ground and we're entrenched. Sir, it will take a lot more than what is in front of us right now to get us out of here."

"Harry won't waste much time putting everything he's got into this," Reynolds said. "Not sure we will be able to hold him with all of my men. But the most important thing is time. If we can hold until late in the day, the whole Union Army will be here by then and we will prevail. This is a battle we can win, and maybe we can drive Bobby Lee all the way back to Hades. This whole war could end right here." He saluted and said, "Nice work, John. Now you hold, and I'll be right back with some infantry." He spurred his horse and went back down the road.

Since early on that same day, the Sharpshooters had been bivouacked just outside a small town called Emmitsburg, about ten miles south of Gettysburg. The camp was full of locals sympathetic to the Northern cause, all cheering and expressing good wishes.

"Everybody just sort of assumes a big battle is about to happen," said Zach to his sergeant.

"Yeah, you can feel the tension. All of these people know the whole Rebel Army is just north of here and just itching to get on with it."

Then the lieutenant ordered everybody to fall in as briskly as possible. They would be heading north toward Bobby Lee.

"Hot damn!" said the sergeant. "Meade is going to take it to 'em."

Rain had fallen in the night and the roads were muddy. Marching was difficult, and the call for quick time made it more so. "What's the matter with these Pennsylvanians?" asked a marcher. "I don't think they even know a road from a cow path."

Soon thereafter, Zach heard horses approaching rapidly from the rear. They stopped near him. "Hey, Harkin, can you ride a horse?" It was Colonel Berdan, who looked like he had been riding hard.

"Yes, sir," said Zach, surprised.

"Well, get on this one," the colonel said, motioning to his lieutenant to give him the reins of a big chestnut they had in tow.

The whole line had come to a stop with Berdan's arrival, and the sergeant walked back to see why. "What's this all about, sir?"

"Orders from way up high. No time now."

Zach mounted the horse as the sergeant held the reins. The stirrups were too long so he started to get off to make an adjustment.

"No time for that now, we can fix those when we take a break," said the colonel. "Let's go."

The horse Zach had been given had an uneven gait that took some time to get used to, especially because Zach could not use the stirrups to soften his ride. They had ridden hard for four miles when they came to an open area in the trees. The colonel led them off, and they approached a group of mounted officers huddled in a circle.

"General, Colonel Berdan reporting as ordered, sir." He saluted smartly. "I've brought the sharpshooter you requested."

"Ah, Berdan," said General Sickles as he turned in his saddle. "None too soon. I'll be right with you." He motioned for them to wait.

General Daniel Sickles, 44, was a Tammany Hall lawyer with a colorful past. He had been made a major general by his friend General Hooker and given the 3rd Corps, now serving under Meade. Without a military background, Sickles tended to act brashly in battle, sometimes ignoring direct orders, but he never lacked in courage.

After he finished his conversation with his staff, Sickles turned his horse and rode over to the colonel and Zach. He dismounted and indicated that they do the same. He walked over to a patch of bare ground, picked up a stick and started to draw a rough map in the dirt. Without waiting to be introduced to Zach, he drew a small circle and said, "Son, here is the little town of Gettysburg, and here is where we are now." He made a dot on the makeshift map. "Over here is Lee's probable headquarters, and this area here is the western flank of the Confederate Army. Now, we have every reason to believe Jeb Stuart is up here," he said as he pointed considerably north of their location. "Lee might not know the Union Army's exact position. If we can keep him in the dark for the next twenty-four hours, we just might have the one tactical advantage we need to rout that old fox and send him back to Richmond."

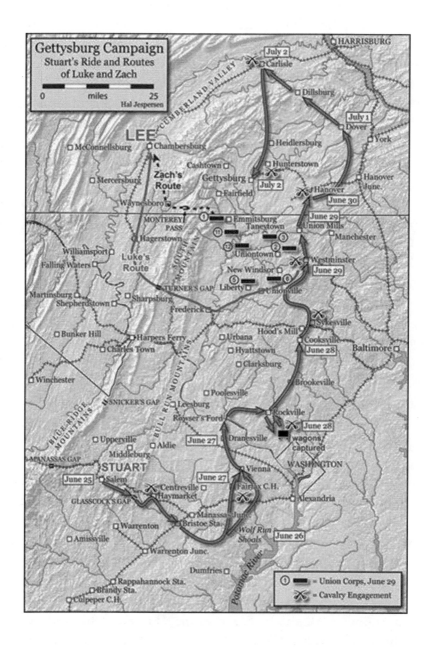

The general paused as the colonel and Zach stared at the map, both wondering what he was getting at.

"This is where you might help us, son," the general continued, pointing to a spot just north of Lee. "You need to get rid of that uniform and sneak into this area undetected. There is a lot of brush and scrub you can hide in as you move. You should go through Monterey Pass here. Then when you get to this point, you'll find a slight knoll. From it, you will be able to see. Your job is to discourage any courier activity from south to north. You will be able to identify couriers because they are usually unarmed and riding fast. Any questions?"

Zach stared at the map. The magnitude of the task and the obvious risk slowly sank in. Even the colonel, squatting next to the map, was speechless, his mouth open.

"Son, do you understand the plan?" asked the general with some irritation.

"I guess so, sir," Zach managed.

"Very well. Time is of the essence. You need to get moving immediately." The general motioned to an aide, "Get this soldier out of his uniform and into some regular clothes, Sergeant. Now."

"May God be with you, son, and good luck," the general said, mounting his horse again.

After donning the ill-fitting clothes provided by the sergeant, and checking his rifle, Zach took off, envisioning the simple map the general had drawn. He felt a rush of adrenaline as he realized he was on his own. All of his concerns about his assignment disappeared. He started to run at a slow pace he knew he could sustain for a long time. Staying low to the ground, he kept heading generally west, suspecting that he might be in enemy territory already.

He stopped in a copse of small trees to get his bearings, looking ahead to pick a path that would afford as much cover as possible. He moved on, then stopped, listened, scanned, moved on and repeated the process. Zach realized that if were to be seen, his rifle with the scope would give him away and he would probably be shot on the spot. Again, he felt like he was squirrel hunting, but this time, if the squirrel saw him, he would be dead. He was not scared; he was thrilled. He thought about how his parents had wanted him to work behind the lines where it was safer. He was behind the lines, all right, but behind enemy, not friendly, lines. He thought about how he used to stalk deer in Tennessee in the fall and how he would go out into the woods and practice walking without making a sound. How he would place each foot, missing twigs and leaves, practicing so that he could sneak up on a deer upwind until he could almost talk to it. As a kid he had often wished he had been born one hundred years earlier, so he could learn from the Indians their ways of hunting.

Following a tree line, he rounded the top of a small rise and stopped cold. To his right was a column of butternut uniforms marching four abreast down a narrow road in his direction. He lay flat on the ground and waited until the regimental-sized column passed. The Rebels were no more that one hundred yards from him.

Up again, angling to the northeast, he slid down a small gully, being careful to keep his gun high and dry. The small stream at the bottom flowed with muddy water, which meant something or somebody had recently gone through this area upstream. At the top of the gully, on the other side, he crouched down and peeked over the top. Seeing nothing, he continued on to a small patch of briars. The briars were impenetrable, so he started to skirt around to his left. He looked ahead and saw a pass between the mountains. It had to be Monterey Pass. Almost around the patch, he stopped suddenly. Horses... he heard horses coming his way through the pass. In the instant, he knew he had no choice. Zach jumped headlong into the briars, which tore his clothes and then his exposed skin. He stayed on his hands and knees, motionless, listening. He noticed his hands were bleeding; blood was beginning to drip down from his nose.

The horses were leading a large column of soldiers. Zach considered it a good omen that, even though they were headed east, they seemed to be in no hurry, which meant they still might not know the Union Army was approaching Gettysburg.

The column passed and after waiting several moments, he started to back out of the briars. It was very painful, but finally he extricated himself, wiped some of the blood off his face and continued. After hiking up and over the pass, he turned due north and traversed the far edge of a thick woods. In front of him was a very long field that gently rose to a crest nearly two miles away. He lay down and brought his rifle up to scan through the scope. As he scanned up the rise, he could see soldiers every-where, some marching and some resting. He scanned further up the hill and on the very top, just under two very large trees, he saw a large white tent. Zach's pulse quickened as he noted a flag flying on the top of the tent. It was Lee.

Zach wondered what in the heck he was supposed to do now. The general's map, and his job, had seemed so simple. He'd thought he understood it. Now he was in position, as ordered, but the actual execution of the task seemed elusive. He was fur-ther hindered by the very limited field of his scope. It was nearly impossible to scan distances nearly beyond normal visual range, because he needed to see an image with his bare eyes before he could find it in his scope.

"Discourage any courier riding from south to north," the gen-eral had ordered. "A courier will be unarmed and riding fast..."

Zach continued to appraise his situation and concluded that if he moved to the western corner of the woods, which was a bit higher, he would be in the most advantageous spot. He was fac-ing north, so that any courier he would see heading toward Lee's headquarters could be the one with a message about his troop's position. "That is good," he thought to himself, "because a rider moving quickly away is a lot easier target than one moving from left to right..."

Finding a large elm tree, Zach lay prone next to it, readied his rifle and started to wait for his prey. Before long, a rider galloping fast appeared on his left heading up the rise. He quickly sighted through the scope, centering his spider lines on the back of the rider, who had an ammunition pouch and a small knapsack. He's not a courier, Zach thought. He felt better. At least he could tell a potential target from one who was not.

Another rider, then another came by, but neither seemed to be a courier. Zach waited. A rider with a side arm appeared. He let him go. Then Zach wondered about what he would do if he found a target and fired. Surely, the Rebs would hear the shot and come for him. How would he escape? He spotted another briar patch growing in swampy ground about two hundred yards in front. That would be a place to hide, he thought. But how could he get there unseen?

Then Zach heard a horse approaching very fast from his left rear along the western edge of the woods. He put his head down flat to make himself less visible. The rider passed within twenty feet. Zach could see him clearly without the scope. No ammunition belt, no side arm, no knapsack. His mount was in a flat out run, with the rider floating on top, moving with the horse like he was part of the saddle. The rider's curly hair blew in the wind behind his cap. Zach drew up his rifle and looked through the scope, centering the spider lines on his target. This is it, he thought. This has to be a courier, and he might have the exact information Sickles didn't want Lee to get. He centered the spider lines again. The rider appeared to be a very young man. Zach suddenly thought about the sniper's diary from several weeks ago. He thought about this boy's family waiting for him to come home. Images of the sniper with the long black hair and shattered jaw flooded in. Images of others he had killed, of families waiting for their loved ones to come home. He had changed their lives forever. Who was he to take this man's life?

He centered the spider lines and took a deep breath. Again, the vision of a family waiting. He held his aim, another deep breath. He lowered the rifle.

He thought about his orders. He had been given an order. An order that could have an effect on the upcoming battle. He couldn't do it. On an impulse, he lowered the spider lines to the left side of the horse's rump and fired. The left side of the horse collapsed, throwing the rider into the center of the briar patch. Zach looked up from his rifle. Rider and horse had disappeared into the thick briars, and all he could hear was the severe thrashing of the injured animal. He waited, hardly able to breathe. He forced himself to take deep breaths to get control of himself.

He laid the rifle down beside him. He stared at the rifle. It looked like a poisonous snake. A lethal killer. The once beautiful hand-crafted weapon his father had painstakingly made for him. The carefully carved stock made to fit *his* hand. The special scope. A viper. He hurled the rifle against a tree and glared at the damaged remains.

The thrashing in the briars stopped after a few minutes. Zach started to look at things rationally again. He could not think about escape. He kept worrying about the young man in the briars. He had been thrown in almost headfirst and must be severely injured. The fact that he was just doing his job never entered his mind. The need to find his way back to his unit never entered his mind, either. He had to find a way to help the soldier, even if it meant getting shot himself. Without thinking, he got up and started to walk toward the patch, casually at first, then breaking into a run. He didn't care if he was seen.

Zach reached the point where the horse had fallen into the wiry brambles. The Confederate soldier, his leg bent grotesquely, lay just beyond the horse. Zach crawled over the horse, avoiding the prickly vines as much as possible, and placed his hand on the young man's forehead looking for a sign of life. The body was still warm. Zach reached for the arm to check the pulse. The beat was fast and strong, and Zach said a silent thank you. He knew the young man would live.

Zach heard a soft moan as he looked at the young man's leg. The broken thighbone had torn through the skin and was sticking up in the air. Somehow, Zach would have to pull him out of the patch and onto open ground before he could do anything. Never having had to deal with such a severe wound before, Zach thought he would lift the soldier out, then worry about everything else. As he picked him up and walked back over the horse, the leg hung down, just attached by muscle and sinew.

Zach laid him down flat on his back and attempted to put the leg back near where it should have been. The young man was losing a lot of blood just above the center of his thigh. He opened his eyes and looked at Zach, "What happened?"

"Your horse went down and you fell."

"I don't feel anything in my left leg."

"You have a bad fracture and you are losing blood." Zach put his hand on the young man's forehead. "Plus you have a nasty lump on your head."

The young man raised his head and grimaced as he saw the fracture. "Are you a doctor?"

"No, and I am not sure help is nearby," Zach said.

"The first thing we have to do is stop the bleeding. Tear a strip off my shirt and tie it just above the wound.

Zach quickly tore off a whole sleeve from his own shirt, because that was the easiest. He thought the rider must have some medical experience; he seemed to be sure of what needed to be done. "Okay, now what should I do? Tie it around your thigh here? he said, pointing at the top of his leg.

"Yes, but tie it real loose."

Zach did so. "Now what?"

"Get a strong stick," he looked to his side. "Here is one right here. Now put the stick between the skin and the cloth and twist it as tight as you can."

As Zach tightened, the rider winced. "Now hold that for a while until the bleeding has stopped. How much blood have I lost?"

"You have quite a puddle back there, but the horse bled a lot, too, and it's hard to tell whose blood is whose. Are you a doctor?"

"No, but I have had some training for these kinds of situations. Never on myself, though."

Zach didn't think the rider knew he was the one responsible for the horse's fall, and he was hesitant to carry on any further conversation.

"Sure appreciate your help. How did you happen to be here when the horse fell?"

Zach avoided the question. "Isn't this too tight?"

"Has the blood flow stopped?"

Zach looked carefully at the wound, "Yeah, seems to have completely stopped."

"Okay, loosen the stick just a little. Where are you from? You must be a Yankee transplant. You sure don't have much of a Southern drawl."

Zach thought quickly, "Neither do you. Where are you from?"

"Crossville. If I've not started to bleed again, you can take that tourniquet off."

"Tennessee?" Zach studied the young man's freckled face. He looked familiar.

The rider winced as Zach unwrapped the tourniquet. "We'll have to set this bone, then put on a splint on it to make it stable. Can you do it?"

"I'll sure try, but you are the one in pain," Zach said.

"The pain won't come for a while, so let's get on with it. We need a stiff tree limb and lots of strips of cloth."

Zach stood. "I'll be right back." He went toward the woods looking for a sturdy stick. He thought about the young man. His size, his freckles, his hair. Crossville. He was so familiar.

"Looks like you have had a fight with a cat," the young man said looking at Zach's lacerations from the briars.

"It's nothing. What now?"

"The upper and lower pieces of the broken bone have to be fitted back together exactly the way it was broken. Then we wrap it all up, attach the piece of wood so it can't move, and we will be done."

For the next hour or so, the young man guided Zach through the process of setting the compound fracture. The rider was in a lot of pain, but amazingly he never lost focus on what had to be done.

After it was over, Zach said, "Now I can go and try to find some help. Will you be okay?"

"I think so, soldier. You are a soldier, aren't you?"

"Yes, I am. By the way, what were you doing in this area?"

The young man thought for a while. "Well, I remember having an extremely urgent message for General Lee, but I can't remember what it was. It'll come back to me soon."

Zach stood up. "I will be right back with some help."

"Why are you out of uniform?" the young man asked.

Zach did not respond as he hurried away. Walking up the rise, he started to realize how very tired he was, and also how he must look, with bloody scratches all over and no shirt. He waved to an approaching rider. "There's a man about half a mile back who is severely wounded and needs help."

"Okay, I'll ride up," the man said pointing up the hill. "Won't take long. What about you? You don't look so good yourself."

"I'll be all right," Zach said.

The rider took off and Zach started walking back to the east. He could hear the roar of cannon fire. Later, he came to a large tree in the middle of a field, sat down against the tree and rested.

"Dear God, Dad may have been right," he thought as he felt the exhaustion in his body pull him to sleep.

Chapter 19

LUKE

Luke had been filled with a strange sense of foreboding these past few days. The June 9th Battle of Brandy Station had ended with neither side able to claim a victory. For the North, just the fact they had not lost was a triumph of sorts. For the South, Stuart's objective had been to keep the movements of the Army of Northern Virginia undiscovered, and he had succeeded. Lee was able to continue his move toward Pennsylvania, where he hoped to end the war once and for all. He still thought Union resolve was weakening. If he could take the initiative to Northern soil, he just might turn popular opinion enough so that Lincoln would have to call the whole thing off and end the fighting.

In late June, Stuart took his forces to the southeast, crossing the Occoquan River then heading north to arrive at Fairfax Station, just a few miles west of Washington D.C. While he considered raiding the Union capital itself, he skirted around it and continued to the north, destroying supply depots, tearing up railroad tracks and spreading as much terror as possible. He planned to join up with Ewell's corps and then meet Lee as he proceeded north.

Stuart's progress was delayed time and again by detours and various skirmishes with Federal cavalry. He arrived in Westminster early on June 29th, shortly after Hampton. After a brief meeting between Stuart and Hampton in the middle of the little town, Stuart decided to send a message to Lee, telling him their location, and informing him they had thus far been unable to contact Ewell.

"We've driven our men and horses pretty hard these last few days, General," Hampton said to Stuart. "Not sure how much longer we can continue at this pace."

The relationship between Hampton and Stuart was cordial but not warm. Hampton was a very Southern plantation owner, reserved, always gentlemanly, steeped in the Southern aristocracy. He avoided the press and shunned alcohol, large parties and social occasions. Stuart, on the other hand, reveled in notoriety and relished large gatherings. They both knew this about each other and understood they would never be close friends, but they worked together well.

"This is the most frustrating expedition I have ever been on, General. What with this heat and the lack of food... It's the raid from hell," Stuart said. "However, we've got to press on. Who is our best courier? Heck, Lee at least should know where his main cavalry is."

"I agree, sir, and we probably should not write a dispatch. If the courier were to be captured," Hampton said, "we wouldn't want those bluecoats to know our plans."

Hampton turned around, looking at the three mounted couriers who were sitting on their horses waiting to be called. He pointed at Luke, "Pettigrew, come on over here."

From his horse, Luke had been studying these two generals and their obvious character differences. Stuart seemed a swashbuckling, bold, brash commander, ready to take chances and gamble on the outcome. He had the countenance of a man who was self-confident enough to think that whatever he decided to do would work out to his advantage. Stuart reminded him of himself – possibly his old self. Hampton, on the other hand, seemed cautious, somebody who would never act impulsively, never take an uncalculated risk even though he had the strength. He reminded Luke of his father.

When he heard Hampton call him, Luke jumped off his horse and ran over to the general, almost tripping in his rush to keep him from waiting. He saluted and said, "Sir."

"General Lee's headquarters is approximately due west of here, maybe ten to fifteen miles," Hampton said. "Your job is to find him and give him this message, 'We are in Westminster, proceeding north, plan to arrive at your location tomorrow, God willing.' You've got that, son?"

"Yes, sir... No problem, sir," Luke said as he saluted again, smartly.

Stuart interjected, "One more thing, Pettigrew. If you run across any substantial Union troop movement, make note. Be sure to report the size, movement direction and other details to Lee. We have been separated from him too long, and I suspect he might be hungry for scouting information."

"Sir," Luke said. "Will that be all, sir?

"And don't take any chances," Hampton added. "If you see Union movements, go around, don't let them catch you, okay?"

Luke nodded.

"Now get going, we are counting on you," Hampton said.

Stuart smiled as he saw Luke back flip onto his buckskin. "I remember when I was that age. Damn, those were the good old days," he said turning to Hapmton. "Don't forget to thank your old friend Paul Perry for sending him over here."

"It must have been quite a sight at Shiloh, that kid riding out of nowhere right into the Union line. I heard his horse was shot three or four times in the rear," Hampton said. "Let's keep an eye on him. Wonder if he can shoot as well as ride."

As Luke started out to the west, he thought about his encounter with Stuart and Hampton. He thought of his father. Luke sat proudly on his saddle and kept his buckskin to a slow gallop, knowing the journey could be long and wanting to spare the horse as much as possible.

Luke crossed a small stream and slowed up to a trot. He was cautious, sensing that behind every tree, rock or hill, danger loomed. Being unarmed, he felt like a prey, like he was being watched. He proceeded at a walk, winding his way through a large copse of thick trees. Exiting the trees, he dismounted just before reaching the crest of a small hill. As he peered over the top, he saw a small group of Union cavalry heading north. He froze. He was several hundred yards from the cover of the trees.

"You there! Halt!" came a voice from his immediate right. It was a Union cavalryman spurring his horse and coming toward him, pointing a pistol right at him. Luke had been so taken by the troops in front of him he had not noticed the soldier on his right.

It was fight or flight, and the decision was instantaneous – flee. He flipped onto his horse and in three steps was at full speed. The pursuer was within thirty yards. Luke bent forward with his head next to his horse's neck to reduce his profile. He waited for the shot. He heard the rapid clump-ditty-clump of the pursuer's mount bearing down. Luke didn't want to look back. To do so would increase his profile, making a larger target. No shot. He let the reins slack between his hands and the bridle, letting his horse know he wanted everything she had. Still no shot. He could hear the man's horse panting. Was he getting closer? He turned left toward some trees three or four hundred yards ahead. The mare made a faint grunt with each footfall. Why didn't the soldier shoot? The trees ahead were mature, long-needled pines. There were some low branches. Maybe, just maybe.

Horse and rider entered the woods. An instant later, the horse behind Luke did the same. The sound of the hooves changed as soon as they hit the fallen pine needles. Luke let the mare pick the way. He saw two big trees with large low limbs in front, and the horse headed straight toward them. Without thinking, Luke took both feet out of the stirrups, held on to the saddle with one hand and hooked his ankle on the saddle horn, lowering his body well to the side of the horse. Clearing the tree limb by mere inches, he instantly moved to the other side to avoid the next limb, clearing it by less than the one before.

"THUMPP" came from behind. He heard his pursuer's panicked scream. The hoofbeats continued. Luke righted himself and stole a glance behind. The soldier had made it under the first limb, but not the second. The horse was veering to the right, still traveling fast. The rider, failing to get both feet out of the stirrups, was being dragged behind. The horse panicked. When it swerved to miss a tree, the soldier swung out. "THUMPP." It was the sickening sound of bones and flesh hitting the tree squarely. Finally the horse stopped. The rider did not move.

Luke exited the woods and continued at a fast pace for a mile or so, then slowed to give the mare a breather. Luke needed a breather, too, as he scanned the area for more signs of bluecoats. He'd thought he was a goner back there. Why didn't the Yankee shoot? Luke had tried not to show him much profile, but certainly he should have taken a shot. Why didn't he?

Feeling safer now, Luke again angled his horse to the west, trying to stay behind trees, or rocks, or whatever cover the landscape offered. He reached around for his canteen, and as he did so, he glanced at his courier pouch, still strapped around his waist and hanging on his back. He thought a moment and it came to him. The soldier hadn't shot at him because he was a courier. He wanted the information he might have had in his pouch, and if the pouch was empty, he would have wanted him alive for questioning. The Union was looking for all the information they could find. He understood it now.

Luke approached a river. He traveled south until he found an easy way to cross that offered limited views up and downstream. He crossed over, the buckskin swimming easily. He rode up a small rise. In the distance, he could see the Bull Run Mountains. Behind them were the Blue Ridge Mountains. And behind that, much farther west, was home and Carol. That warm, glowing feeling swept over him again as the thought of her quickened his heartbeat. Maybe by the end of this year's campaign, this war would be over. Maybe Lee could continue to work miracles and defeat these invaders.

He continued to scan to the west. Several miles ahead, maybe more, large clouds of dust extended for miles right to left. He pulled up. He rode forward several hundred yards, pulled up again. Soldiers! Thousands, maybe tens of thousands of infantry moving north. Who were they? Remembering Stuart's orders to scout out as much information as he could, Luke proceeded slowly forward again, staying in cover as much as possible, only showing himself when he had to.

After another slow walk, he stopped behind a rock outcropping, dismounted and climbed to the top. He lay hidden as he tried to make out what was in front of him. The increased elevation of the rocks helped him get a better view. Blue. The infantrymen were in blue. They were right behind Lee, following him from a distance. Did Lee know it? How could he? His cavalry was ten to fifteen miles east, heading north. Lee was moving blind, not knowing enemy disposition, which was what Stuart had feared.

He then realized delivering this message to Lee's headquarters was of vital importance. His mission had to be accomplished. He had to tell Lee what he knew. He climbed back down to his horse. He started to think about how he could get on the other side of the Bull Run Mountains to the west, then use the mountain as cover to travel north to find Lee's headquarters. How could he get to the other side of the whole advancing Yankee army? If he flanked to the north, the Union cavalry would be everywhere. Not so at the rear. To the north was much shorter and take much less time; to the south, and he probably would not get there until tomorrow. Thinking he had two priorities, the first being to be sure to deliver the message and the second to get there as fast as possible, he chose the safer way. Better to get there for sure than not get there at all. He turned south. A fleeting thought went through his mind. Would he take the safer route if somebody wasn't waiting on the other side of those mountains?

The sun was falling behind some rising clouds and those same Blue Ridge Mountains three hours later. Luke estimated he had traveled twenty to twenty-five miles and was near the town of Frederick. He had stopped periodically, and the dust cloud to his west seemed to be endless. Now, as he looked west, the dust diminished, and Luke thought he might be near the end of the Union columns. He thought the army would stop soon for the night. He did not expect many pickets, because of being in the rear and the perception the enemy was way north. All the better for him to get to the other side. He would use what little light was left to continue south to be sure he was well behind their rear.

In near total darkness, he dismounted by a small brook, filled his canteen and let his mare drink. He washed the dust off his face with his bandana and sat down with his back up against a tree to think about how to proceed. It was too dark to ride. He remembered that night in Shiloh that resulted in his capture and was not going to do that again.

A plan formed in his head. He would wait a few hours until the army ate and settled down, then he would walk up through the gap, rest until daybreak, and then ride hard straight north to find Lee.

He started on his trek around midnight, going forward slowly, cautiously, leading the mare. He could see only twenty to thirty feet ahead, not enough to ride safely. He saw a long line of camp-fires extending north to his right, but there were no fires in front as he proceeded. Going very slowly now, he saw a large object appear in front of him – a wagon. He stopped and listened. He heard snoring.. They were under the wagon. He skirted to his left – cannon, caissons, more wagons, more snoring. They had no pickets, no guards! The mare's steps were muffled by the soft dirt, which had been turned into a fine powder by the marching columns that had passed earlier.

Weaving his way through all the artillery, Luke thought there had to be hundreds of cannon. Lee would want to know that, also. On the other side now, the campfires were receding to his back right. The ground started to rise in front of him, and he figured he was at the base of the mountain. He hiked over to the other side and looked for a place to rest, out of sight, until first light. Finding a nice area between two sets of rocks, he tied the reins to his arm and lay down. He did not want to take a chance that his horse would wander off, or worse, get scared by something and bolt away.

He rested in the cool between the rocks. Sleep was far away, but he was pleased with his progress, knowing he would be able to travel the twenty miles or so to Lee's campt early the next morning and deliver his message. The mountain would be between him and the Federal army and he anticipated a clear ride all the way north.

The next morning as the sun shed light on the far Blue Ridge Mountains, Luke headed north at a medium gallop. The mare could probably run five or six hours at that speed, and they settled into a steady cadence. Stopping only once for water, they made good time. The latemorning air was still cool, and feeling like his mission was nearly over, Luke relaxed in the enjoyment of the ride. The mountain faded to a long ridge on his right, and as he reached the top of a slight hill, he pulled up to scan the horizon in front. Three or four miles ahead, on the top of the next rise, appeared to be a large tent. Soldiers and horses were all around. Luke's pulse quickened as he thought it quite likely that it was Lee's camp.

He kicked the buckskin in the ribs and asked her for more speed. She readily responded with reserve strength Luke did not know she had. Almost at full run now, they passed a heavy woods. He steered the mare to the right of a large briar patch. He heard a rifle shot, then a "thwump," and the mare fell sideways right into the briars. He instinctively removed his feet from the stirrups and as the mare fell, he flew headfirst. He put his hands out in front to break his fall. The last thing he remembered was lightning as his head hit something hard. Then darkness.

He opened his eyes. Everything was spinning. It was like he was looking out from a narrow tunnel. He could not feel anything, like his body was not connected. He heard moans coming from his own mouth, but he had no control. The tunnel door became a little wider. Then he was moving. He was being carried. Was it help?

He closed his eyes, then opened them again trying to focus. A man was looking at him closely. He was young; there was blood on his cheek. Was he a friend?

"What happened? Where am I?" Luke murmured.

"Your horse went down and you had a terrible fall," the bloody cheek said pointing toward Luke's feet.

What does "terrible fall" mean? Luke tried to raise his head to look down. His left foot was pointing up as normal; his right foot was pointing sideways at a severe angle. He tried to focus; the thighbone was exposed. He rested his head back down; the little exertion caused his vision to spin. Then he felt a severe pain in his head. He must have hit his head in the fall.

He realized he was in deep trouble. He was just another wounded soldier now, like the many he had treated back at Shiloh. The man with the bloody cheek seemed to be the only help he had. He tried to think through the fog of his injury. He had no sensation in his right leg. What would John and Big Ed do?

He looked at the young man. He seemed willing to help, but he had admitted that he was no medic. He looked caring, sad, confused.

John and Big Ed would probably just amputate. What would that mean? Carol...oh God, Carol. What would she think? How would he provide for her? Run a farm? Would she be repulsed? Remembering the large numbers of amputees he had seen and how pitiful they looked, he thought, yes, he was sure she would be repulsed.

Still trying to concentrate, he thought back to the hospital tent at Shiloh. He remembered he had been stitching up a soldier when he had glanced up to see Big Ed setting a broken leg. He had used a splint. While that man's broken bone had not been exposed, the procedure could not be much different. Just set the bone, stitch up the open wound and use a splint to immobilize. Yes, it might work.

First, he had to be sure to stop the bleeding. The bloody cheek had told him he probably was losing blood, so Luke asked him if he knew how to apply a tourniquet. No such knowledge. Luke would have to show him how to reduce the blood flow to the right leg.

The young man followed Luke's instructions. He tore a sleeve off his own shirt and then tore the shirt into strips. Luke saw that he was covered in red scratches and welts. He wondered who he was, where he was from and why he was helping. Was he a soldier?

Luke continued to guide the young man, telling him how to set the bone and wrap and close the exposed area. Then how to use a strong section of a nearby tree limb to help hold the bone steady and secure the whole upper leg.

Luke still had no sensation in the leg. How would it heal? He feared the black dot, the onset of gangrene. He again thought about Carol. He realized he probably would be going home. The thought of being able to see her again lifted his spirits.

Just before the young man left, Luke saw that he was looking at him with sadness in his eyes. And something else – sympathy? Maybe guilt? He said goodbye and Luke was sure he saw tears in the young man's eyes.

Luke was alone. His leg felt like it was embedded with hot coals, burning, throbbing, searing, about ready to burst through the wrappings like a keg of gunpowder. His mind was consumed by the pain. He looked sideways toward the briars and saw his buckskin lying there, body contorted. Were those gunshot wounds to her rear? Could his horse have been shot out from under him? If so, by whom? What was his message for Lee? What was his message for Lee?

Some minutes later he heard a wagon approaching. It was an ambulance. "You look like you need some help," somebody said.

Chapter 20

ZACH

The cold, hard steel of a rifle barrel was poking at his shirt-less belly. Zach opened his eyes trying to focus. Three men were outlined on the gray sky above. Two were standing, peering down at him with stone-cold eyes, while the third was crouching, his face close to Zach's. Two of the men had no shoes; their uniforms were tattered, their faces gaunt, their beards unkempt. The third smelled like dirty sweat, his breath like rotten eggs.

"Hee, hee, we've got ourselves a prisoner, boys. This'n is a damn Yankee, sure as tootin'," said the one with the bad breath. "He may have no uniform on, but he looks like one, and if he looks like one, he is one, right?"

The man with the rifle moved the barrel up to Zach's nose and started to push hard. "Yer right, Zeb. Maybe we ought a just string him up right here, damn no good Yankee."

The third man held up a rope with a noose on the end. "I love to hear them squeal when the rope gets tight. Let's do it now. Right here. This'll be fun."

"Git up, you sorry excuse for a Yankee," said the man with the rifle. "Put that rope around his neck and pull it real tight."

Zach watched as they slid the rope over his head. He felt it tighten around his neck. The man with the bad breath jammed the barrel of his rifle into Zach's back. Zach thought it was now or never. In one fluid movement, he turned abruptly, grabbed the rifle by the barrel and jerked it free, then swung it directly into the man's rib cage with all the power he had. The man went down to his knees and Zach quickly turned the gun around and pointed it at the other two.

"So I look like a Yankee to you, do I? Well you three sorry excuses for soldiers don't know your ass from a hole in the ground."

The three of them just stared at Zach, and Zach sensed they were not as brave as they wanted to appear. "What unit are you three bums from, and who is your commanding officer?" Zach asked with authority. "I think he just might want to know where you three jerks are, and why you're not on duty."

Zeb glanced at his two companions, "Hey, man, how do we know? You've got no uniform, you talk like a Yankee…"

Zach interrupted before he could go on, "Not that you have any right to know, but I am attached to the medical corps. I just fished one of our couriers out of that briar patch over there and patched him up. I had to tear my white medical jacket into strips so I could stop his bleeding. The ambulance just picked him up. Notice I don't even have a gun." He paused waiting for the effect. "Now tell me, what unit are you from, and who is your commanding officer?"

"Okay, okay, maybe we made a mistake," one said and pointed to the west. "We are on our way back there now. Gotta get goin'."

The one got off his knees and they started to walk away.

"Better not see you three around here again," Zach said, and not wanting to push his luck started walking the other way up the hill, throwing the gun down when he was out of sight.

Zach decided to take a straight line back to where he envisioned the advance of the Union lines would be, which was not too difficult because of the noise of the cannon and mus-

ket fire to the east. The air started to cool a bit as darkness
enveloped the area and the noise wound down to just sporadic
gunfire. Clouds rolled in, eliminating starlight. He was working his way through the territory occupied by the Confederates and had the advantage that few pickets were placed in
their rear. Always staying in wooded areas, he silently stalked
to the east. He felt a slight breeze from the east on his face,
and then he smelled campfires. He froze. He heard voices of
soldiers being repositioned for the next morning's battle. Ever
so slowly, he crawled to the right of the marching soldiers. He
continued undetected for some time. The leaves, fallen tree
limbs and sprigs were re-opening the cuts he had from the briars the previous day. Then he felt a presence immediately in
front of him. Zach stopped, lying as flat as possible. A man was
slowly moving toward him, maybe ten feet away. Zach tried
to let his body disappear into the undergrowth of leaves and
grass. The man stopped as if he, too, sensed something was
very near. Silence. Zach felt his heart beat in his throat and
closed his mouth to soften the noise of his breathing. Then
the sound of water and a burning sensation on his back, right
on his open wounds. Too scared to feel the humor of the situation, Zach remained still, the splatter hitting the side of his
face. The acrid smell burned the lining of his nose. Finally the
man slowly walked back to his camp and Zach, now able to
breathe, crawled forward.

Back on his feet, he walked until he reached a broad area
devoid of trees and brush. After listening intently for several
minutes, he moved to cross it. Nearing the other side, he heard
voices again and froze. Zach started to crawl around the voices,
but then he could make out some of the words, "...the loss of
John Reynolds today...quite a blow for us...we're holding tough
against Lee...we finally got a general in Meade who can think..."

They were Union pickets. "Don't shoot," Zach yelled. "I'm
Zach Harkin, a sharpshooter coming back from special orders
from General Sickles. Can I approach?"

At first light on July 2nd, Zach found Colonel Berdan's head-quarters and waited for him to come out of his tent.

"Harkin. I see you made it back. Where is your rifle?" he said as he came out of his tent to get a cup of coffee.

Zach followed him to the campfire. "Lost it just outside Lee's headquarters yesterday, sir."

Without asking him any details, Berdan curtly said to an aide, "Get this man a shirt, a rifle and some ammunition." Then he looked back at Zach and said, "Harkin, I am assigning you to Company B this morning. You will be under Colonel Trepp here. I have instructed him to take your company and also H Com-pany forward and probe those Confederate defenses."

"But sir, I don't…"

Berdan interrupted. "Let's get going. Colonel Trepp and I will station you in the spots we need."

The sergeant brought Zach his gear and he hurriedly donned the shirt. The day was already very hot and the heavy cloth rubbed on the open cuts on his back. The rifle was the standard issue for the U.S.S.S. Zach joined the two companies as they marched forward.

Trepp posted each man in a position at the top of a small hill, east of which was a road called Emmitsburg Pike. Then before any action started, Berdan and Trepp hastily left, leaving Zach on the very right end of Company B. Their orders were to act as a picket line and shoot any Rebels approaching their positions. Zach loaded his rifle and waited. Some time later, a few Rebel skirmishers approached from the wooded area just ahead.

"Let's git 'em, boys," Captain Wilson said from down the line, and the firing began.

Zach sighted down on one of the rebels to his left. The sol-dier appeared young. He wore his campaign hat at a rakish angle and Zach pictured him as a self-confident young soldier much like himself, with a father and mother back home dreading the day they would learn of their beloved son's death.

Zach's new rifle had a ball sight on the end of the barrel and a post on the rear. Zach sighted down his barrel, centering the ball on the young man's chest. He took a deep breath, exhaled and took half another, bringing the post up to the ball as if to dot an i. His pulse was racing and Zach had trouble holding the target. He tried again all over. Deep breath… exhale… half-breath… hold. His eyes watered, blurring his vision. He thought of the boy's mother, weeping, distraught, broken-hearted. Zach tried again, but he knew he wouldn't be able to pull the trigger. The rifle suddenly became very heavy and his arms were tired and his fingers would not bend. Shooting went on and on up and down the line.

Zach remained in the prone position. He thought of the sharpshooter on the other side of the river who had shot his friend Myron. Zach remembered how the Rebel looked, his jaw blown off, blood splattered. He remembered the log he'd read, and how the Rebel soldier had planned to go home in a couple of days. It had all ended with one shot, his one shot. He was responsible, nobody else.

An overwhelming sense of grief fell upon him. His eyes were open, but all he could see were reflections from the past.

Late that afternoon, Captain Wilson ordered a withdrawal. They all retreated cautiously back to the Union lines and back to the sharpshooter's camp area. Zach stood his rifle up with the rest of his company's and sat on a log near the campfire, shoulders slumped, head down. The captain noticed and walked up to Zach. "Are you sick, Harkin? What's the matter? I noticed you did not shoot much down on your end, what was going on?"

Zach stood. "Nothing, sir, not used to those rifles; lost mine yesterday."

The captain reached down to Zach's side and flipped open his cartridge box. "You didn't fire a shot today, did you? Every single man out there today came back empty and yours is full!"

Zach did not reply. "What really happened to you yesterday when you lost your rifle?"

"I think I lost my nerve, sir."

"Okay, soldier. Nobody can say you lost your nerve at Shiloh or when you swam across the cold Rappahannock in the middle of the night. Let me talk to the colonel about this."

As the captain walked away toward Berdan's tent the colonel came out. Zach could see them both looking in his direction, pointing and gesturing, talking in whispers. He would be branded as a coward, possibly put in jail or even shot. But he didn't care. He was sick of the killing. He would not, ever, shoot another man, even if it meant being shot himself. That conclusion gave him a bit of solace, something to stand for.

The captain said, "The colonel here tells me you initially signed up for twelve months, is that correct?"

"Yes, sir," Zach replied.

"Well it's been more than that. Considering the circumstances, the colonel and I think you should be mustered out. These things happen. Maybe after you are home for a while you will change your outlook, but whatever the case, you're going home."

The two officers walked away, already discussing something else, leaving Zach awestruck. His heart leaped. Home. Away from the death and destruction. Home, he thought, and peace…

With his discharge papers signed by Colonel Berdan tucked safely away in his pocket, Zach boarded a train in Washington, D.C., bound for Pittsburgh and Cincinnati. From there, he would take the same train he'd taken a little over a year ago, back to Camp Nelson, where he would again borrow a horse to ride to Knoxville. He would be home in ten days.

The rail cars carried many wounded. Stretchers were set up over the seat backs and many of the cars were totally occupied. Zach remembered just a few months ago, when he saw the wounded men on the way to Pittsburg Landing. Very little had changed. Same dirty, disheveled soldiers with the exact same amputations. He felt a kinship to these veterans now. He could see the horror in their eyes like a dark shadow.

Zach walked from the station toward his house. The grass was green, the weather was balmy, and a light breeze was rustling the leaves in the trees. Few people were out as it was suppertime, and many of the town's residents were home for the day. Everything looked exactly the same – the little corner grocery store with fresh vegetables on display in the window, the hardware store.

The shade on the little gun shop was pulled down and Zach softly rapped on the door, his heart pounding. He heard footsteps, and Zach stood straight as his mother opened the door. She looked up at the tall man standing on the porch; her eyes lit up and her mouth opened wide, but all she did was whisper, "Oh my God!" Instantly, her soft eyes welled up and she opened her arms and squeezed him with all the strength she had.

"Tom, come out here!" she said, finding her voice.

Zach returned his mother's hug, crying without embarrassment.

"What's going on out..." Tom said as he rounded the corner and saw Zach. "Son, you're home! You're finally home! We've been dreaming about this day." They continued to stand in the doorway, all three together in one embrace, weeping with joy.

During dinner, Zach told them about some of his experiences – losing his friend Myron, talking with Sherman, working with Berdan and David Stuart and others. He avoided telling his parents the things he had done with his rifle, about the sharpshooter, the cannoneers, Johnston. Whenever the subject came to his sharpshooting episodes, he changed the subject.

The sun was setting with a beautiful red color, indicating fair weather for the next day. Tom looked over at his son, put his hand on his back and said, "Son, we heard about Johnston a few months ago, and we can't help but notice you are not talking about it. Must have been hell. Your mother and I have been worried to death about this war and the damage it can do. I think I understand your pain."

Zach felt his chin quiver, his eyes fill with tears, all the emotion of the last week hitting him at once. He tried to compose himself.

"Dad, when I left here a little more than a year ago, you warned me about what it might be like to shoot another man," he said. "I thought you were wrong. An enemy is an enemy, and I felt those people from the South deserved to die for what they were doing. To be truthful, I have shot men, lots of them. Men who never knew what killed them; men who had families back home; men who had loving parents like I do."

He looked up at his father in the fading light. "Dad, you were so right. I'll never, ever take another's life. A life is too precious."

That night, Zach woke abruptly. Something had awakened him and at first he did not know what it was. Then he looked at the end of his bed. There sat a bearded man with long black hair. His lower jaw was missing. His eyes were sunken and hollow. Sad. He was staring at a picture of a young girl. A girl waiting for his return.

Chapter 21

LUKE

Lying in the back of the lumbering wagon as it slowly progressed up toward the main camp, Luke felt excruciating pain. The driver of the wagon and his helper could hear the moaning, however, after the Battle of Chancellorsville, they were used to such sounds, and they proceeded at their normal pace, forcing Luke to endure the jolts and bumps in their path. Before they arrived at the medical tent, Luke passed out cold.

When he opened his eyes, Luke saw the familiar texture of a white field hospital's ceiling. His head ached. He turned his head without raising it and noticed the tent was larger than the one where he had once worked. It had ten or twelve roughly constructed cots, half of which were unoccupied. He was lying on a thin mattress and covered with a sheet and light blanket. The soldier on the cot next to him was coughing violently, and Luke silently concluded he had whooping cough.

He painfully raised his head and looked down on his leg. He remembered the young man who had so kindly helped him. If it hadn't been for him, he might have bled to death. His bandages had been changed, but blood had seeped through them. He wondered if they had stitched up the open wound. The whole area felt like somebody had put a watermelon under his skin. The doctor had replaced the tree limb that immobilized his leg with a board. When he moved any part of his leg, shock waves seared up his leg and through his whole body. He tried to remain absolutely motionless from his waist down.

"How's the pain?" a man approaching from the rear asked. "You have been out for quite a while." The man wore a clean white smock and appeared older. He placed a caring hand on Luke's shoulder. "You've had a tough time. The doc worked hard trying to get your thighbone reset properly."

Luke grimaced, "Never experienced anything like this. It's almost unbearable. Where am I?"

"You are in a field hospital we set up several days ago. Lucky we don't have much business right now; all of our seriously wounded have been transferred back to Richmond. We have been told we should be ready to move our operation at a moment's notice."

"Are you a doctor?"

"No, I am an assistant. The real doctors do all the heavy stuff. Normally I do the chloroform administration. Had to give you a big dose. The doctor probably wouldn't have spent so much time with you if we'd had a whole backlog waiting to be treated. Chancellorsville was a nightmare. Those poor bastards that just got transferred were the last of them. Where are you from?"

"Crossville, in eastern Tennessee."

"Got somebody waiting for you back there? A young lady, perhaps? You might consider it good or bad, but with your wound, you will probably get to go home after you heal a bit. The doctor will decide."

Luke tried to weigh the significance of what the man just said. Slowly he responded, forgetting the question about the young lady. "You mean this leg might not heal?"

"Didn't say that. All I can tell you is the doctor took an extraordinary amount of time with that bone before he sewed you up. He'll be back soon; you can ask him yourself."

A wave of doubt swept over Luke. What the hell was he talking about? A broken bone is a broken bone, isn't it? Surely it would heal and he would be good as new?

"You have to be thirsty," said the assistant. He walked behind Luke and came back with a tin cup of water.

Only then did Luke realize how bone dry his mouth was. He carefully took the cup, and while the assistant held up his head, drank it empty. "We'll give you some more in a little while. Don't want you to throw it all up."

"Thanks," Luke said handing the cup back.

The man walked away. Luke's body screamed with throbbing, sharp stabs of pain that felt like someone was twisting a knife in his leg over and over again. He was having trouble thinking clearly and closed his eyes waiting for sleep that would stop the pain.

Several hours later Luke awoke to find a short, bespectacled man in a white smock standing next to him. "'Bout time you woke up. You've been dead to the world for three or four hours. Pain any better?" the man asked.

"Worse pain I have ever had," Luke said. "Worse than anything imaginable."

"I am the doctor who tried to set your leg. You have had quite a compound fracture. How did it happen, do you remember?"

The word "remember" toggled Luke's memory, "I have to see General Lee!" Luke said. "I have an urgent message. I have a message from General Stuart and... and..."

"Now slow down, son, you must be hallucinating. Just take it easy. Everything is going to be okay."

"You may think that I am hallucinating, sir, but I am not," Luke said. "I remember it all clear now. I am a courier for Stuart and Hampton, they sent a verbal message to Lee. On the way

here, I saw a large Yankee force moving north, and when I tried
to swing south to get around them, I found out their columns are
more than twenty miles long. It's the whole dang Union Army.
Must be one hundred thousand of them, and I have to tell Lee he
is about to get hit hard."

Luke tried to move. Bolts of lightning shot through him even
though he'd hardly budged.

"Damn it, soldier. You are going to undo all the work I did on
your leg if you don't just lie there and try to relax a little."

"How long have I been here? Luke asked.

"About six or seven hours," the assistant piped in.

"Look, I know I can't move, but you've got to try to give him
that message," Luke said.

"You say there's one hundred thousand bluecoats moving
north behind us?" asked the assistant.

"Yes, sir, at least that many," Luke said.

"I'll go see who will listen," the assistant said walking out.

At this time Lee still did not know the exact locations of the
Union Army. He strongly relied on Stuart to provide him with
intelligence identifying enemy units, artillery, other cavalry and
all the information a commander needs to have an advantage.
The Battle of Gettysburg had begun, and Lee sorely needed all
the information he could get. Lee had extended himself into
Union territory and he was looking for that one big knockout
blow that, in his mind, just might force the already war-tired
North to abandon the battlefield.

The assistant, still wearing his white medical smock, approached two officers idly chatting near the headquarters tent.
He told them of the wounded courier and repeated his message
exactly.

"Is that all? one of the officers asked.

"Yes, sir," the assistant said.

"Okay, we'll take care of it." The assistant stood there, as if waiting for them to go tell Lee.

"Dismissed," the other officer said curtly.

As the assistant walked away, one officer said to the other, "One hundred thousand bluecoats… and cows can fly." They resumed their conversation, dismissing the report.

Back at the hospital tent, Luke asked the doctor about his wound.

"We should know soon," the doctor said. "The problem is that your thighbone splintered when it broke. When I opened it up to reset it, small fragments of bone were missing. I tried to piece it together as well as possible. You are young and the bone should come together and heal, but you need to give it some time. Hopefully, the pain will start to subside as the healing starts."

The roar of cannon fire from the east reached them, and Luke knew what was coming. He was helpless, totally dependent on the doctor and his assistants. He felt vulnerable, alone, weary. He slept again.

An urgent voice and a firm shake woke Luke up some time later. "We're moving you out," the doctor said. "General orders. Everybody goes. They want us to get ready for a lot more wounded. Seems like another big battle brewing."

Then he heard it, more cannon fire, this time closer, like the thunder of an approaching summer storm. Musket fire again from the same direction – steady, intense, even urgent. An expectant pall hung in the air.

"Where will they take me?" Luke asked.

"Probably to Richmond, son," the doc answered. "I think they will haul you in a wagon to Fredericksburg, then they normally put the wounded on a train on down to Richmond."

Luke looked down at his bandaged leg. "Won't be easy."

The assistant came up with a pair of crutches. "You'll have to use these to move around, so let's give them a try and see how you do."

The crutches were whittled wooden sticks pointed on one end with a carved arc-shaped shoulder piece on the other. Somebody had used them before, and the portion where the arcs met the shoulders were smooth from wear.

"Guess that means I have to get up," Luke said as he tried to raise his torso.

The doctor and the assistant managed to get Luke up and turned so he was sitting on the edge of the cot. The pain was excruciating, sending piercing stabs up his body, but it was not quite a bad as before.

"If you want this leg to have any chance of healing, never, ever put any weight on it. Not for a few weeks, until that bone has grown back together," the doctor said.

They helped him off the cot, and standing on his good leg, Luke took the crutches and put his weight on them. They were too short for him, but he thought he could manage. The doctor gave him an envelope, which he stuck inside his cavalry jacket. "Here is a discharge letter, son, signed by me. When you get all healed up and you want to get out of this godforsaken war, just use this letter and you can go home."

They laid Luke in the ambulance wagon with the others and the wagon slowly ambled off.

"Fifty, fifty," the doctor said watching the ambulance move off. "Only an even chance he ever gets home. There was so much dirt and grime in that wound. I wish I could have done more for him. Maybe I should have taken it off…"

They went back to their tent just as the first wagon arrived with the screams and moans of more victims.

The rest of the day and into the night, the ambulance wagon crept toward the south. Lying on his back and sandwiched in between four other wounded soldiers, Luke thought about what his future held. Even though his pain was severe, he could think rationally. In a way, it seemed he'd left home only yesterday. Events merged in a blur. On the other hand, his time at war seemed like an eternity. So many things – Shiloh, Forrest, suturing, Camp Chase, Carol. There was that warm feeling again. He knew he had to see her, to confirm, to reassure. "I loved you from the first time I saw you..." The words haunted him, kept him going. He wanted her; now he needed her. Luke looked up at the stars and thought about those same stars shining on her at this very moment, like they were somehow connected.

He thought about his mom and dad. Somehow, his guilt for his poor judgment had waned. He had sent his pay back to them and that had made him feel better, like he was making up for his recklessness. He would go home, buy a place, get married, try to forget...

From Guinea Station, Luke was transported to the Chimborazo Hospital in Richmond on the daily train bringing wounded from the northern battlefields. Known as the "hospital on the hill," Chimborazo was a vast complex of wooden structures built at the outset of the war as barracks. Several thousand wounded could be treated here at a time, with a staff of several dozen surgeons working around the clock. Daily chores such as feeding and cleaning were handled by disabled soldiers, slaves and a few women.

The ennui of daily existence at the hospital set in for Luke almost immediately. While his pain did not subside as much as he had hoped, each day he would walk on his crutches, gaining strength in his shoulders and learning to move without causing additional pain. Every day, one of the surgeons would stop by and inspect his wound noting any progress. On the third day, the doctor noticed a build-up of pus. "We will have to drain this away," he said.

"I've seen this before. Don't you call it 'laudable pus'? It means it's healing correctly, right?"

"You are exactly right, but we need to allow the fluid to get out. I will make a hole in the bottom of this bandage so your body will void it."

"Sounds good to me, doc, how soon can I get out of here?"

"We are having massive amounts of wounded arriving these days, and we're severely swamped. We must have four or five thousand patients, so we need to free up space as quickly as possible. While I am not happy with the way this wound looks, I will have a nurse apply new dressings with the hole, and if all goes well you should be able to go tomorrow."

"Tomorrow! Tomorrow? That is the best news ever. I'm going home!"

"Yes, you can go home, but in all good conscience, I cannot discharge you. When you are healed, you will be good for service."

Luke did not tell the doctor about his discharge letter. "Sure, doc. It will be nice to go home, if just for a while."

The doctor left and soon a black man came to Luke's bedside. With deft hands, he expertly tore off the remaining old bandages and tied new ones on, leaving a drain hole. Finally he said in a thick voice, "Will mas' be goin' home?"

"Hope to start home tomorrow," Luke said.

After all the thinking, speculating, hoping, Luke was actually going home. He stood on the depot ramp waiting for the train to take him to Danville. He would try to connect with other trains there. He hoped to be able to cross the mountains by rail, then get home somehow.

"How do I get to Crossville, Tennessee? Luke asked the man behind the ticket window.

The man scratched his head, "Over on the other side of Knoxville, right?"

Luke took one steep closer to the window and leaned forward on his crutches. "Yes, sir, between Knoxville and Nashville."

The ticket master looked at a map behind him on the wall. "Looks like if you get to Bristol by taking the Tennessee & Virginia line from here, you can then catch another on down to Knoxville. Don't know how you can get to Crossville from there, but you could walk it if you had to." He looked at Luke's leg. "Then again, maybe somebody could give you a ride. You got discharge papers? You're not running away, are you?"

Luke patted the side of his cavalry jacket. "Got 'em right here."

"The train'll be along any time now. By the way, I hear tell the going can be rough in eastern Tennessee; lots of Yankee raiders around. You wouldn't want them to find a Southern boy with a cavalry uniform. Might be trouble, even though you're…" he looked down at the wound.

"I'll be able to handle myself," Luke said. He exited the depot and sat on a bench next to some other wounded men evidently waiting to go home also.

Munching some stale cornbread the hospital had given him before he left, Luke waited. As different trains came chugging in and out, Luke noticed what poor condition everything was in. The train engines were old and rusty, the boxcars were falling apart. Nothing had been painted in years. Luke wondered if the South could win this war.

The anticipation kept building. Luke had never been away from home before for more than one night, and that was when he fished for catfish all night. He thought about Carol and wondered if she would find his wounded leg disgusting. It would probably be more healed when he saw her. He would be happy to see Jeff, his dog, and go hunting with him.

"All aboard! Lynchburg, Roanoke, Bristol," the conductor yelled.

A crew of old men helped Luke into a boxcar, the floor covered with loose straw, and shortly the train lumbered away to the southwest. Other wounded men were in the same boxcar. Luke found a spot in a corner and lay down. His leg throbbed

from the movement. The others engaged in small talk, but Luke
let the rhythmic noise of the tracks and the sway of the car lull
him to sleep.

Luke was awakened by the screech of the train's brakes,
steel against steel. His sleep had been fitful, but he thought
quite a lot of time had gone by. His leg pain was worse than
the previous day, and Luke reasoned that under these traveling conditions he could not expect a lot of pain relief. He
heard a man approach. "All off for Bristol, does anybody need
help?" He shined his lantern into the boxcar and Luke raised
his hand.

Two men helped him off the train. Luke's pain was intense as
he hobbled to the station building. Inside there was a dim light
over a bench in the corner, and he went over, sat down and put
his leg up so he could see it. He inspected the dressing, which
looked good, then he put his finger down near the drainage hole.
Thick yellow pus was coming out and Luke continued to think it
was a good sign – a sign the wound was healing. He then hobbled
over to the ticket window where he saw a man sleeping at a desk.
"Excuse me," he said, then said again when he received no answer.

The man awoke and looked over Luke. "When's the next
train to Knoxville?" Luke asked.

"Nothing 'til morning," he said and laid his head back down
to sleep.

Luke lay on the bench and tried to sleep as well. His mind
was racing like he had drunk too much coffee. He took deep
breaths trying to relax. Maybe it's the excitement of going home.
He was not far now; one more train ride, then straight to home.
Even though the night air was cool, he was very warm. Beads
of perspiration appeared on his forehead. But he slept. A deep
weary sleep.

"Aren't you goin' to Knoxville?" the man from behind the
window said, shaking Luke's shoulder.

The morning sun shone into the station as Luke woke up. He shook his head trying to focus and it came to him where he was. "Knoxville...yes," he said.

"Well get your butt up and I'll help you to the train. It'll be leaving in a couple of minutes. We called and called but you were not hearing us. Come on..."

The boxcar on this train also had straw on the floor, but the straw smelled like a privy. Luke was the only person in the car; he found a corner and sat down with his back against the side of the car. This is how folks must feel when they've had too much to drink, Luke thought. His head wasn't clear. He looked at the wound. There was no change, but that watermelon feel was there again – as if the dressing would burst from the pressure inside. He tried to eat the last of his cornbread, but wasn't hungry. He was thirsty. Very, very thirsty.

Two men were carrying him when he awoke. They sat him on a bench at the station. "You sure do sleep hard," one said.

"I...I guess so...this Knoxville? Luke managed.

"Are you okay?" the other asked. "What can we do for you? You look like you've had a rough time of it. Did they shoot you in that leg?"

"Water. Give me some water and I'll be better."

They gave him a canteen. The coolness of the water felt like a fire hose being sprayed on a fire. "Thanks, probably all I need-ed. Guess I got a little weak from not drinking enough. Yep, feel much better." He took another long gulp, emptying the canteen.

"Where you goin'," one asked.

"Home. Crossville. Once I get home, I can rest up...be good as new. Won't take long at all."

"I see you're cavalry, how did you get hurt?"

"Rode with Stuart and Hampton, fell off my horse when it got shot," Luke said slowly.

"You say you're going to Crossville? There's no railroad go-ing that way, but there's a freighter that hauls between here and

Nashville. It can be a bit dangerous at times, what with all those Yankee raiders around. He usually hauls non-military stuff, though. Maybe he can help," said another man standing nearby.

"Sure would be nice to get a ride. I don't think I could make the walk," Luke said.

The man said he would check with the freighter. Several minutes later, he returned saying the freight wagon was leaving for Nashville at sunset and the driver would be happy to take along somebody to talk to.

While Luke waited for the freighter, he sat down to take a look at his leg. The pain had actually subsided a bit. However, his spells of chills and fever were becoming more frequent. He thought his symptoms were caused by the lack of rest and poor care. The fluid was coming out of the wound regularly and had a foul smell, but he had seen this before. His skin had some rashes here and there, but nothing abnormal for his injury.

As the eight-mule team pulled the freight wagon up to the train station, the driver jumped off. The man was enormous. "You my passenger?"

"Yes, sir," said Luke, taking care not to move. "I have a little trouble with this leg."

The station platform was about three feet off the street level and the man seemed to Luke like he stood another four or five feet above that. He stepped up on the platform taking only one step, picked up Luke like he was ball of feathers and placed him high on the wagon.

"These bales of cotton should be just fine for you to lie on," he said. "We have a long ride and you look like you need rest. Here are your crutches, too."

"Thank you."

"We'll drive these boys through the cool of the night, and we should reach Crossville late afternoon tomorrow. I've got plenty of water and lots of food. Takes a lot to keep me goin'," he said in a friendly voice.

They ambled off into the setting sun, the teamster cracking his whip, the mules responding, the wagon leaving deep ruts in the dirt.

Through the night and into the next day, Luke slept between spells of chills and fever. During his fevers, his clothing would become wet with perspiration, and when the chills would follow, there was nothing he could do to keep warm. He just had to wait it out until they went away. His pulse was erratic, sometimes throbbing like a drum and other times weak and irregular.

He thought of all the things he would do when he got home. Sleep in his own bed, clean up his filthy body, enjoy his mother's home-cooked meals, sit at the supper table and talk. He had so much to tell this parents. He would get better, see Carol, buy a place, get married, have kids...

In the late afternoon, Luke felt a gentle nudge on his shoulder, "Wake up, son. We're in Crossville. You sure weren't much company on this trip. You nearly slept through the whole thing."

"Yeah, and I feel some better," Luke said. "Sorry I wasn't better company. Must have been more tired than I thought, but I'm rested now."

The teamster lifted him down onto the ground and gave Luke his crutches. "You going to be okay?" he asked. "I've got to get goin'. If I don't have this freight in Nashville by this time tomorrow, I don't get paid."

"Much obliged. I'll be just fine," Luke said as he took a couple of steps on his crutches. "Yeah, I'll be just fine. Just a short walk to our farm from here."

The teamster jumped up on the wagon, cracked his whip and slowly pulled away. "Take care, son, and give that leg a chance to heal. Next time I come through here, you'll be doing somersaults."

The town was practically empty as Luke started to hobble out of town toward the farm. He had about two miles to go, and he thought he could get there well before sundown. He thought this was the very last leg of a long trip that would be over soon.

He would be home. In a few days, he would be rounding up the cows, helping with the crops, doing the things he always loved to do.

The sights were all familiar. He passed the McGraw homestead with the haystack in the back of the barn. He used to slide down that haystack years ago. Their old windmill always had vanes missing, and it was missing a few more now. Sweetest water from that well…

He was out of breath. He stopped, his hands shaking, sweat pouring down off his forehead. I must be going too fast, he thought. The leg feels okay; maybe it's finally healing.

He passed the Bricker place. Their son joined up in '61, fought with Johnston. The house should be back in those trees. Luke realized it wasn't there any longer. Strange, he thought. Wonder what happened.

The fork in the road. Getting close now; maybe I'll rest, he thought. So tired. He sat on a large rock along side the road. He noticed his hands had blistered from handling the crutches. He wished the blisters were the only problem he had.

He wanted to stay there for a while and rest. Maybe he could spend the night and have the energy to finish in the morning. But he got up and started to move forward. He couldn't keep his bad leg in the air any longer, so it dragged along, making a small furrow in the dusty road.

Oh, for a cup of water. Mom will have some when I get there; won't be long, now.

On and on he doggedly plodded. Just around this next bend and down the small hill to home. Small steps. He stopped to catch his breath. Just a few more yards and I'll be able to see the place…

He rounded the top of the small rise at looked down at his mom and dad's spread. A deep, painful scream came out of his throat; shock hit him like a thunderbolt and spread through his whole body. In one split second, he knew he was the only person left on earth. The house and barn were gone; there were just charred remains. Only the kitchen fireplace was still standing. He stood motionless, trying to make sense of it.

He slowly dragged himself down the hill one step at a time. He had no energy. He hobbled over to the old fireplace, his foot uncovering an old supper plate. He sat down with his back against the cold stone. He looked out to the west toward his beloved little creek. Then Jeff, his dog, came out of nowhere. Dirty, pitiful, starving, he nestled his chin on Luke's lap, looking up at him with soft sad eyes.

Neither moved as the sun went down in the west.

EPILOGUE

Hiram Berdan resigned his commission in January 1864. In spite of being generally considered unfit for command, Congress confirmed his retroactive appointment to the grade of brigadier general. Later in 1864, Berdan worked with various gun manufacturers, including Sharps and Colt, to design and construct a breech-loading percussion rifle. None of his designs ever went into production. He died in March 1893.

Ulysses S. Grant was appointed commander of all Union armies in March 1864, when Lincoln became displeased with Major General George Meade's failure to follow up on his victory at Gettysburg. Successfully defeating Lee, Grant would later be elected president of the United States at age 46. He served two terms. A forceful Reconstructionist, he championed the 15th Amendment guaranteeing voting rights to all male citizens. He signed the Amnesty Act in 1871 restoring political rights to ex Confederates. Then he signed the Civil Rights Act of 1875 prohibiting racial discrimination on public property. He died July 23rd, 1885, at age 63.

William Tecumseh Sherman, always a strong Grant supporter, negotiated the terms of surrender for General Joe Johnston's army in 1865, which was the largest remaining Confederate force after Lee's surrender. Fearing that Johnston's army would turn to guerrilla warfare, Sherman granted conditions of surrender that were deemed too lenient by Northern policymakers. The terms of surrender were later renegotiated. Sherman had earlier caused a controversy during his "March to the Sea," when the city of Columbia, South Carolina, was burned. Many blamed him for the wanton fires that burned much of the city, and he was accused of war crimes, particularly by the South. Sherman responded, "If I had made up my mind to burn Columbia, I would have burnt it with no more feeling than I would a common prairie dog village; but I did not do it…" He also said, "In my official report of this conflagration I distinctly charged it to General Wade Hampton, and confess I did so pointedly to shake the faith of his people in him, for he was in my opinion a braggart and professed to be the special champion of South Carolina." After the war, Sherman was promoted to lieutenant general, and after Grant was elected president, he was appointed commanding general of the United States Army. Retiring in 1884, he died in February 1889.

Nathan Bedford Forrest was a self-made man with the reputation of being a fierce and innovative cavalry leader. His exploits of bravery and cunning are found in almost every Civil War book about the Western theater. Some historians doubt whether the wounded Forrest actually picked up a Union soldier during the Battle of Fallen Timbers and used him as a shield as he raced back to the Confederate line, as written by Shelby Foote. The feat seems almost superhuman, especially for a wounded man. However, a man in the heat of battle with adrenaline flowing in abundance could have been capable of such an action. Forrest was a fierce fighter, many times attacking foes of much greater strength. He was very independent and frequently rebelled against his commanders. This characteristic was particularly manifested when he directly said to General Braxton Bragg: "I have stood your meanness as long as I intend to. You have played the part of a ****ed scoundrel, and are a coward, and if you were any part of a man, I would slap your jaws and force you to resent it. You may as well not issue any more orders to me, for I will not obey them, and I will hold you personally responsible for any further indignities you endeavor to inflict upon me. You have threatened to arrest me for not obeying your orders promptly. I dare you to do it, and I say to you that if you ever again try to interfere with me or cross my path it will be at the peril of your life." After the war, Forrest was accused of war crimes surrounding the massacre of hundreds of blacks after the Battle of Fort Pillow. After investigations, he was never formally charged. Forrest died in October 1877.

Pierre Gustave Toutant Beauregard was a French Creole from Louisiana. Graduating second in his class of 1838 at West Point, he went on to become one of the seven full generals in the Confederacy, ranking fifth in seniority (behind Samuel Cooper, A.S. Johnston, Lee, and Joe Johnston), even though he was always bothered by poor health. During the Battle of Shiloh, Beauregard did the major planning for the initial surprise attack against Grant, and was faulted for his poor execution and organization. He later was given command of the Department of North Carolina and Southern Virginia. After the Battle of Cold Harbor, Beauregard correctly predicted that Grant would cross the James River. Severely outnumbered, he was able to hold off the Federals until Lee arrived at what was to be called the Second Battle of Petersburg. To Beauregard's bitter disappointment, Davis replaced him with Joe Johnston, under whom he served for the balance of the war. Beauregard died in 1893.

Daniel E. Sickles was a politician from New York City and was appointed brigadier general of volunteers, then in 1862 was promoted to major general. Just before that, in 1859, he shot and killed Francis Barton Key, his wife's lover. The victim was the son of Francis Scott Key, who authored the Star Spangled Banner. The defense attorney in the case brought against him was Edwin Stanton, who would later become Lincoln's secretary of state. Of interest, his successful defense was based on the temporary insanity plea, and marked the first time that plea was ever used. Sickles was the center of several military controversies. At the Battle of Chancellorsville, as Stonewall Jackson sneaked around Lee's left flank, Sickles incorrectly thought Jackson was retreating and attacked, leaving a huge hole in the Union defense that ultimately resulted in disaster for the North and arguably Lee's greatest victory. At Gettysburg, Sickles disobeyed his orders from Meade and advanced his 3rd Corps into the Peach Orchard (not the same Peach Orchard at Shiloh), causing his whole corps to be severely compromised. Sickles was wounded in his right leg, which had to be amputated. Even though he clearly disobeyed orders, he was still awarded the Medal of Honor for his bravery under fire. Later, he donated his amputated leg to the Army Medical Museum in Washington, D.C., where it is still on display. He died in May 1914.

Albert Sidney Johnston graduated eighth in his class of 1826 at West Point, two years ahead of his friend Jefferson Davis. In a duel in 1837, Johnston received a wound in the right leg that caused damage to his sciatic nerve, resulting in numbness. In September 1861, Davis appointed Johnston commander of the entire Confederacy west of the Allegheny Mountains, making him the highest-ranking officer in the Confederacy. He was shot during the Battle of Shiloh while leading an attack near an old cotton field east of the Hamburg-Savannah Road. The bullet entered behind his right knee and cut his popliteal artery. Possibly because of the prior nerve damage, he did not realize he had been shot until his boot filled up with blood and he became faint. The source of the bullet is widely believed to be from the Confederate side, because he was actually between the two opposing lines and both sides were firing at each other. He died shortly after they had discovered the wound. Later, Davis referred to Johnston's death as "the turning point of our fate." Speculation goes on about what would have happened if Johnston had not been killed. As Davis thought so much of him, would he have reached higher levels of command?

David Stuart, who commanded the far left flank of the Union forces on the first day of Shiloh, may be one of the least recognized heroes of the fighting that day. In November 1862, he was appointed general of volunteers and performed well in several minor battles. The U.S. Senate declined to confirm his appointment as brigadier general, and he resigned from service in April of 1863. He died in September 1868.

James Ewell Brown "Jeb" Stuart would always be haunted by Lee's utterance of "Where is Stuart" during the Gettysburg campaign. Stuart's absence during the outset of the Battle of Gettysburg left Lee and his staff with no idea of where the enemy was. That lack of information was compounded by the fact that they were in unfamiliar territory. If Lee had received up-to-date intelligence of the Union's movements and position, would the outcome of the battle at Gettysburg (and therefore the entire war) have been different? The speculation continues today. Stuart's cavalry was repulsed on the last day of the battle, July 3rd, 1863, and he seemingly never fully recovered. Later, Stuart was fatally wounded by Sheridan's Federal cavalry as he tried to defend Richmond at the Battle of Yellow Tavern. He died May 12th, 1864.

Wade Hampton III served admirably through the course of the war after Gettysburg. Hampton was the military commander of the Confederate forces at Columbia, South Carolina, when Sherman's army approached from the south near the end of his "March to the Sea." Hampton ordered the large cotton stocks to be placed in the streets to deter Sherman's progress, and in the heat of the battle the bales burned, causing vast damage to the city. Both sides denied starting the fires. But Hampton's home was destroyed. Some would say he had failed to protect his home, his hometown and the way of life he so treasured. After the war, he suffered severe financial losses and reluctantly became governor of South Carolina, then a U.S. senator for two terms. While Hampton was in the Senate, John Sherman implied that Hampton was a member of the Ku Klux Klan, which Hampton vehemently denied. Today, a statue of a proud Hampton on his horse stands in front of the South Carolina State House in Columbia.

John Sherman, Tecumseh's brother and a senator from Ohio, went on to become secretary of the treasury under Rutherford Hayes in 1877. In 1880 he had James Garfield nominate him for president of the United States as the candidate for the Republican Party at the party's convention in Chicago. The convention, unable to decide, nominated Garfield instead. In March 1897, he became the 35th secretary of state under William McKinley. He resigned in 1898 because of poor health and died in 1900.

Abner Doubleday, born in June of 1819, moved to Cooperstown to attend a private preparatory high school. He graduated twenty-fourth in his class at the U.S. Military Academy. At he start of the Civil War he was a captain and second in command (under Major Robert Anderson) at Fort Sumter. He aimed the cannon that made the first retaliatory shot in defense of the Confederate bombardment at Sumter on April 12th, 1861. A persistent myth that followed Doubleday was that he invented the game of baseball in 1839 while at West Point. In 1905 a commission was formed to prove that the sport originated in America. They picked Doubleday as the founder of baseball, and because he had lived in Cooperstown, that city became the home of the Baseball Hall of Fame. Doubleday never claimed to have invented baseball and his New York Times obituary did not mention it. Historians generally agree it was a pure myth. He wrote the book

"Chancellorsville and Gettysburg (1863)," which is recognized as an important historical reference of those two campaigns.

Born in 1826, John Buford, a Kentuckian, graduated sixteenth in his West Point class of 1848. Later, in the Civil War, General Buford was given command of the Reserve Brigade, 1st Division, Cavalry Corps. Recognized as one of the best cavalry commanders in either army, he was referred to as "Old Steadfast" by those who fought with him. Just before the Battle of Gettysburg, Buford, knowing a large battle was nigh, recognized the significance of the high ground just south of Gettysburg. He deployed his men on foot northeast of town in an effort to delay the Confederates until help would arrive. For two hours, Buford held off the much larger force of General Heth until John Reynolds' First Corps arrived on the field. Buford's tactical understanding and foresight gave the Union the high ground position from which Lee was defeated. Buford died in December of 1863 just after President Lincoln promoted him to Major General.

Jefferson Davis had the most difficult job: establishing a federal government from scratch and at the same time mounting an army capable of defending against a comparatively huge, well-established, military complex. In many ways, he was extremely successful, but because the South lost, much criticism arose tainting his Confederate presidency. Not until 1881, after the publication of his memoirs, "The Rise and Fall of the Confederate Government," did Southern opinion start to change and his reputation begin to be re-established. In the late 1880s, he strongly advocated reconciliation with the North. Davis died on December 6th, 1889, at the age of 91, having outlived most of his antagonists. His United States citizenship was not restored until October 1978, when President Jimmy Carter signed a Senate resolution posthumously granting him citizenship. Carter referred to the resolution as the last act of reconciliation of the Civil War.

15362711R00152

Made in the USA
San Bernardino, CA
22 September 2014